HIS SECRETIVE MADAM

ENTERPRISING WOMEN, BOOK 3

Peri Maxwell

ARE YOU SIGNED UP FOR DRAGONBLADE'S BLOG?

You'll get the latest news and information on exclusive giveaways, exclusive excerpts, coming releases, sales, free books, cover reveals and more.

Check out our complete list of authors, too!

No spam, no junk. That's a promise!

Sign Up Here

www.dragonbladepublishing.com

Dearest Reader;

Thank you for your support of a small press. At Dragonblade Publishing, we strive to bring you the highest quality Historical Romance from some of the best authors in the business. Without your support, there is no 'us', so we sincerely hope you adore these stories and find some new favorite authors along the way.

Happy Reading!

CEO, Dragonblade Publishing

For Melinda. I'm your biggest fan!

CHAPTER ONE

DRAKE FLETCHER TURNED left, away from Berkeley Square and toward Hyde Park. Gas lights hissed and flickered, bathing Charles Street in a weak golden glow that was still bright enough to dim the stars that had guided him home for years.

Home. The West End, with its wide streets and neat, solid houses, was now his home.

He'd get used to it eventually. After all, it hadn't taken him long to adjust to the noise of London.

Acrid coal oil added to the pollution created by hearth fires, the multitude of horses and dray animals, and the ever-growing population. Regardless, Drake admired the busyness of London, the two faces of it. The clean one it displayed in the daylight, and the dirty one it hid in shadows.

Sweepers worked in the street, trailing carts full of dung. He wondered where they dumped all of it. At some point, a new island would likely rise in the Channel—one no one wanted to war over.

An occasional cab or carriage lumbered past, carrying late-night revelers home from some party or another, or maybe an assignation in Haymarket or Soho. Though most likely it was the pedestrians, flicking past the gaslights with their collars high and their hat brims low, who were rushing home from trysts and praying for no witnesses. Not that they needed to worry. Carriage passengers were in their own worlds, and sweepers were in quite another.

That only left Drake, and he was accustomed to keeping everyone's secrets.

As he rounded the corner onto Charles Street, the first drops of rain thudded against his beaver hat. His new townhouse, at the opposite end of the block, sparked a sense of pride. From the slums in Whitechapel to Paddington and then the West End was quite a climb. But his accomplishment was tempered by the knife hilt nudging his ribs with every step. Regardless of gas lamps and better neighbors, the dark in London was rarely friendly.

He'd ventured from Whitechapel on nights like this, hoping for an easy mark and a quick touch. Telling himself a well-dressed toff wouldn't miss a few bob. It wasn't like he was stealing from the Crown.

Again.

The houses were dark, which made the one on the corner stand out. All the windows were lit in his house. Drake's quickened pace was only half due to the rain. Gavin was even more of a stickler than he was about the boys not terrorizing the new neighbors—at least until they'd fully unpacked. If no one was in bed, there was likely trouble.

"Sir?" The quiet word accompanied a tug on his coattails, nowhere near the pocket. Below him was a boy of no more than five.

Drake eased his hand to his side. "You shouldn't be out in the weather, lad." Though he looked like the water would do him good.

"M' brother is a sweeper, but they say I'm too little to help." His too-large cap made his ears stick out, and his eyes were barely visible under the brim as he craned his neck to meet Drake's gaze. "But Mum sent me anyway 'cause m' sister is sick, and I thought…"

He thought if he could touch a well-dressed toff, he might prove his worth. Still, he hadn't tried to steal it, and his brother was working for his wages. Drake dropped to his haunches, balancing on the balls of his feet, so he could look the boy in the eye. "What's your name?"

"David, sir."

The name was a painful thorn stuck high between Drake's left ribs. Sometimes the sharp sting woke him in the middle of the night, dragged him from his warm sheets, and sent him pacing across a floor that didn't freeze his toes. "And it's you, your brother and sister, and your mum?"

The boy nodded as the rain splattered around them. "Da went off on a ship before Polly was born."

Drake felt in his pocket for a crown, which he held up to David. "Keep it where no one can see it and tell no one you have it, not even your brother." The boy's eyes widened as he nodded, and Drake dropped the coin into his hand. "Find a tree or a shop awning to keep you dry and stick close to the sweepers so your brother doesn't lose you."

Because it was easy to lose track of brothers you should be protecting.

Drake straightened and strode the last few feet home. The door opened, and a man stepped out dressed much as he was, though he had the sense to have an umbrella.

And Drake had the sense not to surprise him. "Gav?"

Gavin Howard, his second oldest living friend, snapped his head up. The closed umbrella came across his chest like a saber in battle. Two blinks later it was at his side again. "Thank God you're home."

Lamps from a passing carriage swept over them, making Gav's white collar a bright slash between his dark suit and his ebony jaw. His grim expression made it squarer, as though someone had begun a statue and stopped after chiseling the basic shape. "Thank you, but if you're going out at this hour, someone *isn't* home." There was only one escape artist under their roof. "Harry?"

"I thought giving him a room in the attic would keep him

from treasure hunting, but he seems to take it as a challenge." Gav stepped clear of the door. "If you want to go in, I'll go get him."

"There's no sense both of us getting wet." Drake beckoned for the umbrella. "Where is he?"

"Likely the White Rose. He's been talking about it all week."

Drake flicked his eyes to the house next door to make certain their windows stayed dark. "What is a nine-year-old doing in a goddamn brothel?"

"He's got a new school chum. Alfie Lane. The boy works for Madam White running errands and such. His brother Tommy is the bartender." Gav heaved a sigh. "As far as what he's up to… I think you know."

The White Rose had a reputation for pretty, clean women and churchlike discretion. As a result, it attracted toffs and politicians like flies. Harry, with his light fingers and keen eye, would be in heaven. Until he was in the workhouse—or worse.

Drake opened the umbrella and swung it over his head. "I'll fetch him."

The rain spattered into puddles and the air smelled of mud and manure. He wanted to be home, his stomach full of whatever Gav had on hand or, more likely, whatever the boys had left him. He wanted to be dry and in his own bed, with a fire in the hearth and a book to read until he was too tired to hold it.

Instead, he was on his way to the last place he wanted to be.

Drake stepped into a puddle that soaked his boot and his trousers well past his ankle. A gust of wind caught the umbrella and knocked it against his hat.

He let fly with a string of curses in a language no one on the street would understand. A childhood at sea had to have some advantages. He snapped his hand in the air to catch the attention of a nearby cab. Marylebone wasn't far if the weather was fine, but damned if he was going to ruin his clothes to haul Harry back in the rain. Besides, it would be easier to lecture him if they were trapped together, sitting down.

"The White Rose," Drake barked to the driver before he remembered his manners. "If you please."

"Sure it'll please you more than me, guv."

The man's jest was muffled as Drake closed the door. He dropped into the seat and let his head fall back to stare at the ceiling as he tried to remember whom he'd met at The Rose when he'd called to tease them with a taste of Amelia's whiskey.

It wasn't Tommy. He'd remember that name—there had been a Tommy that passed through Highcliffe once.

Hugh. That was it. Though he'd looked more like a boxer than a bartender.

And one of the women in the lounge, with her head bent over a book, had looked very much like a grownup version of Jocelyn Kirk, or what he imagined she would look like if she was in a dress with her hair in something other than a braid.

It couldn't have been Jocelyn. Malcolm Kirk would never leave the temptation of the sea, and Jocelyn would never leave her father in Highcliffe alone.

A cold that had nothing to do with the weather ran down Drake's spine. He didn't want to think of Mal in London.

The prostitute's posture had caught Drake's attention. That and the fact that she was dressed in an understated elegance that only the wealthy could afford.

Outside the window, the houses grew larger, the streets wider. The air smelled less of mud and more like wet grass. Drake rapped the end of his umbrella on the carriage roof. "Here's fine." A man walking garnered less attention. He paid the driver well. "Wait for me, and I'll double this. It shouldn't be more than ten minutes."

"If you say so." The cabbie laughed as he pocketed the money. "I'll give you thirty, just in case."

The rain had slowed to a drizzle, but Drake opened the umbrella anyway. It blocked the crisp, damp wind and hid him from curious stares as he strode down the street, intent on his mission.

The brothel was set back from the street behind a fence

draped with white roses, the last of their blooms heavy from the rain. He paused at the gate long enough to smile at the spot where he'd put Amelia's new husband, Richard Ferrand, on his backside. He'd deserved it for breaking the girl's heart.

The still-fresh suspicion that it *was* Jocelyn in The Rose may have given some extra strength to his right hook. He'd spent too many years protecting her to stifle the impulse.

It was ludicrous to consider. Jocelyn would never sell herself. She'd given Davy a black eye for stealing a kiss. Granted, they'd been twelve, and Davy had just finished mucking stables, but she had always worn her self-respect like a fur-lined cloak. She'd carried herself like the richest woman in Dorset whether she was at the market or unloading a skiff in the middle of the night.

The path to the door was almost dry thanks to the large trees overhead. Drake closed the umbrella as he reached the bottom step.

"Fletcher, isn't it? The whiskey merchant?" The doorman was dressed in a suit that would have served him well in any gentlemen's club, but it was cut loose enough that he could swing a punch if necessary.

"Among other things," Drake said as he offered his hand. "Hello, Hugh. I'm looking for a boy. He's—"

The man's affable expression faded as he dropped his hand. "We don't cater to that sort of thing here."

Music drifted from another room. Not the bawdy songs Drake had expected. This sounded very much like a house party. "Nor do I. He's my ward, and I believe he's a schoolmate of Alfie's."

"Harry?" Hugh motioned him in. "He and Alfie are peeling potatoes to keep their hands busy. Follow me."

Drake was halfway to the kitchen when he spied the woman at the door, watching the crowd. Same regal posture and elegant clothing, same dark hair.

"Madam White?" Hugh said. "Harry's guardian is here to fetch him."

"Thank goodness," she said. "The boy's almost finished with the potatoes. I'm not sure how else to keep him occupied." She turned.

Madam White had a scar on her chin, not more than a nick, really. She'd gotten it when they'd been unloading a skiff. He'd been rushing to beat the tide, and she'd dodged the wrong way.

Drake's brain stuttered as his memories of the girl he'd known and the woman in front of him collided. Questions ricocheted until the burning in his lungs reminded him to breathe.

"Jocelyn?"

FOR A MOMENT, just a blink of an eye, Jocelyn Kirk considered reaching into her boot, getting the knife she kept there, and running Drake Fletcher through. Which was silly. Her knife wouldn't go through a full-grown man.

But it could still do lethal damage.

"Hello, Fletcher." She made herself smile. Madam White always smiled when customers were on the premises. "It's been years."

She'd have recognized him anywhere, even though he'd matured from a too-skinny lad to a broad-shouldered man. There was his hair, of course—dark as the bay on a moonless night. But Drake had always had a sharpness in his gaze, like he was hungry for whatever he could find, and a set to his jaw that indicated he'd do whatever he could to get it. Had he sent his light-fingered ward here on purpose?

A smile lifted one corner of Drake's mouth as he reached for her.

Joss stepped back. "You've come for Harry?"

His face reshaped in the blink of an eye, polite blankness covering any recognition. His only tell was the slight gathering of his brows over the bridge of his nose. He'd finally grown into it.

"Yes, of course," he said. "I hope he hasn't caused too much trouble."

"We managed it." She'd managed a lot of things without his help.

Hugh was already leading Harry from the kitchen. The doorman's meaty grip made the boy look smaller and less of a nuisance.

Any thought that Drake was running his own crew in London vanished with his heavy sigh. "Who'd he touch?"

"A lawyer who's one of my best clients." Terrence Macklin treated the women with respect, and he tipped well. He'd been so busy laughing with Edith that he hadn't noticed his wallet was missing until Joss returned it. "I barely caught him before he got to a viscount."

Philip Melton, Viscount Raines, was another frequent visitor. He wasn't as pleasant or as generous as Macklin, and Joss normally wouldn't have minded him losing a few bob. However, one bad report from him could damage The Rose's reputation and send prying eyes her way. The Rose had survived for years because it kept a low profile.

Besides that, she had other plans for the young, talkative viscount.

"What do I owe you?" Drake asked as he reached into his pocket.

She'd be damned if she took his money. "He did his penance in the kitchen, and he worked hard enough to earn his dinner." Elsa, her cook, would have made sure of it.

Drake knelt in front of the boy. "You've had the house in an uproar, lad."

"Sorry about that, Drake." Harry's jaunty posture said he was anything but sorry.

Joss hid her smile behind her fan, but the imp looked right at her and winked.

"Alfie said his house was full of toffs and pretty ladies, and I wanted to see for myself."

"Bollocks," Drake muttered as he put his hands on the boy's shoulders. "You were after treasure."

Rather than hugging the child, Drake ran his palms along Harry's shoulders, back, and arms before sliding them along both legs to his boots. He met the boy's gaze as he rucked up one trouser leg and reached into his boot. Out came one of Joss's silver spoons. "Apologize to the…to Madam White."

Joss didn't know which was more irritating, that he didn't consider her a lady, or that his opinion stung. It shouldn't matter. She'd given up on being a lady long before she knocked on The Rose's kitchen door. Joss took the spoon from him, careful to keep her fingers on the bowl.

"Sorry, ma'am." Harry's wide eyes and cheeky grin reminded Joss more of a twenty-year-old flirt than a nine-year-old boy. "It's just that it was so pretty it reminded me of you, and I wanted a souvenir to—"

She burst into laughter. "Go on with you, Harry."

Even Drake was chuckling as he stood. "Quite right, y' blackguard." He nodded to Hugh before looking to her. "I appreciate your not turning him over to the magistrate."

She wouldn't have had to look farther than her parlor to do it, but there was no way she was sending a child to jail. It was bad enough that she already knew one person in prison. "You're welcome." Joss took pleasure in saying it, especially since he hadn't actually thanked her. She looked down at Harry. "I shall keep a closer eye on you when you visit next." She took pleasure in that too. The dread would no doubt plague Drake for weeks.

"I'm glad you'll let me come back," Harry said. "I didn't make it to the attic, and Alfie says there's a lady up there behind a trunk."

Joss resisted the urge to look toward the parlor. All her ladies had been downstairs from the ring of the gong—unless they'd had a customer, of course. No one had left the parlor alone. "A dressmaker's dummy, I'm sure."

"But he says—"

"Harry, do not discuss the women in this house with Madam White—or with anyone for that matter." Drake pushed him toward the door.

Joss recognized that tilt to his chin, the one that everyone in London wore in the daylight, but only ladies wore at night. The one that said her business wasn't good enough, wasn't honest enough.

They didn't know the half of it.

"Good evening, Mr. Fletcher." Just to irritate him, she winked at his ward. "See you soon, Harry."

The boy swept his cap from his head with a flourish worthy of the stage. Drake put a hand on the latch and looked over his shoulder. His hat stayed square on his head. "Good evening, Jocelyn."

The door closed, and Joss counted to five before glancing through the sidelight. Drake and Harry had reached the end of the walk and turned right. They were nothing but silhouettes in three long strides.

She placed the spoon on the bar. Reaching under the oaken worktop, worn satin smooth from years of use and revarnishing, she closed her fingers around the two-shot pistol she kept out of sight. "Fetch me a lantern, Tommy."

The young man, as fair as his brother Alfie was dark, did it without question. "About Alfie. I'm sorry—"

"This is his home, Tommy. He can have friends visit."

"But that boy and his father—"

Drake Fletcher wasn't anyone's father. The man wasn't capable of caring about anything past his own rather large nose.

"We cannot control what people outside this house think of us." Joss wrapped her fingers around the lantern's wire handle. "I'll be back in a moment."

"But I think Alfie—"

She did not have time for parenting advice. "Tommy, if you believe Alfie and Harry shouldn't be mates, then that's up to you."

Her sharp tone gave her pause. Since the moment the boys had arrived at The Rose, Tommy had been focused on his younger brother's future. "Alfie's a good lad. Maybe he'll have an influence on Harry." She grinned at her bartender's doubtful gaze. "Maybe not. But boys—children—need friends, and if they're here, you can limit the scrapes they get into."

Joss paused again as she passed the parlor. James Mills, her usher and backup doorman, saw her and came to the door. Much like Hugh, James looked every inch a boxer even in a tailcoat and starched cravat. Though he'd have been a middleweight compared to Hugh's bruiser class.

"Is everything going well?" she whispered.

"Poppy just went upstairs."

"Alone?" Joss asked as she scanned the room. All the other ladies were present.

"Mr. Macklin was with her." James slid his finger under his neckcloth. "A woman must've designed cravats."

"Just as a man designed the corset," she jested.

She left the parlor for the stairs, tucked against the wall opposite the bar and wide enough for two people if they held to each other—which was the idea. The second floor, with its lilac-painted walls and violet draperies, housed the ladies' rooms. Hugh had taken a post at a discreet distance from Poppy's room, ready to step in should Mr. Macklin get carried away. The only danger was that the man would overstay his time. Poppy was his favorite.

Joss rounded the stairs, headed for the third floor, and came face to face with two giggling maids, Clara and Lucy. Giggling on this floor was not allowed. If rooms were too quiet, which at times they were, everything became an irritant. Embarrassed clients never returned.

"If you two have nothing better to occupy your time, you can go help Elsa in the kitchen," she whispered to the girls. "Or you can see to the laundry." There were always sheets to iron and fold.

"Yes, Madam White." Both girls scurried away, their steps whispering against the thickly carpeted stairs.

Joss continued her climb to the third floor, where the maids slept. Her room was at the back of the house on this floor, giving her a view of the garden.

She paused at the stairs to the attic. Narrower, steeper. The door loomed down at her. Joss steadied her breath, blaming the shake on climbing in a heavy silk dress. If *ton* women ever climbed to their attics in cotton, fashion would change forever.

But then, she'd wager *ton* women never went into their attics.

Joss considered going for Hugh and making him do it. "Don't be daft, girl. He has a job to do, and this is just a room." Besides, Hugh wouldn't be quiet about anything he found up there. It wasn't his job to be quiet.

And he definitely wouldn't find a dressmaker's dummy. Joss had removed it from the house months ago after one too many frights.

She struck a match and lit the lantern. Lifting her skirts with one hand, she hoisted the lantern with the other. It warmed her knuckles and gave her a small amount of courage.

The door whispered open on hinges that never squeaked.

"It's just a room," Joss whispered. "Just a room."

In the corner, a ghostly presence turned. Tall, curvy, a pale face made whiter by the moonlight that leached the color from her red hair. "Sara, is that you? Is it clear to move about now?"

Joss's breath came out in a *whoosh*. She hoisted the lantern higher and walked into the room, her spine straight. The girl in the corner wasn't one of hers, but the dishes stacked on an abandoned tea cart implied she'd been eating like one. Her dove-gray dress was plain but clean. Her bag was in the opposite corner, next to a pallet made from spring bedding.

The stranger's eyes went wide. "*Shite.*"

Who the hell hid in a brothel? "*Shite*, indeed."

CHAPTER TWO

T HEY HAD A rule at The Rose. Clients didn't stay overnight.
The younger men thought it was a ploy for more visits, and the older men thought it was a quaint tradition. The wives that knew of them appreciated the fact that the girls made husbands go home—though they'd never say it aloud.

They were all wrong.

Joss sat at the desk in her room, quill in hand as Imogen Lloyd took the chair opposite. "What of Melton?"

"The viscount believes his father will sell his country estate to finance his bid for lord high treasurer. They don't have the funds available otherwise." The slip of a girl drew a deep breath. "The viscount is hoping to skim from the sale for the purchase of a racing team."

"Like father, like son," Joss muttered as she finished the sentence with a flourish. She dropped the quill into the inkpot and focused on other things. "He didn't recognize you, did he?"

"He is *too wily to be trapped in ballrooms with marriage-minded chits.*" Imogen pulled her voice into comical impersonation. "So no, he didn't think twice about me. I might as well have been a pillow on the bed."

Which saddened Joss more than she was willing to state. Imogen, who had been driven from the *ton* and her narrow-minded family, deserved more than a life at The Rose. Most of the women who passed through these doors did. They deserved to have someone think only of them.

However, this room was not a place for commiseration.

"He did think it odd that he couldn't have Margot." Imogen walked to the door and stopped. "And she's been glaring daggers since he left."

Margot had stared daggers at Joss earlier as she'd put her coins on the desk. "Let me know if she causes you a problem," Joss said.

Once Imogen was gone, Joss sealed the note she'd just written and scrawled a name across the front. Alfie could deliver it tomorrow.

A brisk knock was the only warning she received before Eleanor Mills, her maid, bustled into the room. "Do you want to see Sara and the attic girl before you dress for bed or after?"

"After, I think. Let them stew a bit more." Jocelyn stood and held out her arms. "I could do this myself so you could get some rest. It's late."

"Madam Madeline would have my ears," Eleanor said as she went to work unfastening the bodice. "Before she left, she made me promise to look out for you."

Eleanor had been looking out for Joss since she'd arrived. The skirt fell to the floor, and she felt a stone lighter. "She likely made you promise that I keep to tradition and remain as mysterious and unreachable as she did."

The words still made her smile. Her predecessor had emigrated from France before the war. She'd carried the French attitude of seduction with her across the Channel.

Eleanor attacked the corset with ruthless efficiency. There was nothing seductive about being undressed by your maid.

The nightdress went over Joss's head, its silk whispering over her skin like warm seawater. The matching robe, made of French lace, made a pretty picture but did little to warm her.

Joss sat at the dressing table and waited for Eleanor to unpin her hair. "Could you please ask Clara to add coal to the stove before she goes to bed?"

Eleanor nodded. "She needs to work on her posture, by the way. And the giggling."

"I know. We should have hired someone other than her sister when that position came open. She and Lucy are a poor combination." Joss looked in the mirror, watching Eleanor work. "James is doing well in his new position."

Predictably, Eleanor beamed. "He's so proud of that evening suit, I fear he'll sleep in it."

"And how is Beatrice?"

"She's far too interested in the parlor and what goes on upstairs." Eleanor sighed. "The more I try to keep her out, the more she tries to sneak in. It was fine for James to be curious; boys are supposed to be. But girls…here…"

Girls were allowed to be curious, too. Joss had grown up listening to the boys in the house talk about the village girls they fancied, but she'd still been shocked by the conversations between the women here. For the first month of her employment, she'd fled every time a customer smiled at her.

Until Madeline had taken her to Paris.

I'm only your bookkeeper.

You are a woman, *Jocelyn. And you are a woman of The Rose, whether you are entertaining or working with the numbers. You should know how to flirt, at the very least. But then, flirting will inevitably lead to other things.*

Instead of satisfying her curiosity, the trip had sparked it, and Madeline had been a thorough teacher. After a month, Jocelyn no longer blushed when a man did anything.

Which was why she'd never suggest taking Bea to Paris—even though it might do the girl some good.

Joss took in her surroundings, still gobsmacked that this was her life. That she had a warm room full of fine furniture and a bed that would fit three people—four if they were adventurous—a closet full of silks that slipped like dry sand through her fingers, and wools that warmed her even on the coldest days. She had a maid, a doorman, a coach, and food on the table or in the larder whenever she was hungry.

She also had a job to do. "We'll do what we can to keep Bea out of trouble. You'd best show Sara and her friend in."

Joss squared her shoulders and lifted her chin in a haughty gaze, doing the best imitation of a madam she could manage, before the girls entered the room.

One of her newest girls, Sara Pearson had arrived at the door with a carpetbag and a black eye. She had the voice of an angel and the personality to match. God only knew how she ended up as a doxy, and it wasn't Joss's place to ask.

It was, however, her place to frighten Sara and her most recent stray into contrition.

Outside the attic, the fugitive was a lovely, tall redhead with a tasteful hairstyle and a creamy complexion. But underneath the poised veneer, her deep brown eyes flitted to every corner of the room. She was so pale even her lips were blanched, and she worried a handkerchief between nails she'd chewed to nubs.

"Let's begin with introductions. I believe you know me," Joss said.

"I'm Connie Hall."

"Connie couldn't stay in her last place," Sara said. "She needed—"

"This is not a stray kitten," Joss snapped. The last of *those* Sara had brought home now lived in the coach house, warm in a haystack and fat from mice. "You cannot bring *people* home with you, Sara."

"But—"

"What in the bloody hell did you think you were doing?" Joss continued. "We promise our gentlemen safety and discretion. You know that. I made it perfectly clear when you arrived that there were rules—"

"Pardon me, Madam White." Connie's voice shook, but she cleared her throat and kept going. "I've worked at the Gold Peacock from the time I was old enough to know what I was doing. It was the best place in town until The Rose opened."

There was a note of pride in the young woman's voice, which Joss understood. The Rose's reputation was why Joss had chosen it, and her ladies lorded their address over their friends. "Then you understand why I'm angry."

"I do, madam, but please don't blame Sara. She was only trying to help."

For her part, Sara was already in tears.

"She can't go back to The Peacock, madam. They'll kill her if she does."

That seemed overly dramatic, but Sara's tears were making Connie cry—though much quieter. Joss would never get answers at this rate.

"Sara, go to your room, please."

The girl only sobbed harder.

"It will be fine." Joss went to the sofa and coaxed Sara to stand and walk. "Dry your eyes and don't talk to anyone about this." She reinforced the command with a stony stare. So far, no one knew about Connie's presence other than Hugh and Eleanor. "I mean it, Sara. No one. We'll work this out."

Once Sara was safely under Hugh's watch, Joss returned to her chair across from Connie and poured two cups of tea. "Tell me everything."

"Are you familiar with Viscount Stratford?" Connie asked in a whisper, as though the man in question was in the room with them.

Her caution was warranted. Lord Alistair Gregory, Viscount Stratford, was rumored to be in consideration for the post of master of the ceremonies. He'd spent his life in the orbit of the royal household, currying favors and collecting them in turn.

But he had a nasty reputation with women, at least the women Joss knew.

"I am. He's a customer of yours?" Joss asked. If he was, it was a black mark against Connie. Stratford could bring powerful friends and worthwhile capital to The Rose, but money wasn't everything. Joss finally had enough of it to be picky about where it came from.

"No, he favored my friend Violet. A pretty girl with dark hair and the sweetest smile. A lot like Sara, she was."

The past tense raised gooseflesh on Joss's neck. *Was* meant one of two things. Violet was no longer a lot like Sara, or Violet was no longer. "Tell me more."

"Violet was a delicate girl. She reminded us all of the fairies we read about in stories." Connie sipped her tea, and when she raised her eyes, her stare was sad. "She saw the good in everyone, and she was delighted when the viscount took a fancy to her."

No prostitute held out hopes for a wedding. "Surely she didn't think—"

"Nothing like that." Connie placed her cup in its saucer like a highborn lady. "She never harbored fantasies of being a viscountess. "He gave fine gifts and paid extra so Madam Price would keep her out of the parlor. Vi always hated that part. Said she couldn't wait for the day that she walked into the room and no one noticed her." The woman looked Joss in the eye. "But we all dread that at some level, I think."

There were old madams, but never old tarts—at least not in houses with posh clients. Women who didn't have coins saved or a place to go were forgotten quickly. And very few families opened the doors to women who left this life. "Go on."

"After a while, we began to wonder if the sounds from her room were all from pleasure. We asked, I swear we did, but Violet said she liked it, and there were never any bruises or marks we could see." Connie pleated her skirt between her fingers until it resembled a closed fan. "Some girls do like it rough. Though I never suspected Vi would be one of them." She grew quiet for a moment. "I should have known better."

The young woman looked everywhere in the room other than at Joss. It would have been easy to assume she was guilty of something. Joss knew better. Terror took all sorts of forms. She put a hand over Connie's fingers, stilling them. "You're safe here,

Connie."

It was a rash promise, given that the girl hadn't finished her tale and there was no indication how involved she'd been. Still, it helped calm her. She drew a deep breath, looked Joss in the eye, and nodded.

"It was during last year's Season. A session of Lords went late into the night, and Vi was bored upstairs. She came down to the kitchen for something and walked back through the parlor—just to see the party. She wasn't there to work. We were entertaining a group of lads from Cambridge—handsome, strapping young things they were. Most were so clean they squeaked when you touched them, and *muscles*. I think they were on the rowing team, though maybe it was football. Mine was—"

"Connie." Joss understood the need to focus on happier things, but her nerves were almost as frayed as Connie's. She needed to hear the end of this story.

The young woman took a sip of tea. "One said hello to Vi. We couldn't be rude to the gentlemen, not ever. She had to speak to him. And he was a gentleman, because when she said she couldn't sit with him, he kissed her hand and bade her goodnight. I think they'd been drinking quite a bit. They were in fine spirits." She cleared her throat. "Viscount Stratford walked in just then."

Connie got to her feet, still grasping the teacup, and paced the back of the room, never nearing the windows. "He was all velvety smooth as he said hello and offered Violet his arm. He was even smiling. Vi fussed over him as she always did, but there was something in her eyes—like when you cross a rabbit at dusk, and they go real still until you pass.

"We all knew, and we kept an ear tuned for danger. I even asked Madam Price to go check on her, at least up to the floor, but she wouldn't. She wouldn't even send an usher up to sit."

The viscount likely paid extra for privacy as well. Many clients asked Joss to do the same, but Madam White had always chosen to protect her girls rather than pad her purse.

"It was quiet up there; I swear it was. We made sure we were upstairs as often as possible, and we made a lot of noise so she'd know we were there—so he'd know, too. But there wasn't a sound. It wasn't until closing that Madam Price knocked on the door. Even a viscount couldn't stay overnight." Tears now streamed down Connie's face. "Vi was naked on top of the coverlet—he hadn't even covered her. And her eyes were all glassy, staring at us like she was begging for help."

Joss went to the girl, removed the teacup from her shaking fingers, and took her hands. A dead girl in The Peacock would have made the news. The scandal would have closed the house. None of that had happened. Despite her sympathy, her heart pounded. "What happened then?"

"Madam Price panicked. She ordered the boys to take Violet to the river and throw her in. Wouldn't even let us dress her in anything but a shift." Connie was sobbing now. "All the while, her head lolled like a broken toy."

That story had made the headlines. A young woman's body had been pulled from the Thames a few weeks earlier. The story had been all the more tragic due to her beauty. Speculation ran rampant that she was a ruined miss who had been jilted by an adventurer.

"Does anyone else know the truth, other than you girls?"

Connie shook her head. "I went to the magistrate, and he said he'd make things right. But I knew he'd believe a lying *toff* over an honest whore. He must've spoken with Stratford, though, because he showed up at The Peacock in a strop, demanding all of Vi's things. Madam Price didn't even bat an eye. His man took everything but the mattresses and the carpet."

Joss led the young lady back to the sofa and poured her another cup of tea, though it was likely lukewarm by now. It gave her time to think. Any report of this wouldn't bear weight unless there was solid proof, other than the word of women the magistrate pretended didn't exist. "They left nothing?"

Connie grimaced over her cup of cold tea before setting it aside. "They took all her jewelry, even the things he hadn't bought her. She had one necklace, an opal cameo on a string of pearls, which was right pretty. She said her mother gave it to her for her last birthday at home. They even took her diary."

A girl who owned pearls and knew how to write was no ordinary prostitute. "You saw these things?"

Connie nodded. "That night. They were on her dressing table. I remember thinking I should take the necklace—she'd always promised it to me. It wouldn't have been stealing."

It was Joss's turn to pace the room. Stratford had items that would tie him to the murdered girl, who was more than just a hapless urchin. She could feel it. The only eager witness was here in her house. If she could get the items *and* the witness, she'd have leverage to move the world.

Or at least the prison gates.

Would you really bargain with one young woman's life and another's reputation?

Why not? Society matrons did it all the time, with much more malice for far more trivial goals.

"You can stay while we sort this out, but it will have to be the attic. I don't want the other girls asking questions." Joss walked to the door. "And after you've rested, you can tell me everything you know about the viscount."

Once she was alone, Joss went to her desk, the silk brushing her thighs with each step. She tore the letter open and plucked another piece of soft, thick paper from her drawer. The quill shook as she held it upright.

"Calm down, you ninny," she whispered. "It'll do no good to get your hopes up again."

She drew a deep breath, then another, all the way to her toes and out. It took her anxiety and frustration with it. She let her hope go, too. This was just another transaction. It was like any other letter. She sent half a dozen of them a day.

Reggie, darling. I am free tomorrow evening and hope you can visit. I've missed you.

As the bold ink strokes dried, she addressed the envelope to

Sir Reginald Spencer, care of Brooks's. No letters ever went to his Mayfair home. Nosy servants and an insecure wife were a bad combination. And the staff in his palace office were just as nosy.

Joss folded the note in half, making its crease sharp enough to slice flesh, and slid it into the envelope. She finished the package with her personal seal, a rose in white wax.

Alfie responded to the bell. "Missus." He yanked his hat from his head as an afterthought. "I'm awful sorry about Harry and him repeatin'—"

"You have nothing for which to apologize." Joss placed a steady hand on his shoulder. "I should thank you for noticing the newcomer. Just…next time, tell me first. Yes?" She smiled when he nodded. "Good lad. Now, in the morning, on your way to school, I want you to drop this at Brooks's. Understood?"

Alfie took it with a wordless nod.

Once she was alone, Joss exchanged the useless lace robe for the simple flannel dressing gown she'd carried from Highcliffe. She'd rolled the plum-colored fabric tight and shoved it into her boot so her father wouldn't tease her about taking on airs or berate her for choosing it over other necessities.

She returned to her dressing table and cleaned her face. A version of the girl she had been re-emerged as she plaited her dark hair. The strands near her face slipped free and hung limply to her too-sharp chin. Freckles, caused by days in the sun, dusted her nose.

She was too plain for this grand room full of fine things. And, if her plan worked, she'd soon get reacquainted with sand and wind. There'd be only her to fetch tea and plan dinner.

She'd miss the luxuries, but it would be enough to know she'd kept her promises and lived up to her responsibilities. Family was rare. It was a treasure to be saved above anything else.

That would be enough.

CHAPTER THREE

Y EARS AGO, DRAKE had lived in a house full of boys.

He'd forgotten how loud they could be. Even when they walked at a regular pace, they were loud. When they all ran together, it was deafening.

But if he bellowed at them for running down the stairs—again—the neighbors' windows would shake.

So Drake waited until they were all in the dining room, and their mouths were full, before he joined them. "Good morning, boys."

Mumbled good mornings came from two of them.

"Good morning," came Ed's greeting a beat later as he returned his napkin to his lap. The seventeen-year-old had been Drake's first rescue. Five years earlier, he'd followed a crowd to a grungy alley, only to find Ed conning the men out of every bob he could wrangle.

The boy was smart, quick, and eager to prove himself now that he had the chance. His easy acclimation to going straight had encouraged Drake and Gavin to find other willing candidates.

Results had been mixed so far.

Drake looked at the empty chair. "Where's Nicky?"

"He's still sick after stuffing all Trudy's cookies down his gullet," Harry grumbled.

Nicky Hughes and Harry Barker had arrived as a pair. They

were usually thick as thieves and the first to stand up for each other. Harry's bad-tempered assessment of his friend meant one thing.

"Are you telling me you ran away to a brothel because of *cookies?*" Drake put his unread paper next to his plate.

"Course not," Harry said. "I ain't daft. And I didn't run away. Alfie said the crowd didn't pick up at his house until after dark, so there wasn't any point goin' until then."

Drake rubbed a finger against his temple. A visit with the schoolmaster was in order, or perhaps he should hire a tutor. He couldn't tell if Harry didn't have the aptitude for grammar, lacked the discipline to use it, or just did it to be funny. "So you climbed from a third-floor window to hare across London in the dark, to go to a brothel? And while you were there, you thought you'd see what you could steal?"

Harry tilted his head while he considered the summary. "Sounds about right."

Drake bit his cheek to keep from laughing with the others at the table.

"I don't see why you're worried. We've all been on the street longer than we've been in a house, except maybe for Ed. We know how to take care of ourselves," Frank said.

Frank Harvey had been in the house less than a year. He had a chip on his shoulder the size of Gibraltar, and he was a challenge even on good days. This morning, he was cleaning his nails with the knife he tended to tuck in his sleeve.

"I worry because I promised you I would." Drake lifted the knife from the boy's fingers. "You've been told to rid yourself of this weapon and that habit. And put all the legs of your chair on the floor."

"All I'm saying is that Harry wouldn't have climbed out the window if Gavin didn't guard the door like a jailer," Frank said.

Drake winced at the use of *Gavin* and *jailer* in a sentence. He was glad the man wasn't in the room to hear it. "Doors are locked to keep people out." Drake looked to each boy as he said it, hoping each of them would learn to choose safety.

"Who broke a chair?" Gav yelled from the kitchen. "Dammit, you louts, we just uncrated these and… Wait, this isn't our chair." He carried the item in question to the door, pieces in both hands. "Who brought this in here?"

There was only one boy in the house who loved to rummage, and he wasn't at the table. They all looked to Harry, the next best source for the story.

"Nicky saw it on our way home yesterday and said he could fix it with a few nails and a good cleaning."

Drake's stomach sank. Their school was less than two blocks away. "Was it on this street?"

"Yes, sir. About two houses down. It made it easy to carry. Something that big would have been pain in the—"

"We get the picture, Harry. Thank you." Drake placed his napkin beside his fork. "Apparently we need to review and amend the rules of our agreement."

He ticked them off on his fingers as he talked.

"No leaving without telling someone. No leaving after dark alone. No skipping school or not applying yourself to lessons. No running in the house, no yelling from floor to floor, no slamming the doors. No escaping from windows, no stealing for fun, no knife play in the garden, and no rummaging through the neighbors' castoffs. In exchange for that, Gavin and I make sure you have everything you need, and we keep you safe. That means locking the doors and making sure you follow the rules."

Everyone but Ed rolled their eyes, and Drake found himself wishing the boy would. Just once.

"I know this is not the same as living on your own, but have a little pity on Gavin. He can't chase after all of you while I'm gone."

"Why does he have to chase us at all?" Frank asked.

"We've talked about this," Drake said. "If the patrols look at one of us, they look at all of us. If they come in this house, they don't just come for your things. They come for everything. If we act like hooligans, the neighbors talk to the schoolmaster, who talks to the vicar, who talks to his parishioners, and then I don't have any clients, we don't have any money, and we are *all* on the street."

Again.

"Besides that, society has rules. Even if it's not the *ton*. You have to learn the rules."

You have to learn the rules before you can break them without getting caught.

The hallway clock chimed half past the hour.

"Get your books and head for school," Gavin ordered them.

Ed led the way, checking his reflection before he opened the door. Harry stopped long enough to shove two slices of bacon between a scone. Frank slouched out last, his books and slate slung over his shoulder.

The house creaked without them in it. Likely from relief, but maybe a little regret was mixed in.

"How is Nicky?" Drake asked.

"He has a sour stomach." Gav sighed. "Maybe a night of miserable puking will finally teach him a lesson."

It wouldn't. Nicky had spent too much of his life hungry and scrounging for whatever he could find. "Should we send for a doctor?"

Gav shook his head. "He'll be fine in about an hour. I'll put him to work tearing out the trellis along the back of the house."

The vine climbing the house was covered in bright blue flowers. It was one of the reasons Drake had chosen the house. "Just have him take the top part down so Harry can't shimmy—climb—down it. Perhaps double the width of the trellis so that it spans the second floor."

"I'll take care of it." Gavin brought his plate and a cup of coffee to the table. "Frank is going to be a challenge for a while yet. I honestly don't know what you see in that boy."

Drake had asked that same question more than once in the past year. The only answer he could find was that he saw pieces of himself at that age. "He has potential if he's willing to learn."

"If you say so." Gavin washed his toast down with a gulp of coffee. "I'll get Harry to clean your boots when he gets home."

"Suitable punishment."

Drake took a moment to look around the room. When he'd left for Amelia's wedding, the house was full of crates and random furniture. Now everything was in its place so that it looked like a home. But it all still smelled new. Even the napkin he'd used for breakfast smelled of straw from the shipping box.

For so many years, that had been the smell of success.

"Joss is in London," he said.

"*Our* Joss?" Gavin asked. "Are you sure? Where is she?"

"Yes, I'm sure. We spoke last night." And it was clear she didn't consider herself *their* anything. She'd looked ready to kill him.

The other man's eyes went wide. "She's not at The Rose. She wouldn't be."

"She runs it," Drake said. "The doorman kept calling her Madam White. I thought I saw her a month ago, but…" Did she really prefer that life over coming to friends for help?

"Drake, Madam White has been in London for donkey's years. There is no way—"

"It is her, Gavin." Drake never expected the best lookout on the crew to grow into a woman that made it difficult to look away. "All grown up in a dress that cost as much as that damned racehorse the old man bought instead of coal."

"Well, if she's here, he's not far away." Gavin tapped the butt of his fork against his plate in a rhythm that matched the ticking clock. "What do you think they're up to?"

Drake had stayed awake far too late wondering the same thing then kicking himself for wondering. He was out of that life. He had built a new one, and if he was worried about her, it was because any scheme of her father's would likely end up a mess. They almost always did.

"I'm not sure I want to know, but we should probably be

prepared." He sighed. "She's seen me, so I can't follow her without getting caught." The girl had eyes in the back of her head. "But she doesn't know you're around. Do you have time?"

"I'll make time." Gavin stood and began cleaning the table. He hated to leave messes for Trudy and her girls.

Drake hated messes altogether. Especially ones he could see coming from across town.

THOUGH IT WAS early in the evening, the parlor was full of laughter and revelry. It always was when Parliament was in session.

"Madam White." Viscount Digby bowed over her hand as he returned from the bar. "I cannot adequately express how refreshing it is to be in a room full of beautiful women who have no notion of marrying."

"We are pleased you could join us tonight," Joss replied, keeping her smile in place. The handsome young man was an earl-in-training and the most eligible bachelor of the Season, small or otherwise, in London or elsewhere. He couldn't be blamed for wanting respite, just as he couldn't be blamed for his opinion. No one thought women in this life harbored hopes of families.

Joss had been of that opinion before she had arrived at the back door. She'd expected bawdiness and laziness, for half-dressed girls to spend the day waiting on leering men to arrive. She'd prepared herself for sadness and resignation.

How wrong she'd been.

The door opened, bringing the cool dampness with it. Rather than retreating to a spot nearer the fire, she turned to greet the new arrivals.

Drake was handing his hat and coat to James, who was serving as footman until the hour grew later—and the crowd rowdier. The young man did an excellent job handling the duty, even though the greatcoat was almost half his height.

Even if she hadn't known Drake's history, she would've guessed he'd spent part of his life on a crooked path. It was easy to see in the way that he scanned the room before focusing on her, in the way he stepped aside, avoiding the open door.

He took her hand, but not like the gentlemen who fawned over it and hoped for her attention. He shook it, his grip sure and firm. It impressed her for a moment, but then she remembered he, of all people, would know she wasn't delicate. It wasn't in him to pretend.

"Jocelyn." His gaze was as direct as his touch. "We need to talk."

The angle of his jaw was as irritating as it was appealing. Joss looked past him to the next arrival, Sir Reginald Spencer, whose determined gaze wasn't as attractive.

"You'll have to wait your turn, Mr. Fletcher. I have an appointment," she murmured.

The stubborn man kept hold of her. "You don't—"

Spencer wouldn't wait. As a chaplain in the royal household, he hated the connotations of meeting her here as much as she disliked him under her roof. Joss gritted her teeth and hoped onlookers mistook it for a smile. "Let go of me and wait in the parlor. Margot would be happy to entertain you."

"How long will you be?"

"Until I am bloody well finished." She pulled free of him and stepped toward Spencer, into the chill of the evening, and lifted her cheek for his kiss. "Reggie, darling. I'm so happy to see you."

His dry cheek brushed hers. "I've missed you too, dearest girl. Shall we go?"

She took the arm he offered and guided him to the stairs, ignoring the sharp gaze she could feel at her back. It went deeper with every step, but she stayed focused on the future. It would have been easier if Spencer was a suitable distraction.

He wasn't a talkative man, which was likely a benefit in his profession, but it was a shame, because he had a deep, rich voice that would lend itself to readings and recitals. The thought of him reading poetry made her chuckle as they reached the second floor.

"Madam?"

"Just a fleeting thought," Joss said as they began the climb to the third floor. It was easier to breathe now—easier to think as she squeezed his arm.

Everything about Sir Reginald Spencer was thin. His hair, which was so blond it was almost transparent, lifted in the faintest breeze. His eyebrows all but vanished against his pale skin, and his mustache reminded her of when Davy had thought he was growing one. He'd spent hours in front of the mottled, cloudy mirror the boys had hung in their bunk room. It barely reflected the light from the windows, but Davy had twisted every which way to catch the glimmer of hair under his nose.

Joss opened her door and led Spencer inside. The moment they were alone, they separated. She didn't need to touch him to deliver the information necessary for the advancement he craved.

"Philip Melton says his father is too broke to pay for his campaign to be lord high treasurer," Joss said. "He's been gambling again, apparently. They're selling the country house to pay for it." Maybe it was only one of their houses. It was hard to keep track.

"It's card night at the club, and the Earl of Wareham is a lousy player and easy to goad." Spencer sat in a chair at her breakfast table and extended his legs to keep his posture dignified in the short chair. "This had better be more intriguing than a peer with aspirations he can't afford. London is littered with them."

She took him a glass of whiskey, full enough to make him appreciative. "It has come to my attention that Viscount Stratford's favorite girl at The Peacock was found dead in her room."

"A dead whore is nothing—"

"He was the last to visit her." Joss was careful to keep her voice even. If Spencer guessed how important this was to her, he'd use it to his advantage.

Spencer paused with the whiskey halfway to his lips and reversed direction, placing it on the table without making a sound. "What proof do you have?"

"I've spoken to someone in the house." Better for him to think the spy was still there. Connie would have been missed already. Any hint that the witness was gone would make her a target. "I'd like to trade it for the release of a prisoner." Joss drew in a breath. Years of gathering tiny secrets had led to this moment. "Malcolm Kirk."

Spencer tilted his head to one side but righted it when his hair began to flop in the same direction. It was like watching a window shutter swing in the wind, but she didn't dare crack a smile.

"Why do you care about an old crook?"

That was all anyone ever saw when they looked at her father. Granted, he hadn't done much—anything, really—to dispel the notion. But he was her father, and he'd loved her the best he knew how. She couldn't visit that prison, watch him grow pale for want of sunlight and fresh air, and do nothing.

"He did my family a great service years ago." She drew in an even breath and kept her gaze on Spencer's as she sipped her whiskey, knowing the fumes would make her blink. "His daughter wrote asking for help, and I said I'd do my best."

"A smuggler in the hand is worth a peer in a bush, especially one with the money for a defense and the influence to ruin my life." Spencer ran his tongue over his lips.

"But surely a witness—"

"Madam, I didn't expect you to be so naïve. The word of a prostitute will never prevail over a peer. You'll have to bring me more proof, something that will lead to his conviction."

It was naïve, but it was also galling. If Stratford's victim had been the daughter of a peer, presented to the queen, and present at every ball during the Season, London would be in an uproar. But doxies went missing every day. Joss walked to the door. "We have nothing left to discuss, then."

"You can't possibly expect to leave after five minutes." Spencer's eyes went wide. "It would rouse suspicion."

Joss kept her hand on the latch. She knew from Hugh and James that Spencer obtained a certain amount of cachet from being the only man she brought upstairs. "Reggie, darling, the only suspicion it would raise is that you're a little too quick on the draw."

He stood and ambled toward her. "I could prove differently."

She evaded his grasp. "No."

He countered and closed his fingers around her wrist. His delicate appearance masked a strong grip, and she hadn't counted on his height giving him an advantage.

"My coin is just as good as any other man in London—better than most," he said, his voice slick, like algae in the shallows. "It could also inspire all sorts of favors."

Would it be so bad? One night and then she could fetch her father at the gate and be gone. She'd never have to paste on a smile for strangers or wonder if a brothel in Marylebone was any different than one in Whitechapel. She could get her father back to the coast, into a little house in a village on a cliff where he could see the sea but not get into it.

Spencer put a hand on her waist and lowered his head, and his gloating smile blocked the light. He was close enough that Joss saw his eyes bulge as she lodged her knee in his softest parts.

"We don't have that sort of relationship, Reggie. Business or otherwise." She moved away from him, not breathing easily until she reached the table he'd recently abandoned. "I'll get the information on Stratford the same way I've gotten everything else."

He straightened before tugging on his cravat. "What do you expect we do for the next thirty minutes?"

It would be much less than that. There was a difference between padding his ego and telling a tale. Joss kept a wary eye on him as she opened a drawer and retrieved a deck of cards. "Since you're missing the game at your club, this seems only fair."

Spencer eased himself into a chair. Joss took one opposite, careful to keep her legs out of his grasp. She shuffled and dealt a hand for whist.

"I hate it when you call me Reggie," he grumbled.

She looked over her cards and planned her first move. "It's all part of the game."

CHAPTER FOUR

FROM WHAT JOSS understood, Horsemonger Lane Jail was not the worst prison in London. It wasn't as dirty as Newgate, and it wasn't as harsh as Clerkenwell—but it wasn't King's Bench, with its merchants and gin shops, either.

Though Joss would prefer not to see her father with nothing to do and ready access to gin, it would be better than walking under the gallows every Saturday afternoon. As she waited outside the imposing gate, the wood carved to resemble impenetrable bars, a chill went down her spine.

It wasn't the idea of heaven looking through the nooses at her. She'd conquered that notion after her first year of visits. Someone was watching her.

Joss called on years of practice, keeping her posture straight and her shoulders square while she eased a pocket mirror from her reticule, using her fingers to block the weak sunshine as she angled it to get a glimpse over each shoulder. Her veil made it difficult to see faces, so she focused on shapes, what wasn't moving, first.

Over her right shoulder, a man stood in the narrow gap between two buildings. Straight and tall, not hiding in the least.

Never hide. It makes you easier to find, easier to remember.

Da was right. She'd have spotted her pursuer easier if he'd been slouched against a wall, out of line with everything else.

Now she could focus on him. Close-cropped hair, dark skin, a wide jaw that left his head almost a perfect rectangle, given the length of his chin.

Gavin Howard. The solid-faced boy with a laugh that made it impossible not to join him. He was hardworking and loyal to a fault. Or, perhaps better stated, to his own detriment. His arrest had hardened the boys overnight.

Joss was half turned, a smile on her face, when the hinges creaked behind her.

"Madam White?" The guard brought the moldering air of the prison with him.

Right. She wasn't here for that type of reunion.

A cart passed. Gavin vanished. He wasn't either.

Fletcher. If he'd found her, he'd probably found Gavin as well. Or Gavin had found him. There had been talk in the house that Gavin's devotion to Drake was why he had gone to prison.

"Madam White? Are you ready?"

Joss refocused on her responsibilities and faced the guard. "Good morning, Cecil." She smiled before lifting her rosewater-soaked handkerchief to her nose.

"Good morning, madam." The young man looked more suitable for university studies than minding criminals, which was likely why his colleagues kept him at the entry gate. "Warden Branford has asked to see you first. I'll walk you up."

He stayed at her elbow, holding each door like he was escorting her to a party rather than through a prison. "Thank you for your advice last week. The flowers did the trick. Jane forgave me. I've saved enough to take her to Gunter's on Monday afternoon."

"That's wonderful news." The smile on the young man's face, the innocence there, made Joss ache. "But it's not a trick. Cecil. It's a way to show Jane she's important to you."

It was a lesson she'd learned the hard way once she came to The Rose, where gentlemen never gave gifts for innocent reasons. She didn't want to teach Cecil to be one of them.

His cheeks flushed. "Of course. My mother would have my

bollocks for earbobs—" His face went bright red. "My apologies, madam."

Joss was glad the handkerchief that masked the smell of the prison also hid her wide smile. "You're forgiven, Cecil."

He opened the last door, and Charles Branford, the man in charge of the prisoners at Horsemonger Lane, stood. He wore a neat gray suit with an intricately knotted cravat. The silk fabric flowed around his gold stickpin like it was a rock in a tide pool.

"Madam White, it's a pleasure to see you again." He came out from around the desk and held her chair.

"Thank you, warden." Joss said it as though they didn't go through this ritual every week. As though they didn't wait for Cecil, or another fresh-faced guard, to close the door.

Once they were alone, he took the seat opposite her. "How are you faring, madam?"

She would never understand the need for small talk during extortion. Still, a game was a game. "I am well, thank you, Mr. Branford. And you?"

"Well, thank you. Better now, though I do wish you'd wear something other than black when you visit."

The glint in his eyes, the way they moved over her body, told her he'd prefer she be in nothing when she visited. After her first visit, she'd soaked for hours in as much scented water as her tub would hold, as hot as she could stand it, to rid herself of the feel of that leering stare. Shortly afterward, Madeline had taught her how to handle men like him. That, combined with the lessons she'd learned from her father, put iron in Joss's spine.

"I assume your family is as well. As a matter of fact, I've learned your daughter is recently engaged to Lord Preston's heir."

She'd learned the gossip from Margot, who had entertained that same heir last week. The young man was less than enthusiastic about his new bride, whose mother was the second daughter of a baron of an insignificant village near enough the Scottish border that most spoke with a brogue.

In front of her, the warden's smile froze. "Yes. We're very happy."

"And your son. He's serving as a page for the prime minister this term, isn't he? What a promising start for a young man."

"It is." Branford fidgeted in his chair.

"And your wife… A charity board appointment, I believe."

That tidbit was something she'd read in the paper this morning over tea.

"The Duchess of Waverly, yes. Maude is quite proud of the association."

From her seat across the desk, Joss took satisfaction in watching Branford pause as understanding dawned. His gaze flicked first one way, and then the other. Maude would be less proud if the *ton* learned her husband was taking bribes from the madam of the White Rose, where her future son-in-law spent the night in bed whining about having to marry her daughter.

Joss pulled a pouch heavy with coins from her reticule. The weight gave her pause. It wasn't a great deal of money when her father's health and comfort were at stake, but the total was mounting. If she couldn't free Da soon, Branford would be a wealthy man, and *she'd* be choosing between the life of a working girl or going to debtor's prison.

She dropped the pouch into Branford's hand and stood. "Until next month, then, warden."

"Until next month. I'll have a guard show you down. Someone a little more stalwart than Cecil."

The man who escorted her to the cells was a walking wall of muscle who hulked in front of her on their way to the last cell in the row. Branford claimed the location offered more protection, but Joss doubted that motive as she walked the gauntlet of prisoners pressed against the bars.

Some made lewd suggestions and others begged for help. Joss never looked right or left. Torn between cowering behind her guard, who might be as dangerous as the men behind bars, and running for her father's protection, she chose instead to grip her reticule in shaky hands and let the words bounce from her cloak and veil.

"Here now! Leave the lady be."

Joss remembered the times when her father's shouts had rattled the rafters and sent the boys scurrying for cover. This scolding accomplished nothing. If she hadn't been so near, she likely wouldn't have heard it at all. Worry quickened her pace.

Malcolm Kirk was waiting for her, arms wide, as the guard opened the door. She walked into his strong embrace. He smelled of tobacco and apples, his favorite fruit. His wool coat snagged her veil as they separated.

A traveling circus had come to Highcliffe once, and she and all the boys had sneaked into the tent one at a time. They'd let her go first so she could see more of the show. Well, second, because Drake had insisted on making sure the way was clear. All evening, she'd been fascinated by a particular lion. Dark-maned and muscular, he'd prowled his cage searching for a way out.

Her father had always reminded her of that lion.

Now, his great mane was thinner and silver white. He was lean and fit, but the bones of his face and fingers stood in stark relief under his skin. It would be the same under the coat.

"Take the chair, dear." He sat on the neatly made bed. "There may be lice in my sheets."

She lifted her veil to get a better look at him and the space. "Branford should—"

"No amount of money will keep pests from traveling, Joss. It's what they're born to do." He balanced one ankle on the opposite, bony knee. His pants were worn, but they weren't threadbare yet.

"Tell me what else you need." Jocelyn swept her cloak from her shoulders and draped it over the back of the chair.

"There isn't much to tell. My meals are improving, and I have less trouble from the guards." His gaze swept over her. "That blue suits you. It reminds me of the summer sea."

Which was why she'd worn it. "It's a lovely day out."

He squinted up at the window overhead. The sun cast feeble shadows of the bars across the floor, stretching toward Joss. She tucked her feet under the chair.

"It seems to be nice for November. It is November, isn't it?" He looked at her and smiled when she nodded. "Tell me of the world outside."

She related every entertaining story she could remember from the week before leaning in to whisper, "I believe I've found the way to garner your release. A scandal worthy of trading."

"That's my girl." He reached forward and squeezed her knee. "I knew you could do it."

It wasn't done yet, but Joss stopped short of warning him against high hopes. The approving light in his eyes was addictive.

The shouts in the hallway told her that the guard was returning. Her time was up. She lowered the veil over her face and swept her cloak over her shoulders. "I almost forgot. Drake Fletcher is in London."

"You're certain?"

She nodded. "He came to—"

Her father's grip on her shoulders was bruising, and her veil distorted his face into a snarl. "You stay away from that man. He is *nothing* but trouble for us."

The keys rattled in the door as Joss nodded. She pressed a kiss to her father's cheek. "I'll see you next week, Da." The harsh smell of the prison's washing powder burned her nose.

"Fletcher is no good, girl. Stay well clear of him."

It was likely an unnecessary warning. Drake hadn't even waited for her to return downstairs.

Joss nodded again before she left. The door clanged closed and the lock slammed home. The gauntlet was as bad leaving as it was arriving. Every brush of fabric on her skin had her imagining vermin crawling over her skin and into her hair. She pressed her handkerchief to her nose. God help the first man who brought her roses as a peace offering. She'd even be hard-pressed to leave the bushes in the garden after today.

She would do whatever it took to free her father before another payment was due. She wasn't paying another cent. She wouldn't subject herself to this any longer.

The guard escorted her to the gate and through it, and Joss dragged in a deep breath of air that was at least fresh, if not entirely clean. Tommy was waiting with the carriage, and Alfie already had the door open. As Joss climbed in, she caught a glimpse of Gavin ahead of them, climbing into a cab.

"Tommy. Follow that carriage."

THE FRONT DOOR closed with a *snick* that might have been mistaken for a tick of the clock if it hadn't been for the smell of the street that came in on the breeze. The carpets muffled Gavin's heavy steps. It had to be Gav. The boys were never that quiet, and thieves wouldn't come through the front door in broad daylight.

"I have your answers," he said from the door.

Drake set his ledgers aside and leaned back in his chair.

Gav took a seat nearer the fire. "I visited with my contact at Horsemonger Lane." He unwound his neckcloth as he spoke. Its cream color exactly matched the silken ivy splayed across his maroon waistcoat.

It said a lot about Gavin that he'd gone back to the jail that haunted him simply because he'd been asked. "Thank you for doing that."

The man shrugged it off, but he wouldn't meet Drake's eye. "He says Joss visits every week."

"He knows it to be her?" How could he recognize her in the veil unless she removed it once inside the gate? Perhaps the warden was a client. What better way than prison to hide an assignation?

"He knows it's a well-dressed, dark-eyed woman in a black

cloak and veil who carries herself like a duchess and visits the same prisoner every week." Gav raised an eyebrow. "Sound familiar?"

It did. Joss had used that disguise more than once.

No one looks at a widow, and the cloak covers my trousers.

His irritation doubled when Gavin's description conjured the image of her leading that balding fop upstairs the night before. "Whom does she see?"

Gavin considered him for a long moment. The silence allowed Drake to fill in all sorts of blanks. A husband, perhaps. Maybe a lover. Whoever it was, she clearly cared for the man. She sought him out in the foulest of places when she wouldn't even share a drink with Drake.

"Dammit, Gavin. Who?"

"Malcolm."

Malcolm Kirk was alive. Drake had assumed the old man to be dead because no living father would see his daughter walk into a brothel. Not a respectable father, in any case. Which explained a great deal. If Malcolm had fallen, he'd have taken everyone with him.

"Is anyone else there with him?" Drake recalled the faces and names of the boys he'd left behind. They'd be men now, hardened by a life in the shadows. If they were alive at all.

"They didn't exactly open the roll books for me," Gav scoffed. "And I didn't wish to see the old man. Not like that."

Drake didn't wish to see Malcolm at all, though he had the urge to wring the bastard's stiff neck.

He walked to the window and stared out onto the quiet London street. Even here, in his new home with quality carpets and a full pantry, with a fire in every room, he knew that the house across the way had a space under the stairs, perfect for stashing loot, and that the alley two doors down had a spot that would block the wind.

The police patrol walked by, glanced toward the window, and tipped his hat in greeting—just as the clock chimed two. He'd do it again at four. A crew could move a lot of freight in two hours.

Malcolm had taught him that.

"Don't go down there, Bat."

Drake had hoped Gavin had outgrown the need to use the ridiculous nickname. "You haven't called me that in years."

"Because you haven't had that look on your face in years, not unless you're scanning ledgers. And they can't come to any harm." Gavin handed him a tumbler half-full of whiskey, the liquid almost gold in the light. "If you go see Malcolm, you'll regret it."

Drake didn't think he'd regret seeing the old man's face when he learned what his daughter was doing—what she'd been forced to do to feed herself. "He should know she's—"

"What makes you think he doesn't?" Gav asked. "What makes you think they didn't cook up this scheme together?"

Because Joss would never have agreed to this, and Mal should have at least one limit. "In what world would the old man work this far inland on purpose?"

Always have a clear path to the sea.

"And in what world does sticking your toe back into that mess leave you anything but dirty?" Gav asked.

"Here now!" Trudy's good-natured scolding was all but buried under the tramp of heavy steps and laughing jibes. "You four..."

One of the boys landed against the stairwell wainscoting and gave a rowdy shout before another walloped the wall. The books shimmied on their shelves.

Drake walked to the door, intent on calling an end to the roughhousing before they ruined the plaster and brought the chandelier down on their heads. Laughter made him pause.

Ed and Frank were in a pile, grappling for an upper hand. Nicky and Harry danced away from the combatants' flailing feet, Nicky eating a scone and cheese as he did so. The scene reminded Drake of wrestling with Gavin and Davy on the beach, the sand silver-gray in the starlight.

"You take it back," Ed growled. "You shouldn't tell tales."

"Is it a tale, though?" Frank teased, his voice muffled by the carpet. "If you make us walk past the park every day?"

"Keep your mouth shut." Ed's boots slid over the marble floor as he wrenched Frank's wrist higher. "You don't know anything."

Frank's laughter tightened to a grunt at the end, and Drake stepped forward to separate the boys. Brotherly arguing was a good thing; breaking limbs was not. "That's enough, Ed. Go into the library with Gavin and cool off."

"Aww, Drake. It was just getting fun," Harry and Nicky said, though Nicky's protest was half smothered by scone crumbs.

"*Fun* is in the eye of the man on the bottom of the pile." Drake helped Frank from the carpet and tested his elbow, ensuring nothing was amiss. "Besides, there's to be no fighting in the house." The words came back to him, and he heard the loophole. "Or outside—with each other or with anyone else."

Certain Frank was fine, he looked to the younger boys. "Harry, put your schoolbooks away and change. You have work to do with Gav in the cellar. Nick…" He sighed. "Clean the crumbs from the floor and your clothes. Use the broom from the kitchen—without taking another scone."

"Yes, sir." Nicky's face fell.

Drake remembered what it had been like, never knowing how long he'd have to wait between meals or how large those meals would be.

Malcolm Kirk might have been a greedy wanker, but he always made sure his boys ate. At times it was little more than cold beef on stale bread, but Drake's belly had always been full. Men were less desperate when they weren't hungry.

He put a hand on Nicky's shoulder and squeezed in a way he hoped was reassuring. "Dinner *will* be on time, and there will be plenty for everyone. I promise. In the meantime, after you've cleaned up, go finish your lessons." He tilted his head to whisper,

"And keep an eye on Frank."

"It's not my fault Ed can't take being ribbed about a girl," Frank grumbled as he went upstairs.

Drake returned to the library, and Gavin left to supervise the work in the cellar. Ed faced Drake, pulling his hands from his pockets at the last moment. "I'm sorry for fighting."

Drake waved off the apology. He'd been teased mercilessly for years over one thing or the other, usually by boys larger and meaner than Frank. "He likes to get a rise out of you."

"And Nicky and Harry fall right into step behind him." Ed sighed like he had the weight of the world on his shoulders. "He never takes anything seriously."

Drake suspected Frank was more serious than anyone knew. No boy survived on the street for long simply by being up for any fight that came his way.

"Gavin says your studies are going well." He sat in the nearest chair and pointed at its companion, irritated that Ed had to be asked to sit in his own home. "And that you'll be ready to sit for exams next month."

The house would be a little rowdier with Ed at Cambridge, and Gavin would feel the added weight of shepherding the remaining three, but Drake was proud that he'd given Ed an opportunity to expand his horizons past a grubby alley in an increasingly dingy town.

The young man was quiet for a long moment. "What if I wanted to sit for Oxford rather than Cambridge? I'd be closer to ho—London that way."

"Oxford would be fine." Drake searched his brain for a connection he would have to that university. It wasn't as direct as having a duke recommend the boy to Cambridge, but perhaps one of the other managers in the lending circle could do it. Perhaps Augustus Chitester wouldn't hold his daughter's secret distillery business against the man who had helped it succeed. "But if you're worried about being on your own, I go east regularly. And with the planned rail service, you could come back for visits easily enough."

"I know you've been looking forward to having one less of us." Ed stared at his boots. "But I would like—"

"Wait." Drake sat his drink on the reading table nearest his chair. "I have never said you were banished, have I?" He waited for the boy to shake his head. "You are welcome here, in your home, whenever you would like for however long you wish. It's just that when we spoke of university, we've always talked of Cambridge. What has changed your plans?" He thought back to Frank's taunt. "Is it a girl?"

The bell rang, and Drake trusted someone else to open the door. The house was full of people, after all.

Ed looked him straight in the eye. "No."

But he'd waited too long to answer, and he was far too still when he spoke. He was lying.

Perhaps Ed *was* focusing on something other than his studies. Drake was torn between relief and worry. Ed had come so far that it would be a shame to lose his chances due to an indiscretion.

How did one even bring up a topic like that?

The bell rang again, this time followed by an insistent knock that, given the criminal pasts of everyone under his roof, was far too familiar. Drake quelled the urge to bolt for the nearest exit to avoid arrest.

"Dammit." He hated that feeling, and the best way to deal with it was to face his fear. "I'll return in a moment. Don't move."

Drake strode to the door and swung it open, sure to have one brow arched so that he looked as peevish as he felt over the interruption.

None of that mattered to Jocelyn as she pushed her way over the threshold. She brought the faint stench of prison with her. She must have followed Gavin from Horsemonger Lane.

"Gavin lost sight of me before he could ask me for tea." She thrust her hat into his hands. "I thought I'd save him the trouble of finding me again."

Rather than her black cloak, she was dressed in sky blue, and her hair was caught up in a twist that called attention to her high cheekbones and flashing eyes.

Drake closed the door. Gavin would hate this. The boys would likely be smitten. Drake wasn't sure how he felt about it at all, but he wasn't prepared to toss her out on her ear. No telling what she would do.

"Please do come in, Miss Kirk. I'll ask Trudy to set another place for tea."

And to make some. If they had any in the house.

CHAPTER FIVE

"**T**HANK YOU FOR the tea." Joss touched the corners of her mouth with a serviette, careful not to leave lip rouge behind on the pristine white fabric scented with cedar.

She refolded the cloth and ran her nail lightly over the deep, sharp crease it exposed. She didn't need to look toward the end of the table to know Gavin was watching. He'd watched her hands from the moment she had walked in the door, a frown carved into his long face.

"I'll see you out." Drake stood with her, though he didn't rush to hold her chair. He didn't have to. Gavin was already pulling it from beneath her.

"Thank you for the hospitality, Gavin." Joss returned the man's unrelenting disapproval. "Allow me to return it. I go to Surrey every Saturday afternoon at one. Next week, I'll fetch you on the way. It will keep you informed and out of the weather."

She left without a backward glance, pausing only to allow Drake to open the door for her. She was a lady, dammit. It didn't matter what they remembered of her, or even what they thought of her now. She remembered just as many things about them and had made her own judgments long ago.

Drake's touch on her elbow stalled her flight. "Where is your carriage?"

"Likely back at The Rose. I prefer to walk in the air after I visit the lane."

Even though Gavin had likely divulged where she'd been and whom she'd visited, Joss didn't wish to say it. She didn't want to give him the satisfaction.

"Your cloak and veil are there as well, I suppose." He fell into step beside her.

"Yes." She'd deliberately left them after changing in the carriage. "Walking in such attire draws more attention than simply showing my face, even in the polite part of town." Not to mention how much lighter she felt in her indigo-blue coat and hat with matching feathers. "You do not have to escort me."

"Any gentleman would see a visitor safely home." He said it like he was reciting a passage from a schoolbook. "Even a lady with a knife in her boot."

"Thank you." She said it because a proper lady would have.

They walked in silence to the end of the block, he with his hands behind his back, she with both hands on her parasol. The quiet weighed on her. The suspicions she'd had after meeting Harry had reignited after meeting the other young men in Drake's house.

"Why are you collecting boys?"

For several steps, Drake stared at his feet as he walked, hiding his thoughts as well as his lack of conversation. It had been maddening when they were younger, and Joss was just as vexed now.

"Never—"

"I'd like to give them an alternative to growing up criminals, I suppose."

The girl in her—the one who had cried as the constables led Gavin away in shackles and screamed in the dark as Davy drowned—understood that sentiment. They'd lost the same friends to the dangers of their job. But Joss had learned to read using pilfered cargo manifests and spent many evenings as a lookout while teenaged smugglers had worked in the dark.

"I have a girl at The Rose who does the same thing with

kittens," she said. "Perhaps I should bring you one of those. It might soften Gavin's disposition."

"He wouldn't be so huffy if you didn't poke him so." Drake's face was stern, but humor flavored his words.

Joss didn't see the joke. Places where she could be herself were few and far between. Old friends were even fewer. "He was huffy before I arrived, and I haven't seen him for years."

"He doesn't like being near the prison. Too many memories."

She understood that all too well. She didn't like being there, and she was just visiting. And her father, cooped up in there without a view of the sky, was a constant shadow throughout her day. "I didn't ask him to be there, now did I?"

"No, that falls squarely on me."

"Then you can stop asking him to follow me, and he can stop staring at me like I'm the only criminal in the room. And don't say he doesn't, because he kept waiting for me to pocket the silver. I'm shocked he didn't search me before I left."

"He looks at you and sees Malcolm."

Joss was accustomed to that. In Highcliffe, the glances had swung between suspicion and pity, sometimes in the same conversation. In London, she was just a face in the crowd—unless she passed a client on the street. There was something about a man's wary glance as he tipped his hat that left her taller as she passed. "Then I need to find a new way to do my hair."

"If only it were that simple." Drake's rumbly voice carried even over the rattle of carriages and carts on the street.

"It wasn't Da's fault that Gav was snatched. It could've been any of us, at any time. We knew that when we signed on."

His frown didn't waver. "You make it sound voluntary."

"He didn't kidnap any of you and chain you to the walls," she retorted.

"No, it was a choice between stealing and starving."

"Exactly. It was a *choice*." She was weary of people who made decisions and then complained about the results.

"It was not Gavin's choice to be left behind in favor of a

shipment." Drake came to a stop. *"Livelihood over lives,* remember?"

Her father had said that once when Joss had been much younger. She had never taken him seriously, though many others had. She faced his latest accuser. "At least Gav is still on this side of the dirt."

"And I wish every day that Davy had the luxury of prison," Drake snapped.

Her ragged breathing shivered in time with her trembling legs, but it was her hair sticking to her neck beneath her coat collar that indicated how fast she'd been walking. Something she should keep doing. The sooner she was rid of Drake Fletcher, the better she would like it. "I have no more need for an escort. You can go…back from whence you came."

She was not going to tell him to go to hell in the middle of the street like a fishwife deprived of a farthing. Given the way Drake's scowl deepened, he understood her meaning anyway.

His hand shot up as his sharp whistle split the air. Three separate carriages made their way toward them, too slow for Joss's liking.

Drake seemed to share that opinion. He was reaching for the door latch before the first carriage had come to a full stop.

"Drake? Is that you?"

The lady approaching them was tall, slender, and carried herself with an elegance money couldn't buy. Curiosity stopped Joss mid-escape.

"Blast," Drake muttered. He reshaped his face into a smile and greeted the woman as she neared. "Hello, Tavie."

Their familiarity raised dozens of questions Joss would likely never get answered. By the time Drake bowed over Tavie's hand, his smile was as natural and charming as any Joss could have hoped to receive.

From anyone else, of course.

"Mrs. Octavia Foster, may I present Miss Jocelyn Kirk." His touch on her elbow lured Joss away from her cab and closer to his side.

"It's a pleasure to meet you," Octavia said as she extended her hand. She was older than her posture made her appear, and the red hair peeking from under her hat was an orange that was closer to peach. Her grip was firm, and her eyes were bright. Curiosity sparked in their green depths.

"You as well, Mrs. Foster," Joss replied, returning the woman's direct gaze.

"What brings you to Charles Street, Tavie?" Drake moved her aside so a delivery cart could pass.

She offered an envelope with his name flowing over it in bold strokes. "I intended to invite you to dinner on Sunday evening like a civilized Society lady, but now you've caught me on the street and saved me the steps." Her smile encompassed them both. "Bring Miss Kirk."

"Tavie, this is not… She isn't… You don't…"

For a moment, Joss considered letting him drown in politeness. But no matter how angry she might be, he didn't deserve that fate. "That is very kind of you, Mrs. Foster, but—"

"Tavie. I insist."

"Tavie." Joss began to realize why Drake liked this woman. "I am grateful for the invitation, but my evening is planned."

"Tea, then. On Monday." Tavie put up a hand. "I'll not take no for an answer." She made to leave but hesitated. "Don't tell Martin I was out without a carriage. He worries."

She was gone before Joss could formulate an excuse. "Who was that?"

"A client." Drake opened the cab door and held it for her. "And if you don't join us, she'll never give me a moment's peace." Despite his grumbling, he was still smiling. "I'll call for you on Monday afternoon."

She could come up with an excuse by Monday, certainly. Joss took the hand he offered as she stepped into the coach. "Thank you, but I'll find my own way."

"As you wish." He gave her the address and closed the door.

Joss sat with her back against the squabs, facing forward and away from her past.

When they rounded the corner, the turn sent her hand to the window to maintain her balance. It was the only reason she saw Sir Reginald Spencer speaking with Viscount Stratford. They were near enough to an alley to hide in the shadows, but far enough toward the street so as not to be skulking. Gentlemen never skulked.

Gentlemen also didn't discuss political business on the streets. Parties were made for business. Shadowy streets were suitable for schemes. And there was only one scheme Spencer and Stratford could be discussing.

A chill slipped down Joss's spine. She rapped her parasol against the roof of the carriage, demanding haste.

She had a woman to get out of London.

IT HAD BEEN years since Drake had been uncomfortable in Tavie's home. Not since he'd first rung the bell in his only suit, a cheap one that had depleted his savings. But here he was, trying not to fidget in his chair while his tea grew cold.

He'd been dreading this afternoon since Tavie had issued her invitation. Despite his hopes and almost prayers that Jocelyn would have come to her senses and sent her apologies, she had arrived promptly at two dressed like a proper Society lady. The only thing missing in her disguise was a chaperone.

"What was Drake like when he was younger?" Tavie asked as she served him a tiny sandwich he hadn't yet requested. It was slivers of bread pasted together with something that tasted of dill and cucumber. He would never understand Society's obsession with tiny food.

And gossip. Tavie loved nothing more than talking, and it was generally good-natured and purposeful. She gleaned more business information from a party than anyone Drake had met. He'd educated himself at her elbow through countless seasons.

But he wasn't her business. He was her business*man*. And Jocelyn wasn't the most reliable source for information on his past. He ignored the sandwich and waited, prepared to rebut any assessment.

Jocelyn was quiet for a long moment. The longer she considered Tavie's question, the more anxious Drake grew. Then her gaze met his, and the twinkle in her eyes told him she knew he was uncomfortable, that she was doing it on purpose just to tease.

She could hide behind dresses and deceptions, but those eyes… He'd recognize them anywhere. They were the color of tide pools after a storm.

"He was always quiet. Observant." Jocelyn put her cup in her saucer without making a sound. "So when he did speak up, everyone paid attention. His input was always sound."

Dear God, she made him sound like the most boring boy in the house. "There was fun, too. I seem to remember hunting for shellfish." That was one of his fondest memories of living under Malcolm's roof. He'd had friends his own age for the first, and last, time.

"You swiped my bucket of clams as the tide came in." Jocelyn's lips twitched as she looked to Tavie. "He could be a wicked boy when he wanted."

"Oh, I have no doubt," Tavie said. "It's one of the traits that makes him good at what he does."

"What is that, exactly?" Jocelyn asked. "He said you were a client, but we didn't discuss particulars."

He wouldn't talk about Tavie's business. It was unprofessional to disclose others' secrets, especially when they were in the same room. Drake uncrossed his legs and leaned forward, putting his empty cup on the table and his head between theirs. "Perhaps we should—"

"Did he not?" Tavie refilled his tea and put two biscuits on the saucer before returning it to him. "I thought he intended to invite you into the Circle."

Jocelyn's blue-green eyes narrowed over the rim of her tea-cup. Her fingers were as fine as the china, but he knew how strong they could be. "Circle?"

"The London Ladies Charity Circle. We help each other and other worthy candidates in establishing and operating successful businesses," Tavie explained. "And along the way, we may help a few men get a new start as well. Drake is invaluable in my efforts."

Jocelyn kept her cup to her lips for an extra moment. She had to be curious—no one enjoyed tea that much. If she was curious, maybe there was a way to help her after all.

"How?" Her quiet, measured question was directed at him. Drake recognized suspicion when he heard it.

"I cared for Tavie's horses at the stables near the park. One day she asked me to ride with her, and we began talking. Before I knew it, she'd invited me for tea. Before I left, she had offered me a job."

"He's oversimplifying out of modesty." Tavie reached for a scone, and Drake put the marmalade next to her plate. She slathered the spread over the biscuit as she continued her tale.

"We spent the entire ride discussing business articles from the newspaper and gossip he had gleaned from eavesdropping at the stables, because you know how *ton* men are loud on purpose to make themselves important."

Jocelyn struggled not to laugh as she swallowed a mouthful of tea.

"He impressed me further on his second interview, during that tea, so I followed my instincts and hired him as my man of business."

Jocelyn's eyes widened as her cup clattered against her saucer. Drake wasn't certain if he should be amused by her reaction or proud that he'd proved he was worth more than salt water and what he could steal.

"And now he represents several other businesswomen as

well—my niece, the Duchess of Rushford, is one. So is that lovely distiller, Amelia Ferrand. Though I always think her bubbly demeanor would be better served if she made champagne. Maybe we could convince that handsome husband of hers." Tavie finally stopped to draw a breath. "But I digress, something to which you grow accustomed."

Drake liked to think if he'd had a dotty aunt, she would have been like Tavie. He hated disappointing her. "Jocelyn isn't—"

Jocelyn put her hand over his. Her palm was warm. "I'm honored you would consider me a candidate, Tavie, but I own a business already."

"Really?" Tavie practically bounced in her chair, and Drake's stomach began an anticipatory drop. "Because we welcome established businesswomen as well. You could make a difference in London and mentor young women who need a fresh start."

He had to put a stop to this. "Tavie—"

Jocelyn squeezed his fingers. "I do that now, of a sort." Her smile shook at the edges, but she kept her gaze direct and her spine straight. "I'm Madam White of the White Rose."

It was almost impossible to shock Tavie Foster. Drake had tried to do it a few times over the last ten years. Jocelyn had succeeded in fewer than two hours with fewer than ten words.

"If you would prefer I go, I would understand," Joss said, her voice still quiet and level.

Where was the pugnacious little girl who had done her best to push him down when he'd tugged her fraying braid? Or even the woman from last week who had brazenly left him staring as she escorted another man upstairs?

Tavie brushed the statement aside. "You are very kind to be concerned, but if I were worried about Society, I'd be sitting in the corner at Almack's with a bottomless glass of ratafia." She leaned forward. "You're not old enough to be Madam White. She arrived in London while I was newly married."

"I'm the latest incarnation," Jocelyn disclosed in a conspiratorial whisper. "Madam Madeline chose me as her successor, as someone had done for her, and someone for her." Joss drew a circle with her fingers, hinting at a cycle that had repeated itself for decades.

Drake wasn't certain he wanted to know the promotion requirements. He hoped Tavie didn't ask.

"Much like me," Tavie replied. "I'm hoping Thea, the duchess, takes my place leading the Circle soon. I'd like to be just another board member."

The statement surprised Drake, but it also made him take a longer look at the woman who'd put her faith in him when no one else would have. He always saw her as the red-headed dynamo who had teased him about racing in the park, but the years were catching up to her. A few more gray hairs, deeper wrinkles at the corners of her eyes. Her posture was still straight, but her steps had slowed.

"We should go." He stood before offering Tavie his hand.

She kissed his cheek before reaching for Jocelyn and doing the same. "Now that I know where to find you, expect an invitation for tea. On our own next time. I have *so* many questions."

Her laughter took years from her face. Drake had known he and Tavie could be friends the moment he heard her laugh, an unguarded peal that had him sharing in the humor.

Jocelyn's laugh had a different effect. The quiet, deep chuckle brushed his skin, recalling the breeze that always came when the moon rose over the sea.

It made sense. They'd spent their childhood on the edge of the ocean.

Martin, Tavie's devoted butler, brought their coats and helped Jocelyn into hers. The dark wine color made her skin glow. Drake remembered her dressed as a boy, trousers rolled to her knees and the sea to her ankles.

Until that dreadful night with Davy.

Tavie came to Drake and straightened his collar. From anyone else, it would have been too intimate.

"She is surprising." She kept her voice low. "I like her for you."

No wonder Thea sometimes complained about Tavie's intuition. "It isn't like that."

"That's unfortunate." She brushed lint from his shoulder. "For both of you."

"I'll see you on Friday for our meeting." Drake kissed her cheek again. "Alone."

He took his hat and nodded goodbye to Martin before offering his arm to Jocelyn. She took it. He blamed Tavie's comment for his awareness of such a simple touch.

"Thank you for a lovely afternoon, Tavie," Jocelyn said. "I look forward to seeing you again."

The satisfaction he took from her gracious manners was Tavie's fault, too.

Once on the street, Jocelyn made to move away. Drake covered her hand to keep it on his coat. "I was certain you'd cry off."

"I had every intention of doing so, but I like Tavie and I was curious about your connection." She sighed. "Besides, no one respectable ever invites me to tea."

"You had tea on Charles Street less than five days ago." Her arched eyebrow should have irritated him, but instead it made him smile. "Point taken. Gav and I aren't exactly respectable."

"And I invited myself so I could dress you both down, which you stymied by introducing me to the boys and keeping them in the room until they could no longer sit still."

They had behaved much longer than he'd anticipated, likely because they'd all been smitten by a lady in the house who looked nothing like their motherly maid. He couldn't blame them.

Drake stepped closer to her, letting the hem of her coat brush his calf. He had questions, and he didn't want to shout them from six paces away. "How did you get here?" He tilted his head toward hers. "And I don't mean the carriage."

CHAPTER SIX

J OSS OPENED HER parasol and returned her hand to Drake's arm.
Not because she liked it there. She needed to touch him like she
needed the shade of a parasol on this dreary November day.
However, she did like the privacy. And he smelled of cinnamon
and the forest.

"Necessity, I suppose." She didn't think long about how
much to tell him. If he didn't get enough information, he would
never stop pestering her, but he didn't need to know every detail.

"They moved Da's trial to London." There was no need to
hide her father's situation. "So I followed."

"How did they catch him?"

"He chose the wrong vessel." Da had seen the manifest and
hadn't bothered to look at the vessel's owner or where the
shipment was headed. He hadn't seen the crown on the seal.
"They caught the boys, who were terrified of everything, from
paddling to hanging, to going to the devil while still breathing."

Not that she blamed them. But if Drake and Gavin had still
been at Highcliffe, Da wouldn't be in prison, and she wouldn't be
in London.

"Where are they now?"

"I found all of them places before I left." There were young
men from Highcliffe sprinkled all along the coast, working in
dockyards and butcher shops, or at smithies and farms, left in the

care of friends or friends of friends.

Drake walked beside her, and the noise from the street filled the space between them.

When she'd been in Highcliffe staring out the window and waiting on the boys to come home, she'd imagined living in London. Following her father had given her a guilty thrill, which had faded after the first night. The incessant noise created by so many people, by the maintenance required to care for so many people, was a never-ending swell crashing against the sand. Even this wide street, bordered by tall houses, was full of people and sound.

"Did you go straight to the White Rose?" He asked the question without looking at her.

Of course, because women arrived in a city and knew where every business was located, how to get to respectable neighborhoods and safe havens. "When you arrived in London, did you go straight to Tavie?" She knew the answer, but she wanted him to see the parallel.

"No, but I didn't have a friend in London. *You* did."

Joss wasn't going to argue the definition of a friend in the street. Instead, she nodded to one passerby, a man whose eyes widened under the brim of his hat. He looked remarkably like a customer of one of her girls, Maisie. "Because you would be so easy to find. And for all we knew, you were in Australia."

"I don't sail anymore," he muttered.

Despite herself, Joss squeezed his solid forearm. These days she, too, was happier near the water rather than on it.

"Why *there*, Jocelyn? You could have worked at a hotel, or as a maid, or as a—"

"Do you think I didn't try?" As much as his question irritated her, she was more annoyed that he wouldn't look at her as he spoke.

She planted her feet and let her hand slide from his arm, past his elbow, and into the cool air. Finally, Drake faced her.

"You had the benefit of a strong back in a city that needs

workmen," Jocelyn said. "Try being a young woman with no references. Try dealing with assessing gazes that have nothing to do with housekeeping." She had another thought. "And that's assuming I wanted to do housekeeping in the first place. I had done enough laundry at Highcliffe to last a lifetime."

"So you knocked on the door of a brothel." He kept his voice to a whisper as the crowd skirted around them.

She had arrived at the White Rose in the middle of a downpour, her heart pounding in the cold and her stomach growling. "The kitchen door, yes."

It had been Da's first night in prison as a convicted man, and Joss, who had been certain of his acquittal, had spent the last of her coins for breakfast the morning before. She had been too heartbroken to care where she landed or what she did, so long as it was safe, dry, and near her father.

Elsa, the cook, shocked by the shivering mess of a girl, had summoned Madam Madeline to the kitchen. The regal woman, whose austere bearing made her appear twice her size, had taken one look at Joss's simple dress, which was already two seasons old, and her lopsided shawl that had run out of wool before the end of the pattern, and declared Joss hopeless as a prostitute. At which point Joss, though relieved beyond words, had dissolved into tears.

A maid. We can hire you as a maid, child. Please stop crying. Sit next to the fire. Elsa, fetch a plate.

"Madam White hired me out of the goodness of her heart."

So Joss had ended up doing laundry anyway. The job had been simple enough, and since maids and employees lived on the premises, Joss used her wages to pay her father's barrister and to keep him as comfortable as possible while he served his sentence.

"Once she discovered my talent for numbers, she promoted me to managing the finances."

"You were always good with keeping us going," Drake said. He offered his arm again.

She took it. Mostly because they were drawing curious stares.

"I'm good at most things."

Being at The Rose had been difficult at first. Skirts had been a challenge, and women fought over different things than boys—and differently than boys. But the work was mostly at night, which she was used to, and Madeline had filled her days with school, or at least education. Some of the topics would have made even the most nontraditional schoolmaster blush.

However, as the years dragged on and life in crowded London stretched before her, she needed another plan. It had come in a surprising offer.

"Which is why Madeline asked me to become the next Madam White."

"How does that work, exactly?" Drake asked. "I assume the name is more like a title."

Drake Fletcher didn't need to know *exactly* how anything about how decisions, retirement or otherwise, were made at The Rose. "Using the name makes it easier to fade into the countryside when one wishes to do so."

"So you've been…successful at The Rose, then?"

The tightness in his words matched the flush climbing his neck toward his jaw.

Joss had loved the freedom she'd had in Highcliffe, but it had come at a price. A life in trousers meant being treated as a boy who happened to have braids. Even if she'd worn a skirt, the village boys would have never approached a girl surrounded by ten watchful lads and guarded by a father who valued her chastity but not her reputation.

This was likely the first time Drake had seen her as a woman. Given his question, he definitely didn't see her as a lady.

"The girls are healthy and well paid. The customers stay healthy and happy. The house is safe and warm. I'd call that successful, wouldn't you?"

After all, that was what he had.

They'd reached the park, and Joss saw a familiar form. "Is that Ed there against the fence?"

Drake scanned the fence line. "Doubtful. He's supposed to be ensuring the others get home."

"It certainly looks like Ed." She steered Drake that way. Honestly, how could he not recognize the boy? He had the same lean, hungry stance that Drake had himself at that age. But not the awareness, because the boy didn't see them approaching. Only one thing could hold a young man's attention that completely.

Joss followed his gaze to a young lady on the arm of an older gentleman. Even from a distance, she recognized Sam Goddard's sable hair and sparkling smile. Given the girl's age, she was likely Grace, the daughter he spoke of so often during his house calls at The Rose.

The two were engrossed in the few flowers that were still blooming in the fall. Sunlight gilded her hair as she touched every petal with careful fingers and brushed her gloved hands along the bark of trees that were raining their leaves onto the grass.

Ed followed her every move like he was a starving man, and she was holding a pie.

Drake pulled Joss to a stop. "Wait. Don't embarrass him."

She hadn't been raised with many manners, but she'd been a quick study. Ed needed an introduction.

"Trust me." She freed herself and never looked back at him as she approached. "Hello, Dr. Goddard."

"Mad—" The man looked to either side. "Mrs. White. Hello there."

She lifted Ed upright, then made him take her arm and walk her through the gate. Drake had no choice but to follow them. "May I present an old acquaintance, Mr. Drake Fletcher, and his ward, Edward Ross. Mr. Fletcher, Mr. Ross, this is Dr. Sam Goddard and his daughter, Grace."

As the older men greeted one another, Ed saw only Grace. Joss, with nothing to do, found herself envying the young girl's blush and shy smile, the glow in the young man's eyes.

Young love. Fascination. Hope.

After a quick visit, Drake came back to her, his face far too grim. "Dr. Goddard has offered to let Ed walk with them until I get you home, since he'll see you tomorrow."

So much for gratitude.

They were silent for the length of the block, which was just as well, because he was walking so fast that she was too winded to talk. When it became too much, she grabbed his arm, but it was no use. "What the hell is wrong with you?"

"I'm sure you thought you were doing a good thing," he said. "But I don't want you introducing Ed to your clients."

Joss stuttered to a stop and blinked. Twice.

Sex can be for fun, dear. And if you aren't one of the girls, then of course you don't have to be paid for it. You could choose who you prefer. That, by the way, is a benefit of being a madam as well.

Joss shut her parasol to make it easier to whack him with it. "You arrogant bastard." He reached for the lacy weapon, but she parried and poked him in the chest. "*I* pay Sam to care for my girls, and he's enough of a professional and a gentleman to realize they deserve to be safe and healthy."

"How was I to know that?" Drake shouted back. "Every other man on the street has stared at you like you were naked the entire time we've been walking."

"And their behavior is my fault?" she countered. "Your assumptions are not my responsibility, and you have no right to be this judgmental of me or my girls. Not when you're doing exactly the same."

His face reddened. "I do not."

"Really? You have relationships with women based on lies. Where you pretend to be something you aren't, and they pay you for it." The thrill of being right shot through Joss, and she glared into his bright blue eyes. "That makes you a gigolo."

Drake shoved a finger toward her nose. "I am a businessman."

She batted his hand away and kept pushing him from her path. "And I'm a bookkeeper who can see herself home."

Drake watched Jocelyn until she turned the corner at the end of the block, using the time to calm his thoughts and slow his breathing. Even as a girl, she'd had the ability to twist the logic in any argument to her favor. Watching her do it to someone else was fun. Being that someone was infuriating.

Almost as maddening as seeing the stares of every third man who had passed them.

He walked back to the park and stopped to search for Ed. The young man's height made him as easy to spot as the sun glinting off his white-blond hair. He was walking between the doctor and his daughter—talking to the man instead of the girl.

Daft boy. He was wasting the opportunity Jocelyn had presented him with the introduction. One Drake hadn't realized he needed.

He'd given the boy a home and an education, yet assumed he'd only be attracted to shop girls.

Drake walked through the gate and toward them, hoping he appeared to be strolling instead of late for a meeting.

"I apologize for being late," he said as he rejoined the group.

"Not at all." Sam Goddard never stopped walking, yet somehow he slowed enough for Ed and Grace to take the lead. "It didn't take you as long I as expected."

"Jocelyn realized she had another errand."

That sounded much better than *she whacked me with her parasol and left me gaping in the street.* Her name also sounded better than her title.

"I notice Miss Goddard has a love of plants." Drake hoped he was right. He was better at math than helping young men court.

"She inherited my scientific mind, poor girl." Sam smiled. "It seems to be something she and Ed have in common."

Was it? Drake searched his memory. Had Gav told him about Ed's interest in science and he'd forgotten? "They do seem to be getting along quite well."

Ed was keeping a respectable distance, but their shoulders occasionally touched. Grace's parasol sometimes hid them both, but the sunshine cast only her shadow through the cloth. Regardless, it was impossible to miss the excited tones of their conversation and the way Ed's words rushed together.

"I am glad Jocelyn introduced them," Sam said. "Grace tires of having only me to talk with."

Drake found it difficult to believe the young woman didn't have friends or other suitors, but then, Ed didn't have others in his life either. "I believe Ed feels that way about his brothers."

"University will help," Sam said. "At least, it helped me." He stared ahead at his daughter's shadow. "I wish Grace could have that option."

At last, Drake could add something useful to the conversation. "I've heard a group of women are opening a university in London. It will be a few years, but perhaps that would be an option."

"Perhaps, but she would need to be more thoroughly prepared than her governess can manage." The doctor sighed. "My wife always looked after Grace's education. After her death, I found governesses rather thin on the ground."

"I have a client…" Drake regrouped his words. Representing any client well was a challenge. Adding that his clients were predominately women was another layer altogether. "I have a client who is acquainted with the Duchess of Rushford. She is beginning a preparatory school for young ladies in her husband's county seat in the hopes of helping those such as Grace."

Sam walked a distance in silence, staring at the horizon. "It would be difficult to have Grace all the way in Norfolk." He chuckled. "I sound like her mother instead of her father, but she has become even dearer to me since Hope's death."

"I spend a great deal of time in Thetford, where I have part ownership in a freight depot. The doctor there is aging, and I believe the duke would welcome a younger man in that post. The school is to be built there."

Sam's wide, easy smile took years from his face. "I'm assuming you can make an introduction?"

Drake nodded. "When you are ready."

"Then I owe Jocelyn thanks for introducing *us* as well."

"How long have you known her?" Drake asked. He couldn't help but like the doctor, but something about him, about hearing Jocelyn's name on his lips, made Drake's ears hot.

"Madeline, the previous Madam White, invited Hope and me to tea—at a very respectable tearoom. She was looking to hire a new doctor to keep on retainer, and she wanted to assure Hope that, should I accept, there would be no *sullying of my character*. I believe those were her words, anyway. Jocelyn was there. She is actually the one who discussed my salary and took notes on what would become our contract. Even then, Madeline made it quite clear that Jocelyn was to be her successor."

I'm a bookkeeper, she'd said. Perhaps she was. But then again, he didn't think Sir Reginald Spencer took her upstairs at The Rose for investment advice.

"What about you?" Sam asked. "How long have you known her?"

Drake had arrived at Highcliffe at age eleven, or at least that was his best guess. That would have made Jocelyn eight. He'd thought she was another one of the boys until her hat had fallen off in the garden. He couldn't be blamed for that. Her father dressed her as a boy, worked her like a boy, and even called her a boy's name. He would have cut her hair if she hadn't hidden in the stables until he'd grown distracted by another plan. "Since we were children."

The bell tolled four.

"We should be off home, Grace."

The girl returned to her father without complaint, but her smile seemed sincere. "Thank you for a lovely afternoon, Mr. Ross. It was a pleasure to make your acquaintance, Mr. Fletcher."

"Thank you, Miss Goddard."

She was a lovely girl. Her blonde hair was the color of wet sand, and the smattering of freckles over the bridge of her nose complemented the twinkle in her brown eyes.

Sam shook his hand and then reached for Ed's. "You are welcome to walk with us any time, Ed."

The boy watched them leave and beamed when Grace looked over her shoulder to wave goodbye.

Drake was content to continue walking in the park. "You lied to me," he said as they topped a small rise. A large pond sparkled under the sunlight, and Drake veered to the path that took them in the other direction. "You said there wasn't a girl."

"Since I hadn't spoken to her, it wasn't actually a lie." The young man heaved a great sigh. "It doesn't matter, does it? She's far too good for the likes of me."

"Bollocks." In the move to Charles Street, Drake had secretly worried about the boys mixing in Society only to have those people look down their noses. But to have Ed feel less about himself wouldn't be tolerated. Half of success was believing you could succeed. "Today went well. You build on that tomorrow." Perhaps not tomorrow. The boy shouldn't be a pest. "Or next week, perhaps."

But that led to a larger discussion. "But I would caution you against changing your education plans simply because she is in London. That may not always be the case."

"And if it was for more than that?" Ed asked. "If I wanted to pursue a medical degree?"

He wanted to be a doctor? "The last time we spoke, you wanted to study architecture." What had changed his mind? "Is this because you admire Dr. Goddard?"

"No." Ed stopped in the path, forcing Drake to do the same. "It's because the human body is a marvel of design, where everything is connected, and one failure can create chaos. Finding that failure is like solving the ultimate puzzle." He drew a deep breath. "And I haven't told you because you've been busy with other things, but also… I was afraid you'd think I'll fail."

"What?"

"The boys who test into Oxford have either spent years in prep school or they already have a spot because of their fathers."

Ed had neither of those, and Drake had no idea what a father, or even an older brother, should say in times like this. He was adrift with only one rope to grasp—a version of what he'd heard from his mentors aboard ship when he decided to leave the sea behind.

"Ed, you are a fine, intelligent young man, worthy of any university and any young lady in town." He swept his hand through his hair and scratched the back of his head, working out what to say next. "And your changing your mind shouldn't surprise me. I've done it several times in my life." He looked the boy in the eye. "It also shouldn't be a secret you keep out of fear I won't support you. If this is what you want, we can investigate both schools and see how we can manage."

Perhaps he had a few connections who were Oxford men. Jasper Warren came to mind, though their relationship was tenuous at best.

They began their walk again, this time toward home.

"It was kind of Madam White to introduce us," Ed said. "Should I send her a note?"

Jocelyn would enjoy that. She'd always loved to see the post arrive. "We both should."

CHAPTER SEVEN

JOSS STOOD IN the shadows outside Parliament, marking time until the foot traffic subsided. The tide of coaches and drivers had already waned. The reporters were the last to go in. After all, sunlight banished scandal, scheming, and gossip.

It would shock most women in London that *she* did not burst into flames while crossing the street. She might have been slightly shocked herself.

"Hello, miss." The usher held the door. "You may watch the proceeding from the balcony."

"Thank you." Joss nodded as she passed, using the wide brim of her bonnet to hide most of her face and her self-satisfied smile. The man was a regular visitor to The Rose, and he hadn't recognized her. True, she had dressed for town rather than for entertaining, and she'd used a light touch on her cosmetics. But he also wouldn't expect to see Madam White here, of all places, in a pelisse and a feathered bonnet.

The balcony was half full of women similarly dressed, some with young boys who were clinging to the spindles, craning their necks to see the floor.

"David, darling," one of the women said. "Step back from there before you embarrass your father."

Or fall. Why did every *ton* mother consider embarrassment the worst fate imaginable? Joss knew a boy who had clamored for attention and suffered much worse for it.

But then, Davy had sought the attention of the wrong person, hadn't he?

"I don't know how they expect those boys to sit here all morning and behave," whispered a young lady as she took the seat beside Joss. "They ought to be out in the sunshine."

"Perhaps they're training them to be disappointed early," Joss replied, using her fan to muffle her voice. It was surprising how easily sound carried.

"A day at Lords would be an efficient tool." The woman paused. "I've not seen you before. I'm Victoria Yorke."

It was her name as much as her smile that made her familiar. Victoria Yorke was the daughter of Edward Cust. Her wedding to Welshman Steffan Yorke had been the talk of London.

"It's a pleasure to make your acquaintance, Mrs. Yorke." Joss dipped her head. "I'm Jocelyn Kirk." It was as unfamiliar to use her real name as it was to have women smile in her direction. "I must admit surprise at seeing you here. I thought you and your new husband would be on your wedding trip."

"Steffan wanted to stay and lend his voice to Father's bid to be master of the ceremonies. He's facing a conniv— considerable—opponent in Viscount Stratford."

He was facing a murderer if Connie's tale was to be believed—which Joss did. It was the only reason she was here.

"After this, we're back to Errdig for a summer in Wales. We'll travel to Italy after harvest."

"You don't seem the least bit disappointed over summering in Wales." Joss immediately wanted to recall the tease. She spent too little time in polite society.

But the new Mrs. Yorke laughed, her eyes sparkling. "Steffan's—our—home there is large enough that we could get lost and simply pretend we were in Italy, except for the Alps, of course."

Order was called in the chamber, and the balcony quieted. Even the rowdy boys sat, though it was on the front row at the edges of their seats, their necks craned so they could see the occasional crown of a powdered wig.

As expected, they began with the marshal debate, and Mr. Cust, as the elder and ranking courtier, took the floor first. Joss found herself imitating the boys.

Cust was an unassuming man. His words were kind, but his voice rang with the authority of a commander who expected to be obeyed. It was easy to imagine him in charge of foreign dignitaries and in the presence of the queen. The pride in his daughter's posture was touching.

The longer he spoke, the more spectators entered the balcony, men now as well as women. Joss's toes twitched in her shoes as she fought the urge to turn her face.

Below them, the chamber erupted into applause.

"He acquitted himself quite well, I think," Victoria Yorke whispered as she relaxed. "Would you agree?"

"He would have my vote," Joss said as she gathered her handbag and stood. "Were it possible."

"Were it possible, I believe some of us would be on the floor rather than in the rafters." Victoria looked up from her seat. "Are you leaving before Viscount Stratford speaks?"

"Unfortunately, I have somewhere to be." *And that somewhere depends on Viscount Stratford speaking.* "It was a pleasure, Mrs. Yorke. I hope we meet again."

"As do I Miss Kirk." Victoria winked. "Perhaps at Father's celebration."

Joss nodded as she passed, careful not to return the stares she could feel as she left the balcony. Viscount Stratford's voice rang behind her as she hurried down the hallway. If he was a smart politician, and everything she knew of him indicated he was, he wouldn't hold the podium long.

Following the directions Alfie had given her, Joss traversed the maze of hallways lined with doors that all looked the same. She kept her steps swift and quiet and stayed close to the wall so that her green pelisse and brown skirt lent camouflage. Viscount Stratford's rooms were near, on a dead-end hallway, close enough to the floor that she could hear him speaking.

After finding the correct door, Joss dropped to the floor and pushed her bonnet from her head. She pulled her lockpicks from her reticule.

"What the hell do you think you're doing?"

Her tools clattered to the tile, and she spun on the spy, heart in her throat. "None of your damned business." She matched Drake hiss for hiss, searching for her picks without taking her eyes from his. "Bugger off."

Rather than obey, he bent double and swept the silver tools from the floor. "I suppose you have a good reason for breaking into a viscount's rooms. In Parliament."

"I do." But Joss would be damned if told him. Instead, she thrust out her hand.

Viscount Stratford droned on as she and Drake stared at one another. With a quiet swear, he dropped his hat into her lap and hitched up his trousers. "Move aside."

"I don't need your help." Even as she said it, Joss made room for him in front of the door.

"Of course you don't." He knelt to see the keyhole and slid one pick inside, rolling it in his long fingers first one way, then the other. "But I'm faster." A slow smile lifted one corner of his mouth as he used the second pick much as the first. "Try the knob."

The door swished open, whispering against the thick rug, and Joss ignored the hand he offered. Instead she grasped the doorframe and pulled herself upright.

Drake sighed as he followed her inside. "What are you hoping to find?"

"Proof of something." She went to the desk and tried each door, not surprised when she found all but the center drawer locked. She ran her hand inside, going up to her elbow before her fingers closed over a square item that was cool to the touch. It was too small to be a jewelry box and nothing at all like a diary. "I'd like to think he had nipple clamps or a riding crop in here." Or maybe a piece of rope. "Anything useful."

Drake frowned. "You can't be serious."

"You never did have a sense of humor." Joss shuffled through the papers stacked on the desk but stopped halfway through. Stratford wouldn't keep evidence out where anyone could see it. She moved on to the bookshelves, checking only the books that weren't square or where dust was lacking.

"I fail to see anything funny about this." Drake followed behind her, straightening the papers and nudging the books back into place.

Joss cast her gaze about the room, looking for other hiding places. It would help if she knew what she was looking for. Gregory likely didn't write *Kill my mistress today* in his diary. There might be letters, perhaps jewelry, maybe a risqué sketch or two. Joss knelt and ran her fingers under the edge of the carpet. "Make yourself useful. Check under the cushions."

"For?" Drake drew the word out, clearly hoping for a hint.

He was smart enough not to need one. "Anything that doesn't belong there."

Joss turned up nothing. There wasn't even a safe behind the sole painting, a war scene that was likely meant to celebrate a victory. She found it grisly. Across the room, Drake lifted every chair cushion and did a thorough, efficient check of the cabinet there.

His suit was well cut, and his watch chain matched the gold pattern stitched across his navy-blue velvet waistcoat. She remembered when his trousers had never been long enough, and his socks were always slack around the tops of his boots. Those days were behind him now, given the sharp crease that broke over his knee when he walked and the starched white collar that followed the strong line of his jaw.

Voices grew louder. Men were debating—in the hallway rather than in the chamber. *Damn.* She'd been ogling her lookout instead of making sure he was near the door. "You're losing your touch, Fletcher. Grab your hat."

It had been a small chance that the viscount would have kept anything here tying him to Violet, but it had been the easier place to access. It was likely at home, where he could keep an eye on it. She needed an excuse to get in there.

Joss went back to the desk, opened the drawer, and dragged out the only personal item she'd found. It was a snuffbox, likely shoved there when Stratford had stashed his diary in the evenings. She pressed the clasp and thanked her lucky stars when she saw his initials engraved on the underside of the lid. She shoved it in her reticule.

"Jocelyn, you can't steal that."

"I have done." Joss shoved Drake into the hallway and flipped the lock before she closed the door. The stairwell creaked. Their way out was blocked.

Dragging in a deep breath, Joss pushed Drake against the wall, wrapped her hand around the back of his neck, and pulled his mouth to hers.

THE ONLY THING more surprising than kissing a prostitute in Parliament was that the prostitute was Jocelyn Kirk.

He'd never considered kissing her. But here he was, her lips pressed to his, her breasts against his waistcoat. He didn't need to see them to imagine her cleavage. He'd gotten a good look every time she'd knelt lower than her waist.

Her grip on his neck threatened bruises. Drake rested a hand on her waist, reassuring her that he understood the plan. Though God only knew how he was going to get them out of this.

Jocelyn's ribs curved under his thumb, and her hip flared against his palm. God, she was delicate. Her warm breath fanned his cheeks, leaving peppermint lingering in its wake. Her lips were as soft as the cotton blouse teasing his fingers.

It had taken months of life in London for Drake to rid himself of the briny scent of life in Highcliffe. Jocelyn smelled of salt, just enough to be buried under the smell of bluebells, violets, and lavender. Just enough to be tucked under the warm odor of moss.

He'd expected roses and musk—the scents of a bedroom. He got the wildness of a bluebell wood after a sea-fresh storm.

Jocelyn's tongue was hot and slick against his, tasting him, and her soft sigh reached through him to stiffen his body in indecent places. Her soft curls clung to his fingers, and the shell of her ear led him to the curve of her jaw. The bone there was fine, but the muscles beneath it were strong and sure.

"Ahem. Sir!"

It took a moment for the words to breach Drake's thudding heart and filter to his brain. He dragged his lips from Jocelyn's and forced himself to ignore her dazed stare. Using his body to block her from view, he looked over his shoulder. Viscount Stratford stood at the end of the hall, flanked by a peer who was much more amused by the situation.

"My apologies, sir. What did you say?" Drake asked.

Stratford's eyes widened. "I asked, what the devil do you think you're doing?" Though his words were indignant, he craned his neck in an effort to see Jocelyn.

Drake drew her closer with one hand while he used the other to free her fingers from his hair. They left a shivery trail in their wake. Her lips were wet from their kiss, and he could still taste her on his tongue. "I think that would be obvious, your lordship."

He pressed a kiss to her knuckles—only to make him more convincing as a besotted lover. It wasn't that he liked her this close, that he couldn't bear to let her go. Her knee grazed his inner thigh as she shifted. Then she did it again. After the third time, Drake moved out of reach.

Men got killed by being this distracted.

"But I do regret the intrusion." He cleared his throat. "We needed a private place in a public venue, away from…entanglements." He hoped Jocelyn would hear the pause and guess his plan.

The viscount's raised eyebrows told Drake that the other man had taken the intended bait.

The rest of Drake's false confession stuck in his throat as

Jocelyn put her warm hand in the middle of his chest and winked.

"I am married, your lordship." Her deep whisper charged the air between them. "I know this is wrong, but my husband is ill, and his family…" She muffled the words in her handkerchief as she dabbed her already dry eyes. "They are looking for any reason—"

They were drawing a crowd. Peers of the realm angled for a better view, reminding Drake of Ed and Frank gawking at the first girl they'd seen in a corset.

"I just wanted a moment of happiness," Jocelyn wailed, her eyes sparkling.

"There's no need for hysterics," Stratford said, still trying for a glimpse. "I see no reason to expose you." He paused. "Unless your husband is a peer?"

"He's a tradesman, your lordship," Drake snapped, irritated by the double standard. It was fine if he dallied with someone's wife, so long as it wasn't one of *theirs*. "We thought this was a safe place to meet because so many had come to hear your speech, and I am here often enough to avoid suspicion. But the spirit of the discussion was contagious."

Jocelyn's laughter quaked through her in a silent ripple, but her tiny excuse for a handkerchief wouldn't contain it for long. He pulled her against his shoulder, and her corset buttons teased his thumb, because of course it fastened in the front.

He was weary of talking with his back to a crowd of strangers, and her scent was making it difficult to concentrate. "If I could just escort the lady—"

"I *have* seen you here before. You're in service to—"

God, this would never end, and Drake was bloody well tired of toffs thinking he was a servant. "I am *employed* by the Duke of—"

"Drake? Is that you?"

Damn and blast. What had possessed him to follow Jocelyn into this mess?

"Rushford." Drake gritted his teeth and looked over his

shoulder. "Oli—Your Grace."

Oliver Hawkins, the Duke of Rushford, skirted the edge of the crowd. His robe and wig made him part of the group, but the breadth of his shoulders and the color of his skin, both due to hard work and life outdoors, made him stand out. "Did we have an..." He trailed off as he came nearer, his smile widening as he glimpsed the top of Jocelyn's head. "Oh, I see."

Hell. Drake was in hell. He'd been struck by a carriage crossing the street, and he just didn't know he was dead yet. "If I could just get her out of this blasted hallway," he whispered.

"The door to the back stairs is to your left. Come up after you've finished." Oliver blinked. "Or whatever." He turned to go but reversed course and leaned in to whisper, "And you might want to straighten your hair."

Oh bloody hell.

Oliver faced the crowd and motioned like he was clearing chickens from his kitchen garden. "Gentlemen, we have better things to do, I think."

Drake waited until Stratford had closed the door to his rooms. Then he pushed Jocelyn to the stairwell and followed her down, running his fingers through his hair as they went. It wiped the tingle of her touch from his scalp.

"That's not how I planned my exit." Her giggle echoed in the stairwell and shot through his nerves.

"That debacle was a plan?"

"It would have been fine if you'd stayed out of it." She stopped and faced him. Her bonnet was still hanging down her back, and her dark hair soaked up the sunshine. Her curls made his fingers twitch.

"What exactly did you have in mind?" He waved his hand across the stairwell, from rail to wall. "Because you didn't know about this." If she had, she'd never have kissed him. Because had he known of the stairwell, he'd have avoided being trapped with her.

Wouldn't he?

"Why does that matter to you? Why are you even here?" Jocelyn's chin tilted at an angle Drake recognized from every time he'd assigned her to lookout duty rather than haulage.

"I was going up to Oliver's rooms when I saw you." Drake's careful preparation gave him the ability to look her in the eye while he lied. It was galling, and slightly admirable, that she held his gaze.

It shouldn't have surprised him. She was Mal's daughter, after all.

"You're on a first-name basis with a duke?" Jocelyn asked, her eyes narrow. "What's the game?"

"No game." Drake put his hand on her waist, encouraging her to descend. They needed distance between her and the viscount. If Stratford noticed anything amiss, he knew exactly where to find them. There'd be no hiding, and no witnesses, in this narrow space. "Unlike you and that trick with your knee."

Her laughter rippled through his fingers, past his wrist, to his elbow.

"You enjoyed that, and you know it." She leaned in, her breath teasing his ear. "I certainly do."

"Enough, Jocelyn." They'd reached the ground floor, and Drake ushered her into the hall. He kept her moving toward the door. "Lord and Lady Rushford count on me for my discretion."

She nodded her thanks to the usher who held the door for her. "You just implied that parliamentary debate is an aphrodisiac. I believe discretion has gone out the window."

Drake smiled in spite of himself. "If that gets out, there won't be a seat left in the gallery."

"And debates will grow much more heated." Jocelyn shuddered. "Heaven forbid." Her smile banished the wariness from her eyes.

The air cooled Drake's skin and pulled away her tempting scent. Her retied bonnet shaded her face. She was just another woman on the streets of London. If she had a basket, he'd almost believe she was headed to market.

The urge to kiss her again lay heavy on his tongue. He cleared his throat and kept his distance.

"Be careful, Jocelyn. If Stratford had caught you, there would have been nothing I could have done."

"*If* he had caught me, I would have handed him my calling card and invited him to visit." She lifted her skirt and descended to the first stair. "The viscount has a *penchant* for dark-haired doxies, as luck would have it."

He liked other things, too, if Drake's sources could be believed. He grabbed her arm before she could retreat further. Their height difference, the green ribbon decorating her bonnet, her useless lace handkerchief—all of it combined to make her seem more fragile. It might have been a disguise, but all Drake saw was a twelve-year-old in trousers and braces, her hair shoved under a cap.

"Stay well clear of him."

"This isn't the beach, Fletcher." She pulled free, her mouth a firm line under the bourbon-brown bonnet. "You aren't the boss."

She continued down the stairs, only to look back when she reached the street. "Come for breakfast tomorrow. Nine o'clock. I'd like your help with a personal matter."

Drake watched her go until she was part of the crowd. No one gave her a second glance. She was just another woman in London.

He returned to Westminster and took the stairs two at a time to reach Oliver's rooms. The exercise did him good. By the time he reached the door, he wasn't thinking of bluebells or corsets, or the feel of her knee against—

Damn.

Oliver looked up from his paperwork, a smile splitting his face.

Drake dropped into the nearest chair. "Don't tell Thea about this." He pushed his hand through his hair. "And for God's sake, don't tell Ferrand."

CHAPTER EIGHT

DRAKE LOWERED HIS hand from his cravat and relaxed his grip on his walking stick. There was a fine line between prepared and preening.

There was also a distinction between helping and gloating, which he tried to remember as he rang the bell at the White Rose. As a precaution, he took a step back from the door and turned away to face the front garden. In the daylight, in the shade provided by the covered entry, this could be just another home in London. The roses were well tended, even though the last of the season's blooms were fading. Autumn companion plants mounded under hedges and circled the base of the fountain, the marble of which gleamed in the sunshine.

Drake had paid little attention to it on his previous evenings, stopping just long enough to hear water gurgle and splash and dismiss the unfamiliar shape as an ornament rather than an enemy. But now it was impossible to overlook.

Young lovers were frozen mid-reunion, an endless stream of water trickling from the half-forgotten urn the woman held at her side as she raised her lips for a kiss. He, though he could hold her forever, was doomed to be a breath away for eternity. The piece was finely carved, leaving the impression that today's wind had caught the woman's skirt as she ran into his arms, and that her hair was soft against her lover's fingers. For his part, the marble man had a tight grip on his lady's backside, given the dents his fingers left in the stone fabric.

Much like when Drake had held Jocelyn outside Viscount Stratford's rooms in Parliament. His body heated in a too-familiar way, much as it had every morning since, when he woke with the sheets tangled around his legs, hard as the marble man in the garden. He envied the lover his eternal embrace, but at least Drake had gotten a kiss. Though Jocelyn's taste would likely haunt him for years.

"It's a lovely piece, isn't it?" Jocelyn said, her voice too close to his ear.

Blast. The woman could distract him to the point of foolishness. "It is finely carved, and much more sedate than I would have thought. Who is the artist?"

"I'm not certain, though it's likely in the records somewhere. Madeline saw it in Paris and bought it without giving thought to how water would be piped. It sat dry and quiet until she could bring the artist over to install it properly."

Drake listened with half an ear as he schooled his thoughts and his expression, looking anywhere but at the stone sculpture as she spoke. Her quiet tone wove a spell that had the two of them very much alone in a very public house in a very noisy city.

"You expected naked virgins in an orgy with horned satyrs, didn't you?"

"No." He drew a breath to object further and was assailed by bluebells, which were out of season in autumn. It drew his eyes to her, and her impish grin disarmed him. "Perhaps."

"And you're disappointed, aren't you?" she whispered, waggling her eyebrows. "Admit it."

Drake rolled his eyes. "Jocelyn."

She dissolved into giggles that erased her age, whisking him back to the days when they'd all escaped to sunshine and sand and let the sea foam tickle their toes, where they'd forgotten that salt water was for work rather than play. His laugh felt as rusty as it sounded.

"We can't go scandalizing our neighbors in the daylight." She looked over her shoulder as she turned toward the door. "Are you coming in?"

She was fresh-faced, and her braided hair was pinned to her head in a simple circle. Its darkness contrasted with a pressed white shirt with a crisp collar. It looked much like his, except it was open at the throat, the neckline leading to a row of pearl buttons. Even her dove-gray skirt was simply tailored. Her narrow waist drew his hand like a lodestone as they crossed the threshold.

She pulled away with an efficient grace that left him both amazed and bereft.

"It was good of you to come." She took his arm, winding her hand up his biceps until they were elbow to elbow, her breasts dangerously close.

Drake bent his arm to keep her a safe distance as she led him deeper into the house. "Thank you for the invitation."

They stopped at a conservatory dominated by the dining table. Fourteen seats awaited occupants. "I thought we'd be meeting alone."

"We can discuss our business after breakfast. The house always gathers in the morning, and I prefer to start my day with a view of the garden."

More like *in* the garden. The wide-leafed potted plants arranged at the edges of the room contrasted with hedges and heaps of flowers that lay beyond windows so clean it seemed possible to step through them. Golden autumn leaves dotted the lawn like scattered treasure that tempted you to pluck it as you walked.

"Expecting more scandal?" Jocelyn asked as she tapped a maple wood mallet against a silver gong.

"I may need the name of your gardener." Despite the fact that he'd chosen the house on Charles Street because it lacked a garden.

"Madam might not hire herself out for someone else's flowers, but Tommy and I would be glad to give you a price."

The businesslike proposition lost some of its credibility when Drake had to look almost to his waist to find the speaker.

The boy, with hair the color of Yorkshire mud, held out his hand. "Alfie Lane."

Drake returned the greeting, careful not to smile too wide. "Drake Fletcher, Mr. Lane."

The boy's eyes widened. "You're Harry's master, ain't ya?"

"*Aren't you*, Alfie," Jocelyn whispered.

Drake bristled at *master*, but he was never sure what to call himself. He technically wasn't a guardian, and he definitely wasn't a father. "Harry and I have an understanding."

"I like Harry. He knows all the good places in town." The boy pointed out the window to a cart heaped with soil. "Someone tossed that cart just because it had lost a wheel."

Drake followed Jocelyn to the buffet but put Alfie between them. "How did you get it home?"

"It weren't easy." The boy reached for a scone. Jocelyn put tongs in his hand.

Drake didn't bother to hide his laugh. No wonder Alfie and Harry were friends.

The boy reached the end of the buffet with a plate heaped full of fruit, eggs, and bacon. The scone teetered for a moment before tumbling toward the carpet. Alfie caught it with the ease of a veteran fielder. "You let me know when you want me to look at your garden. Just because Harry and me are mates don't mean you won't get a good day's work."

Drake found himself wishing he had something for the boy to do. "I'll keep you in mind."

"You have school," Jocelyn said as she urged the boy to the table. "And Tommy already has a job."

As more women entered the room, Drake let them in front of him to fill their plates. He took the extra time to study the garden. Apparently, Jocelyn still enjoyed growing things. She'd spent hours fussing over her scraggly vegetable garden and scrawny rosebushes at Highcliffe. It cheered him to know she'd found better soil in London. It also gave him an idea. If she enjoyed flowers as a pastime, perhaps there was a way to capitalize on it.

Something nudged his middle, and he looked into the shy smile of a lovely blonde who could have graced any ballroom. A plate lay between them.

"Thank you, miss."

"Imogen." The girl's dark eyes sparkled. "It's been a long time since anyone's called me miss."

They would if you were in a different line of work. The words lay heavy on Drake's tongue as he stepped forward to fill his plate. As a guest, it wasn't his place to point out the obvious to Jocelyn's staff—if that was what one called them.

He noticed Imogen took only one slice of bacon, where everyone else had heaped their plates full. "You don't care for the pork?"

"Oh no, sir. Elsa is the best cook in the city, but there's not much left, and it's impolite the rob the guests of treats." She gifted him with another sparkly smile. "You should have gone through the line earlier."

Men likely queued up around the block for an hour of her time, not to mention her treats, but Drake couldn't help returning her smile. "But then I wouldn't have met you."

"Madam will have her hands full with you, Mr. Fletcher."

"You know me?" Surely their paths hadn't crossed. She would have stood out like a pearl in a puddle.

"Madam told us you'd be visiting this morning so we wouldn't be surprised. We don't normally have men in the house this early unless it's Dr. Goddard. And he's already here."

As she spoke, Sam entered the room. From his brown tweed suit to his buffed boots, everything about him was conservative, except for the redhead clinging to him like a vine. He led her to the buffet and placed her behind Drake.

"A solid breakfast will do you good, Margot," he said in a quiet voice. "I need to speak to Madam White."

"But Sam, you should eat—"

"Grace will be expecting me for breakfast." He lifted her hand from his arm, never losing the fatherly smile that creased his face all the way to his graying temples.

Though his eyes stayed kind, the rest of his features reminded Drake of the expression he'd seen women wear when faced with unwanted attention. He offered the new arrival a plate. She accepted without removing her eyes from her companion, who did not look back.

"Imogen," Drake said. "Allow me to help you to the table."

He led the young woman to the empty place beside Sam, who was now in deep conversation with Jocelyn. Margot's gaze, and frown, followed them from her spot near the sideboard. In silk and chiffon, she seemed more suited to reading social invitations in bed while sipping chocolate than serving herself breakfast.

Without looking up, Jocelyn placed her hand on the spot to her left, indicating where Drake was to sit.

"Sam, I don't want you to be uncomfortable," she said. "I'll take care not to call on you about Margot again."

"No. I *want* to see her if she's ill, but it seems her main goals have become more personal in nature." The man looked up as if shocked to see someone next to him. He nodded to Imogen before casting a relieved glance at Drake. "I suppose I have you to thank for the intervention, Mr. Fletcher."

"It's the least I could do after your kindness to Ed in the park. How is Grace?"

"Fine, thank you, but she's dreading her lessons this morning. I'd like to visit with her governess before they get started. She needs to challenge Grace more."

Jocelyn blotted her lips with her serviette before she pushed back from the table. "Let me pay you."

"Nonsense." Dr. Goddard motioned for her to stay seated. "I'll not take payment for an unnecessary visit. But I'll see you in a fortnight."

"Very well, if you insist. Until then." She smiled at the doctor. "I hate to ask you to see yourself out, but the gentlemen are busy with another task."

That's what was missing. Drake cast a glance around the room and out into the rear garden. None of Jocelyn's male employees were in sight. From what he'd seen during previous visits, Hugh was practically Jocelyn's shadow.

"I can do it," Alfie said as he scrambled from the chair next to Drake. "I'm done—finished—eating, and I can make sure Tommy and the boys have had a plate."

"And then you can help Elsa with the dishes," Jocelyn said. "Before the tutor arrives."

The boy blinked. "But I thought I'd be helping upstairs."

"Just because you're staying close to home doesn't mean you're staying uneducated," Jocelyn replied with a wry smile. "You'll be down here with the ladies learning geography and grammar, since your schoolmaster seems to skimp on the latter."

Breakfast continued, and the conversation grew in volume. Laughter spilled over the table, soothing Drake's nerves along the way. If he didn't think too hard, he could be at a lending circle meeting before business began.

"Thank you for accepting my invitation," Jocelyn said in a quiet voice. "Though I hate to admit it, you're the only man I know in London who is qualified to help with this matter."

"I appreciate your confidence." Drake put his cutlery beside his plate and removed his serviette from his lap. A young maid cleared his place with silent efficiency. Another did so for Jocelyn. The young ladies, however, carried their own dishes as they left the room.

"People take care more with things for which they are responsible," Jocelyn said as she followed his gaze. "Whether it's clothes, rooms, or dishes."

Drake wondered where she'd learned that lesson. It certainly wasn't from her father.

"There are several businesses which would be easy to start,

with the right investor," he began. Her trembling smirk unnerved him. "But a florist might be the best fit, since you already know so much about gardening. Fresh flowers would be more difficult to stock. The investment would be higher, but if you grew your own, after a few years, you should—"

"And you think the women of London would buy flowers from someone who takes their husbands' coins every evening? That their husbands would stop for nosegays to take home to the mothers of their children sold to them by a former soiled dove?" Jocelyn's lips twisted over the last two words.

"Then don't stay in London. Go to a village where no one knows you. You've moved before. You weren't always…this." He waved his hand to encompass the now empty space, save for her holding court at the head of the table. Despite the pretense, despite the trappings, she was something he never thought she'd consider.

She was better than this.

"I see." She rolled her lips together. "I apologize that the invitation was vague and that the context of my compliment was misconstrued." Her eyes flashed. "But I have a business. A damned successful one. In London. Where I wish to live."

A chill ran down his spine. If she didn't need his help getting out of the sex trade, then she needed his skills in the only other thing he knew. "Then why am I here?"

She paused for so long that he thought—hoped—she had reconsidered. Finally, she drew a deep breath and leaned close enough she could whisper. "I need to get someone out of London."

He would not help her break Malcolm out of prison. The man was exactly where he belonged. "Who?"

"A young lady who saw something she shouldn't have, and who will be in danger if she's found."

People were in danger every day, and they left London regularly. "Then put her on a coach, or aboard a ship. Hell, she could walk—"

"Do you think I didn't consider that before I asked you? The ports are being watched, as are the stations and the gates. She wouldn't last a moment, and it's *vital* that she does. She's a witness to a crime."

Half of London saw crime on a daily basis, some multiple times. "Jocelyn—"

"She saw her friend murdered by someone who will never see justice unless the *ton* is forced to mete it out."

Drake stared hard at her, trying to read her face. A flicker of acknowledgment darkened her eyes.

"Stratford." He breathed. "Bloody hell, Jocelyn. He's seen you."

"No, he's seen you."

Blast. She was right. For all he knew, Stratford had men watching his home. Someone could have followed him here. Someone could be trailing the boys.

His life had been fine before he came to this blasted place. He should have chosen the Gold Peacock for whiskey sales. He should have just left her to her own devices.

She placed a hand over his, warming his knuckles. "I'm sorry, Drake. Really, I am. But this girl, Violet—You've met Imogen today. Imagine she was the victim. I suspect they're very much alike. And Stratford will get away with this because he can. To everyone else, Violet is just another doxy in the river."

The image she created wrenched his conscience, and Drake wasn't certain if she'd done it on purpose. He wanted to believe she wasn't manipulating him, that she was as sincere as she sounded. "Where is your witness?"

"Likely pacing the attic."

"She's *here?*" Drake pulled away from her as he lost the battle to stay quiet. "Dammit, Jocelyn. Do you realize how dangerous that is?"

"Why do you think all my male employees are guarding the property from upstairs windows?" she countered. "Why do you think I'm asking you for help?"

"And why the deuce did I even come?" Even as he said it, he knew the answer. He'd been prepared to be her rescuer. Though it wasn't how he intended, she still needed one. For that matter, he might need one as well. It would be best to deal with this situation head-on.

He traced the damask pattern etched on the tablecloth as he considered his options.

"I have a shipment of wine to deliver. It's routine enough no one would pay attention." But he couldn't take it to Thetford directly. If Stratford was watching, it would lead him to Thea and Amelia. To the freight depot. To the children. He needed to warn Oliver. Ferrand would need to be alerted as well, though it galled him to admit a mistake in front of the Frenchman.

"We could go to Highcliffe," she offered.

There was no *we*. She wasn't getting more involved in this than she already was, and he wasn't setting foot in Highcliffe again. "There isn't anyone there to offer her protection from a viscount."

The Marquess of Ramsbury might help. Jasper was almost always on the fringe of scandal. However, there was scandal and there was *scandal*. Drake's connection was too tenuous to count on unilateral support, and he wasn't certain of Jasper's political loyalty. They could knock on his door and be turned away—or turned over the constables. "I'll call on someone tomorrow. Now, how do I get her out of town?"

"We can dress her as a man," Jocelyn offered. "She could ride next to you."

Drake did a mental inventory of the women at the table. All of them could have served as models for Botticelli. Trousers would do nothing but call attention to their figures. They'd have to hide her. And they couldn't stuff her in a barrel. "I'll think of something."

He stood, as did she. At first glance, she looked as though they'd been debating the price of ham in the market. But she was worrying her bottom lip between her teeth like she'd done years before when the sea grew rough.

Drake didn't realize he'd reached for her until her hair tickled his nose. He pressed a kiss to the top of her head. "I'll send word tomorrow, somehow. It's likely best if we aren't seen together until this is over."

She nodded against him, a quick jerk against his topcoat before she pulled away. "Agreed."

CHAPTER NINE

"THE MARQUESS IS in his office. Follow me."

The new Marquess of Ramsbury's household was managed by a man not much older than Drake himself, and he moved with the grace of one familiar with his body and what it could do, someone who had pushed that same body to its limits more than once. As he turned the corner to the stairs, he drew up short and swore as he put a hand on his knee.

"Old injury?" Drake asked.

"In France," the man answered. "You'd think two countries could eventually just agree to coexist. It's always the same argument, wanting more when you already have enough."

"Just so," Drake answered. Greed for wealth and power, regardless of the scale or the stakes, was a waste. No matter their ages or the weapons they chose, the skills they employed, young men lost lives for someone else's honor, another man's gain.

War, injury, relative youth... He reevaluated his assumptions of the man next to him. "You aren't a butler."

"You catch on quickly."

The words raised the hairs on Drake's neck. At least he'd ignored Society rules and carried his knife with him. Two, actually. Though if this was a trap, he wasn't sure he could fight them both.

If it was a trap.

His escort opened the door and announced him. Jasper Warren stood, his blond hair glinting in the shaft of sunlight cutting through the open drapes. "Fletcher."

"Lord Ramsbury." Drake clasped the hand that was offered. "Good of you to see me."

"According to my cousin, you are the brother she never thought to ask for, and I am to give you any help you require."

Trust Amelia Ferrand to call in a family favor before Drake knew he'd need it. "She is a determined and redoubtable young woman. I'm honored that she considers me so."

Jasper waved his hand to a chair before the fireplace, and sat in the opposite one, slouching into the corner so that he half faced the fire while his elbow rested on the arm. "My uncle will likely corner you with more questions when you see him next. Helping her begin a distillery under his nose was a bold move."

Drake took the chair but didn't unwind. He'd met the marquess only twice before, and this was a large favor. "She'd already begun it. I simply helped her succeed more quickly." He noted the bottles displayed on the tray nearby. Even without reading the labels, he knew Jasper displayed his cousin's work with pride.

Following his gaze, Jasper poured two drinks and handed one to Drake. The scent hit him before the taste. Thetford wheat and peaches blended with the raspberries he'd helped her buy two summers earlier. It seemed like a lifetime ago.

"Which was easy to do," Drake stated. It was important for Amelia's family to accept that her success was hers alone. Money was nothing compared to talent and drive.

"Indeed." Jasper stared steadily as he sipped. "How can I help you, Drake?"

He'd rehearsed this request all morning as he worked in the carriage house, yet nothing had sounded right. It still didn't. Sometimes the best way to request a difficult favor was simply to ask for it. "I need to get a young woman out of London, somewhere she'll be safe."

Jasper coughed over his whiskey. When he regained his composure, his smile widened. "And you thought of *me*?"

"She's not a sheltered Society miss." Drake waited, hoping Jasper would understand without further explanation. When he nodded, Drake continued. "She's the sole witness to a murder committed at her former place of work by a man who will remain untouchable should she disappear. Perhaps even if she doesn't."

Jasper was no longer lounging in his chair. His elbows on his knees, he dangled his hands in front of him. His pale blue eyes were sharp. "You've spoken with her?"

"I've spoken with someone who has spoken with her." Jocelyn would never have called for help, especially from Drake, unless she believed the tale.

"So a doxy saw a peer murder another doxy, and you need me to hide her until the furor subsides." Jasper paused, waiting for confirmation. "Why me?"

"Because your properties are far out of London, and a marquess outranks a viscount."

Jasper raised his eyebrows. "Norfolk is a good distance from London, and a duke outranks us both."

Drake shook his head. "I won't put my friends and their families in danger. Besides that, your connections are older."

"Fine answers." The marquess sipped his whiskey. "Which viscount?"

Drake had prepared for this question, but he paused nonetheless. The revelation would seal everyone's fates, which was why it had to be made. "Stratford."

The name rocked Jasper back in his chair. He was silent for a moment, but the glint in his eyes was unmistakable. "You're certain she can be trusted? That this is valid?"

"I am."

Jasper stood and strode to the bellpull, yanking it hard enough that it should have tumbled to the floor in a pile. Unease pooled low in Drake's belly. Amelia had trusted her cousin with her largest secret, but a distillery was no match for a peer who was a murderer. And *considered* family was much different to *being* family.

The faux butler reappeared, straight and tall. "Yes?"

"Kit, bring a map, pins, and coffee," Jasper commanded as he cleared his desk. "We have work to do."

Drake exhaled a long, deep breath. "Thank you, my lord."

"Don't thank me." The man spread a sheaf of maps and notes across his desk and then placed his glass in the far corner, out of the way. "There is a larger game in play, and I have been searching for a way to get Stratford off the board." He looked up. "If we're going to do this, you'd best call me Jasper."

DRAKE LEFT JASPER'S townhouse long after nightfall, shaking his head to clear it before he began the shadowy trek. It seemed Amelia and her cousin shared the same unrelenting focus and drive. He'd gone in requesting a favor and come out with a fully formed plan.

Caution dictated that he hail a cab, but Drake preferred to walk. He didn't want to deviate from that behavior. Besides that, walking gave him a view of the street that a cab did not.

He had just made his turn onto Charles Street when a tug on his coat drew him up. He made himself relax, half expecting who would be there. An assassin wouldn't ask for attention. He turned and looked down. David was there with another, older boy, who kept looking over his shoulder. His hair was well over his collar, but it was clean.

"Hullo, sir," David said. "This is my brother, Charlie. We wanted to tell you that we noticed a man." He raised his hand.

Charlie batted it down. "Don't point him out. We don't want to borrow trouble." He looked up at Drake. He couldn't have been much older than Nicky, who was in the house trying not to overeat. "You paid my brother a pound for nothing, and I thank you, but our debt's repaid, sir. Watch out for that man down one and across the street from your door, just outside the lamplight.

He looks like a brawler."

Drake nodded his thanks and reached into his pocket. When Charlie shook his head, Drake persisted. "If I don't give you something, the lout will be suspicious."

Charlie looked at the coin glinting in his dirty hand. "This is too much, sir."

"Not from someone who values the lives of those in his household. Thank you for looking out for me. If you ever need anything for your family or yourself, come to the door. You won't be turned away."

Charlie tipped his hat before leading his brother away. They returned to the line of sweepers, David dutifully following behind his brother, keeping in plain sight.

Drake kept on his path, careful not to look to the side, though his skin crawled with apprehension. He didn't slow, or breathe, until he was behind the door. He locked it with a vicious shove. "Gav?"

His friend came from behind the stairs, a dishtowel in his hand. "We need to talk."

"In a moment. Are the doors and windows locked?"

"Yes." He slung the dishtowel over the stair railing. "Do I need a pistol?"

"It might be wise for the next few days." Drake plucked the mallet from its resting place and rang the long-ignored gong, wincing as it reverberated through the house more loudly than he'd expected. However, the boys all came to the upstairs railing.

"Come down here, lads," Drake commanded. "Sit on the stairs." He'd put the house, their house as much as his, in danger.

Gavin joined them, looking over his shoulder as he climbed. "I told you not to stick your toe back into that mess."

Never mind his toes—Drake was soon to be in this up to his neck. Once they were all settled, he sat with them. "I have been asked to help a friend with something very important, but…there are some who would rather this not occur. The house is being watched."

Frank looked to the door, his smile too feral for a lad his age.

"Let's just go out there and get him. There are six of us and one of him."

"They'd send someone else, or more, bent on darker things," Gavin said. "It's best if we go about our business until this is over. But I'll be walking you all to school and home for a few days, just in case. No haring off without me, and no stops until we get here."

Ed's disgusted sigh filled the hall.

Drake nailed him with a hard stare. The boy had never been spoiled, and he'd spent too much time on the street to be soft. But he'd always been alone. "Ed, you are in this mess because of a decision I made, and though it is for a good reason, I'm sorry. But if you give these people an idea that someone might have necessary information, they will be in danger as well."

The young man's eyes went wide, and Drake kicked himself for getting them into this scheme. He'd promised them all a safer life—a chance at a life. Instead, he'd brought danger home with him.

"I need go out for a few minutes, but Gavin will look out for you until I return. Go on up to bed."

"We're not babies you have to take care of," Frank shot back as he climbed the stairs. "I'm sleeping with my blade under my pillow. Everyone better knock before they come in."

Nicky nodded in agreement. "I'll keep my cricket bat nearby."

Once they were back upstairs, Drake turned for the library. "Where did Nicky get a cricket bat?"

"He likely plucked it from a refuse pile. And that's what you want to talk about?" Gavin followed in his wake. "The boys are sleeping with weapons, and I'm carrying a gun into the kitchen. Tell me you're not daft enough to break the old man out of prison."

"Of course not." Though Drake couldn't help but wonder how Jocelyn's father was involved. He unlocked the safe and reached for a packet of papers he'd hoped to never touch once he'd written them. He thrust them at Gavin. "This is everything you'll need should something happen to me."

Bank letters, deeds, letters of introduction. There were a few very personal goodbyes. His whole life was summed up in less than a dozen sheets of paper.

"Well then, they're safer where you had them." Gavin put them back in the safe, closed the door, and twisted the lock. He returned the key to its hiding place. "Be careful, Bat."

"Always." Drake clapped his oldest living friend on the shoulder. "I won't be long. I should talk with Jocelyn before this goes further. I'll be back to relieve you on watch within the hour."

Gavin snorted a laugh and shook his head. "You are the only man I know who'd go to a brothel to *talk*." He walked past, out of the library. "I'll be upstairs when you come back. Sing out so I don't shoot you."

Drake itched to go to the window, pull the curtain back, and get a look at his hulking shadow. But the man would be just that, and he'd know he'd been spotted. They'd go to ground. Any hope of executing this plan would be lost.

"Is this why there's a cart full of wine in our carriage house?"

Drake whipped around, his hand halfway to his hip before he recognized Ed in the doorway. "Don't creep up on me like that. Ever."

The boy's throat spasmed in a deep gulp, but he didn't budge. "Is it?"

"You should be upstairs." Drake sighed as he dropped back against the edge of his desk. "We all should."

He put his fingers to his temple, hoping to soothe the dull throbbing that had become a persistent rhythm over the last week. What had he been thinking, putting these boys at risk like this? Why had he even offered them safety when he knew how easily it could vanish? No matter how far he climbed out of the tide, it was always there waiting to suck him back under. "I need to work out how to hide a person in there. A girl."

"How big is she?" Ed asked as he approached the desk on noisier feet than before.

Drake didn't know which of The Rose's employees he was to rescue, but he could at least average the ones he'd seen at breakfast. He touched his shoulder, "About this tall, likely nine stone, perhaps ten. I thought I could build a false bottom in the cart, but the barrels will sit too high. And I can't put her *in* a barrel all the way to—" It was best no one knew their destination. "Wherever."

"Put her in the box," Ed suggested.

Drake lifted his head, his guilt fading as the boy's words sank in. "What?"

"Even if they check the cart, you have to stay in charge of the horses. Drivers never leave the box." Ed's words gained momentum as he pulled a piece of paper from the sheaf. "We did it once with a pig." He dipped a quill in the inkpot and talked as he drew. "You should reinforce the top so you can get rid of the braces in the middle, and you need to ensure air can get in. If you chisel a few holes, it looks like wear."

Jocelyn had compared these lads to helpless, docile kittens. He'd even treated them like that. They were anything but.

Drake looked from the sketch to the boy, who was tensed for criticism. "This is fine thinking, Ed. Thank you." He tapped a finger on the corner of the hastily made diagram. "We'll build this tomorrow, you and I."

The young man flushed with pride, but his eyes still held questions. "Why did Gavin call you Bat?"

Drake would've given almost anything for Ed to have never heard that name. Now that he had, he deserved the truth. "Because a long time ago, I only went out at night and didn't let anything get between me and what I wanted."

"Like now."

Exactly like now. The man in the shadows thought he was dealing with a *ton* dandy who would cower at the first sign of violence. Drake curled his fingers into a fist. That man and the one who'd sent him had no idea what they'd awakened.

CHAPTER TEN

JOCELYN SAT IN her parlor, near the fireplace in a straight-backed chair that gave her a perfect view of the room and the front hall. Her back hurt, and she was losing the battle against fidgeting, but it was her own fault. She'd deliberately chosen a chair spare enough to not impede her if she needed to move.

Though the crowd might get in her way.

It had taken her months to grow accustomed to the noise that filled The Rose each night. The parlor was always full of music and laughter, be it over a song or a game of cards. Even the back rooms were busy. Pots clanged in the kitchen and plates clattered. At the bar, ice crashed into crystal glasses, and seltzer bottles hissed.

Other than that, it wasn't much different from life in High-cliffe, where work had been done from dusk until dawn. She'd spent too many of those nights keeping watch in a quiet house, reading by the lamp that guided the boys home or mopping their muddy tracks from the floors—anything to distract herself from staring out the window looking for their shadows to come trudging up the hill.

"Madam White, would you do me the honor of a dance?"

Joss forced herself to smile at the young viscount who was blocking her view of the door. "Thank you, Lord Raines, but I'm playing chaperone this evening." She looked across the room and caught the eye and the nod of an idle girl. "Maisie is available, though."

The younger version of herself would be disappointed to see her refuse a dance. She had pestered her father for months about going to a dance in town. Only after he'd relented did she realize she didn't own a dress suitable for dancing. It was probably why he'd agreed in the first place.

It had been a relief when her father sent her out to fill the gap when they were short-handed, when she'd been one of the group trudging up the hill. The challenge of stealth had made her blood sing, and the scent of the sea on her hair had brought her peace.

Until the night she'd washed up on shore, coughing up salt water, and stayed huddled on the beach while rain made it impossible to see anything past the shore. She'd screamed until her throat was raw, calling for Davy and then begging Drake to get out of the wild sea.

If she could survive that, she could survive a few hours in a stiff chair. Though her corset, which was chafing just below her shoulder blades, might do her in.

No one ever died from sitting straight.

Madeline's voice rang in Joss's memory. It had taken exactly two days of wearing silk and a corset to make Joss long for the baggy trousers and oversized shirts she'd once loathed. And while it had been easy to cinch in her waist, it had been almost impossible to rid herself of the poor posture she'd cultivated to hide in plain sight.

And now, here she was, in teal silk, in the middle of a brothel, waiting for her enemies to come at her. Which they would, because they thought women were weak.

The door opened, and Joss held her breath. It came out in a relieved exhale when she recognized Drake in the hallway. Beads of water trailed down his top hat and pooled in the brim, much as they slid down a window. They fell from his coat as he removed it, as though the wind had shaken a tree.

His clear blue gaze swept the room before it landed on her.

The intensity of it, the set to his mouth and the angle of his jaw, was as familiar as the butterflies in her chest were foreign.

It was the adventure they were sharing. Nothing more.

Joss stood as he approached, and the crowd parted before him like the sea yielding to a ship. She stretched her hand to him in the hopes of keeping him at arm's length, as she did all visitors to The Rose save for Reginald Spencer.

Drake kissed her knuckles, his breath warm even through her silk glove. His firm grasp sent sparks to her shoulder. The shock of it eroded her resolve to keep him away.

"We need to talk," he whispered. "Now."

He had tucked her hand into his elbow before her senses returned. Madam White only took one man to her rooms. It was crucial that nothing disturbed that pattern. She stepped away from them and opened her fan. "It's not possible, Mr. Fletcher. I'm chaperoning this evening. But Imogen is free."

The young lady, hearing her name, came to his side. "Hello again, Mr. Fletcher."

"I do not want Imogen." Drake glanced to his side, a grim twist to his lips. "My apologies, miss. Under other circumstances—"

"There can be no other circumstances. I am not free." Joss kept her voice low as she held his gaze, hoping he could see the secret there. "Imogen is well prepared to see to your needs."

After a moment, his thunderous expression smoothed to glass. He offered his arm to Imogen. "May I?"

She was still giggling as she led him to the door. They made a lovely couple, her dainty features and light hair juxtaposed against his dark broodiness. As they vanished up the stairs, his laughter tumbled down.

Joss returned to her uncomfortable chair, glad for the warmth of the fire. It soaked into her leather slippers, promising to keep her toes comfortable when she left the room. Maisie departed with Viscount Raines, and Poppy was in an animated conversation with Terrence Macklin. The man couldn't stop smiling at her.

The clock pendulum swung, counting off every second since Imogen and Drake had left the parlor. The ticking echoed louder with every stroke.

Across the room, Margot was attending to the card table, either delivering drinks or perching on the players' chairs. She was careful not to flit from player to player and only move between hands to avoid complaints of distraction and accusations of cheating. Sarah was hanging on every word from a nervous young man who couldn't possibly be that interesting. Edith was already upstairs with his companion, likely either his father or uncle.

Imogen was upstairs as well.

The only young lady not working tonight was the one in the attic, the golden goose who was turning Joss's world on its head. There was no other reason for her to keep glancing at the ceiling while the minutes crept past.

The half-hour chimed, and Joss stood. Surely five minutes was long enough. No one was watching her anyway. Rather than taking the front stairs, she went to the kitchen. Eleanor was at the table, watching Bea do her schoolwork. Elsa was at the workbench, kneading dough.

"More bread?" Joss teased as she filched a biscuit. "We won't be able to eat it all before it molds." Elsa had been baking since the night Connie had been discovered in the attic.

"I'm not sure I mind." Eleanor placed her fork on her plate. The dark crumbs were laced with bits of carrot. "That's one of the best cakes I've had."

"I can stop if you'd prefer it, Joss." Despite her words, the cook kept working. "It's just that I like to keep busy."

"And I'll not get in your way," Joss said. "What we can't eat, we'll donate. I'm sure your mission can use it."

The kitchen was her favorite room in The Rose. After a life of staying up until all hours, sleep frequently eluded her. She always ended up here, listening to Elsa and Eleanor gossip in the warm room that smelled how a home should smell. Elsa had taught Joss to bake, and Eleanor had tried every disastrous result. They were as close to aunts as she would ever have, and they were two of the few who remembered that *Madam* wasn't her first name.

"Are you ready for me, then?" Eleanor stood and smoothed her skirt. "I'll confess, I feel odd going out there."

Bea's head snapped up from her book. "I'll do it."

The girl was a lovely fifteen-year-old. In a few years, with cosmetics and silk, she'd stop conversation in any room. Maisie and Sarah had done her up as a lark a few months earlier, and Tommy had damn near swallowed his tongue. Eleanor had kept Bea in the cottage for a solid week.

"You'll finish your studies and go to bed." Eleanor pointed to the book for emphasis.

Joss stopped on her way to the back stairs and put her hand on her maid's shoulder. "Thank you for doing this."

"Whatever gets that girl out of this house and James back where he belongs." Eleanor shook her head. "I never thought I'd wish to see him in that parlor."

Joss didn't have the luxury of feeling guilty about everything the older woman's statement implied. No one ever woke wishing they worked in a brothel. But when this was over, when she had more time, she'd sit down for tea with Eleanor and have a long conversation.

"Call for Tommy if you need him."

The narrow stairs kept her focus on her feet rather than the fact that she'd left her business in the hands of a maid, a cook, and a bartender who was barely old enough to shave.

Hugh sat in his usual chair on the second floor, though he'd moved it closer to the front stairs. With Maisie and Edith both entertaining, the moans and sighs were doubled. Even though the thick doors and wall tapestries helped stifle most of the sounds, the softness of them touched Joss's skin as she walked to Imogen's door.

She raised her hand to knock but paused. *What if some of those sighs are from Imogen? What if that deep groan is Drake?* She didn't think he'd take Imogen to bed, but he did have a smile he saved only for her.

Thoughts of Drake naked on the mattress sprang to mind. Joss had taken his arm enough times to know he was well muscled, and his trousers clung suggestively to his hips and thighs. His penchant for stitched waistcoats drew attention to his broad chest, and now she wondered if it was smooth or covered in the dark hair that contrasted with his fair complexion.

How he'd escaped his life on the sea without freckles was beyond her understanding. Perhaps he had them somewhere else.

Joss closed her eyes to banish her imagination, but all it did was put her in Imogen's place, exploring his body to answer all her questions as he kissed her until she was dizzy from it. A rapturous cry had her on her back foot, ready to run, before she realized it had come from across the hall.

An ache built low in Joss's belly as she stared at the door. "I never should have kissed him."

"What's that?" Hugh asked from behind her. "Is anything amiss?"

Blast. The man had her talking to herself. "I asked how you stay out here all night and stay sane."

It was not Drake who was driving her to distraction. It was the situation. Once Connie was hidden, he'd never have to darken her door again. As soon as this mess was over, she'd leave London with her father and never look back.

"You get used to it." He used the wood in his hand to indicate the selection of knives spread across the small table beside him. "It helps to have something to do."

Joss made a mental note to keep the smaller pieces of kindling to support Hugh's hobby and knocked on Imogen's bedroom door.

The young lady, still fully clothed with her hair neatly swept back, opened the door, and stood aside as an invitation. The lock *snicked* home.

Drake stood near the window, peering past the curtain into the darkness.

"That doesn't look suspicious at all," Joss said.

"There's a man across the street watching the house."

She went to him and pulled on his elbow. It was akin to uprooting a tree. "And you in an upstairs room paying more attention to the street than to the lady with you will only encourage him to keep doing it." She heaved an exasperated sigh. "Do try to play along, Fletcher."

He let her lead him away, but veered as they approached the bed. He chose to perch on Imogen's dressing table chair instead. He didn't look out of place in the finely curved chair, but he didn't seem comfortable either. Joss expected him to crash to the floor with his first deep breath.

Imogen stayed positioned by the door, leaving Joss to sit on the edge of the bed. "What have you worked out?"

"We'll be ready to go tomorrow evening. Have your man bring the girl to Charles Street at dusk. We'll leave from there."

She nodded in agreement, impressed but not shocked that he'd arranged things so quickly. "We'll be there."

"Not *we*, Jocelyn. *They*." He glowered from under his brows, his mouth firm as he pointed to the window. "This is not a game. There is a man at my home as well."

"And I'll not abandon the young lady when her life is at stake."

"So you'll care for her while leading others, like Imogen, into debauchery and…God knows what else."

How dare he look down his nose at her. "Says the man who was a thief for most of his life." Joss tightened her fingers into a fist and wished he was close enough to strike. She'd knock him from that foolish chair. "I didn't *lead* Imogen anywhere. You can thank the randy son of a marquess for that, and her priggish parents for tossing her onto the street. Not to mention an education system that prepared her for nothing but parties and managing staff."

"She could have worked—"

"Society wouldn't accept her as one of their own, and they wouldn't take her as a servant. Even as a governess, she would have been prey. So, yes, I suppose she could have worked for a shilling a week in a dressmaker's shop or making hats for her former friends." Jocelyn arched an eyebrow sharper than any blade. "Instead, here, she makes two pounds a week, and gets a useful education."

"And spends her evenings—"

"Doing *exactly* what she would be doing in any ballroom during the Season. The men pay for her time. How she *chooses* to spend that time is up to her. If she *chooses* to enjoy sex with them, that is up to her."

"You cannot be that naïve," he scoffed.

"And you can't be so much of a prig to not even consider that women can enjoy sex."

His blush irritated her. After everything he'd done in his life, it was maddening that he would find pleasure embarrassing. That he would look down on her for pursuing it while she had the chance.

"But she could be more than this," he said.

Was this still about a more legitimate trade? Was he still angry that Joss wouldn't leave The Rose behind in favor of a *flower shop*? "And if I took you up on your offer, left this life behind, and opened a more acceptable business, if I hired all the ladies here as staff to wait and cater on Society wives, they'd still be subject to the whims of men on the streets, who saw them as less because they were shop girls, who took what they wanted without paying anything at all. We'd be fighting off landlords who expected extra consideration."

"Not if I were your landlord." His statement was quiet, but firm.

"I do not want that life," Joss stated flatly. She did not want to be in his debt any more than she already was.

"Could you really do that?" Imogen whispered from her spot

at the door. "Perhaps with hats rather than flowers?"

Joss had forgotten that she was even in the room. Given his expression, Drake had as well. However, his shock melted into a smile. "I could. I have a space on the high street in a lovely Norfolk village that is in desperate need of a new milliner."

The hope in the girl's eyes tore at Joss's heart. "I'm sorry, Imogen. I never considered—"

"No, madam. Nothing you said was incorrect, but I know that it's only a matter of time before I must choose between my purse or entertaining men I once avoided having on my dance card. Or, worse, when no one wants me to entertain them at all."

Joss nodded. Over the last few years, she'd had similar conversations with many of the ladies. Even Madam White had spoken of it before her retirement.

"Can you make hats, Imogen?" Drake asked in a voice that was kinder than Joss could have imagined outside this room.

"I can. It was once a favorite pastime. I've made a few, and mended many more, for the ladies here." She looked to Joss for confirmation. "I'm quite good at it, aren't I?"

"She is." Joss glanced at Drake, expecting to see gloating triumph painted across his face. It wasn't there. "She's very talented. She gifted me my favorite hat one year for Christmas. I get compliments every time I wear it."

"That settles it, then. As far as financing, I'd be happy to draw up a contract and provide all the initial investment—"

"She has money of her own to invest." It was important to Joss that they continue the lessons Imogen had learned here. While she didn't doubt the girl's commitment, she also knew the difference that caring for your own business brought.

Drake quirked an eyebrow. "Good, then." He stood and went to Imogen, shaking her hand. "We'll discuss this in more detail next week. I'll visit during the afternoon when you aren't occupied."

His manners with Imogen rubbed the edges from Joss's anger. He treated the girl with respect and spoke to her like the intelligent and talented young lady she was. His smile transformed the geography of his face, erasing years of worry and care. It was rare to see, and even rarer to see *here*.

He didn't want anything. He wasn't charming, and he didn't try to be. It all worked to make him more attractive than any titled dandy downstairs.

Imogen practically danced from the room, leaving Joss alone with Drake and her heart softening like driftwood tumbled over the sand.

"I do hope she remembers not to go back to the parlor without you. It will raise eyebrows."

"She's a smart young lady." Drake offered his hand to her, palm up, fingers curved, as though he was asking her to dance rather than helping her rise from a mattress in a brothel.

Joss stood as though she wasn't imagining toppling him to the bed and messing him up a little. "You thought I keep all the money she makes, didn't you?"

"In Whitechapel…" He cleared his throat. "But we aren't in Whitechapel, are we?"

"Good of you to finally realize that." Joss could smell the mint on his breath and feel his heat through her bodice. "You should at least go downstairs looking a little worse for wear."

He reached to muss his hair, but she beat him to it. The inky strands were as silky as she remembered, but his lips were softer than last time. His breath filled her like a warning before his tongue came in search of hers. Heat slid through Joss's middle, leaving hunger in its wake. She drew him deeper, begging him to fill her and gasping when he did. One hand rested on her waist, temptingly close to her backside, while the fingers of the other curved to her ribs.

Drake's lips might be soft, but nothing else was. His jaw was heavy against her thumb as she curled her other hand around his waist and up his back. Every line of his body was hard and solid. Even his behind was firm.

His hands left her body to claw at the knot on his cravat,

making it more difficult for them to kiss. Instead, his lips found her ear, and then her neck.

"Finally," he muttered before sweeping back to devour her mouth. His open collar gave her access to skin so velvety and warm it was a shame to keep it covered.

His deep groan undid her.

"Madam?" Imogen called through the door. The sharpness of it hinted that it wasn't the first time she'd called out. "I nearly forgot Mr. Fletcher." The knob rattled.

Drake's mouth left Joss's, and he curled her to his shoulder like he'd done at Parliament. The thought of him shielding her from scandal here, of all places, brought on a fit of giggles.

"We'll be out in a moment, Imogen." The shake in his sex-rough voice tempted Joss as much as the pounding of his heart against hers.

He stepped away from her and looked down at their bodies as if amazed they were still clothed. It was the first thing they had shared in years. Joss would gladly stay here and find other things between them.

The second knock was louder. "Madam?"

Hugh. *Damn.* "I'm well, Hugh. We're on our way out."

She went to the dressing table and smoothed her hair. Her kiss-swollen lips and dazed expression matched Drake's as he joined her, and she noted with pride that he was having trouble with his cravat.

"Tie it in a simpler knot. It will help sell the illusion."

"And how messy should my hair be?" he asked.

Unable to resist, she combed her fingers through it, leaving it presentable but mussed enough for the men downstairs to believe Imogen had shown him a good time. But it hadn't been Imogen he'd kissed breathless, and it wasn't Imogen's body that craved his touch. Creating this fiction was dangerous. "There. That should do it."

Joss walked with him to the bedroom door, keeping her hands to herself. His stayed behind his back as she turned the knob.

"One last thing." Drake swept down and kissed her quick and hard, then he pulled back and winked. "I was right about the hat shop." His back was straight as he went to the top of the stairs and offered Imogen his arm.

Laughter filled Joss's hollow places as she returned to the room to muss the bed.

CHAPTER ELEVEN

"WHY CAN'T I go?" Frank groused. The wine cask under his hands dropped into place with a wobble and a *thump*. "I'm a good hand in a fight."

Which was exactly why he wasn't going. "This won't require fighting. It's a boring drive to…the country and back." Drake still wasn't comfortable divulging the location to anyone. Gavin knew, but that was only so he'd start searching in the right direction. "And you have to be in school tomorrow."

"Ed got to miss today."

"Because he's doing well with his lessons." Drake grunted as his barrel reached the apex of the ramp and sloshed drunkenly while it teetered between finishing its journey or crashing to earth. Nicky guided it forward with a hand that was steadier than his age predicted.

"I'm not stupid." The knife hilt flashed under Frank's coat as he caught the cargo that Nicky had pushed into his hands like it was a pillow rather than something twice his weight.

"I never said you were." Drake nodded his thanks to Nicky and went back for the last of the shipment. "But you are behind, especially for consideration at Cambridge in a few years."

"What if I don't want to go to Cambridge?"

Everything with Frank was an argument, but Drake should have known he wouldn't want to go to Cambridge if Ed was going there. The boy made everything into a competition. "Oxford, then."

"Maybe I don't want to go to university at all."

Drake's temper flared. It had been a long, difficult day, and he was going to spend the night on pins and needles while he sat atop a stowaway half of London was hoping to find. "Even if you apprentice to a blacksmith, you'll have to know maths and grammar."

"Maths, anyway," Nicky joked as he swung from the cart in a graceful arc. "I've never seen a smithy who could conjugate a verb."

Drake and Frank barked a laugh in unison. Though the boy still held his jaw at a determined angle, the fight left his eyes as he stepped down.

"Thank you for your help." Drake clapped both boys on the shoulder and steered them toward the house. He wanted them out of the way before his real cargo arrived. Given the way each of them froze in their tracks, he'd failed in that objective.

Jocelyn stood in the doorway in the black cloak and veiled hat she always wore to the prison. Beside her, a young man about Frank's size stood with slouched ease, or perhaps his ill-fitting coat ruined his posture. Drake stared harder. The woman in black had auburn hair. The boy had a familiar scar on his chin and a challenge in his eyes.

Drake removed the peaked cap and revealed hair the color of rich coffee in a topknot so tight it was a wonder she could blink. "No, Jocelyn." The first time he'd told her to stay home, her father had overruled him. Mal wasn't here now. This was his job. "Absolutely not."

"Well, I'm not leaving her in your care alone." She put her fists on her hips, which called attention to her shape.

It wasn't the first time Drake had seen her in trousers, but that had been before he kissed her. Now he felt those curves in his dreams. "Fine. We won't go at all." He was not carting her all the way to Berkshire thinking about her backside. They'd all be dead by sunrise.

"Is this where you want me?"

The fugitive had removed the cloak and hat. She was dressed simply, and her carpetbag was small. Flanked by Nicky and Frank, she was already standing in the box, looking at her feet. She was taller than he'd expected. "Will you fit?" he asked.

Without a word, she sank to her knees and then disappeared altogether.

"I may walk stooped for a few days, but it should be fine," she called out. "Will I be able to breathe once you've closed the top?"

"There are holes chiseled discreetly, and Nicky has ridden in it to test the design."

"I suggested the blankets in the bottom." The boy beamed. "It was a blasted miserable jostling around on those planks."

"Nicky, watch—"

The boy pulled his hat from his head. "Beg your pardon for the language, miss."

"It was a lovely suggestion, Nicky. Thank you." The young lady looked to Drake and then Jocelyn. "Are we going, then?"

They were already late departing. "Please go home, Jocelyn. I swear to you that I'll watch out for her. But I can't have both of you along."

"And I can't go home without her, since half of London walks past here."

"You walked to my front door? With some blackguard watching the house?" He massaged the bridge of his nose with a finger and a thumb. He thought she was smarter than this. She had *been* smarter than this.

"I didn't have another coach because I sent Imogen dressed as me with Tommy by her side, and Eleanor dressed as me took a cab on Hugh's arm with Alfie along as their tiger. All of us dressed the same, all with the same carpetbag. So if I go home on my own now, it will look odd."

This shell game was exactly the confusing mess Mal would suggest. "And how is it going to look if you walk in the door with her and then ride out on the box with me?"

She blinked. "Well, it's dark enough that no one—"

"It isn't dark enough."

At least if she was dressed like this, he could banish thoughts of kissing. He needed all his imagination to think of a plan.

After wasting precious minutes, Drake hated what he devised, but he didn't have a choice. He couldn't send her home without an escort, and her house was unguarded until the others returned. Plus, he didn't trust her not to follow them on her own.

"Frank, change coats and hats with her." He looked up at Nicky. "How will that cloak fit you?"

The boy blinked. "Sir?"

"One of you has to be the girl. Frank can pass as your escort, but you're going to have to wear the hat and cloak. Put them on and try."

Nicky tossed the cloak over his shoulder and plucked up the hat like it was a spider before he climbed from the cart. Then he tried them on. It would be passable if no one stared too hard or too long.

Drake offered his arm and showed Nicky how to take it. "Come with me. Keep your steps small so no one sees your trousers. Follow behind, Frank."

"This is bloody awful," Nicky said as they walked.

"I dunno, you look pretty good in that hat," Frank teased. "Maybe you should keep it."

"I'll keep it and stuff it down your throat, you—"

"Quiet," Drake commanded in a whisper as they reached the street. He hailed a cab. "Go to Parliament. Have the driver drop you near an alley. Dispose of the disguises and then vanish into the crowd—but stay together. Get back here as soon as you can."

He put them in the cab and watched it leave. As soon as the coach turned the corner, he strode back to the carriage house, sickened by the hope that the shadow would take the bait and follow Frank and Nicky rather than him and Jocelyn.

Gavin was waiting, holding the team that was stamping and

snorting, eager to start. Jocelyn was already on her seat, hiding their illicit cargo.

"Did I just see Nicky in a lady's hat?" Gavin asked, a frown creasing his brow.

"You did. I sent him and Frank to Parliament. They should return in a few hours." At least, Drake hoped they would. "You know how Nicky hates to miss supper."

Gavin flicked a glance at Joss. "Be careful."

"Always am."

Drake took the reins from her without looking and urged the team forward. They lumbered toward the street. "I'll be back by noon tomorrow at the latest."

Or they'd all be dead in a ditch.

HE HADN'T SPOKEN since they had left the house on Charles Street, and Joss was content to let him sulk as he guided the draft cart through the busy streets. But then they stopped at a pub two blocks south of their starting point.

"Step down and go balance the ramp against the cart so we can unload a barrel." He climbed down without looking at her.

Joss did as she was told. This was a job, after all, and people stayed safe if they didn't stop to question the boss's orders. Inside, though, she was seething with familiar resentment. He couldn't see past his very large nose and admit that she could be helpful. Her plan hadn't been *his* plan, but that didn't mean it was terrible. Not altogether.

Drake passed by her and clapped her on the shoulder hard enough to rattle her teeth as he climbed the ramp in two long, powerful strides. He was clad all in black, even his shirt and cravat.

"Catch this as it comes down. Brace your feet or it will roll right over you."

"I know how to do it," she muttered as she squared her shoulders and locked her knees.

Even so, the weight nearly bowled her over.

"Roll it to the pub's back door." Drake pointed the way but didn't descend to help her.

It was awkward work until the liquid gave up fighting itself and all went the same direction. But that made it more difficult to stop when she reached the pub steps. Once it was still, Joss stared at it, praying it would right itself by magic.

It didn't. Praying never helped anyone who didn't work hard.

Left with no other option, she curled her left hand around the upper rim and braced her right hand against the lower one. Her work boots slipped against the cobbles and her knees shook, but she finally got the barrel high enough to wedge her elbow under it, then her shoulder, and used her body weight to force it upright.

She bounced on the balls of her feet, quite proud of herself. All Drake did was twitch his head in a silent command to come back to the cart.

"I thought I did that well." She climbed into the box and took the seat beside him. Beneath the cap, sweat soaked her hair and tickled her scalp. Muscles she hadn't used in years screamed in protest. "Especially since—"

"Be quiet." Drake looked over his shoulder as he guided the cart back into the street. His leather gloves were stretched tight over his knuckles; his spine was ramrod straight. When he faced forward, his jaw was just as rigid.

As he drove, he tilted his head in small adjustments. From the back, it might look as though he was talking or fidgeting under the weight of his wool coat on a warm evening. Joss knew better.

Gavin had nicknamed him Bat years ago, and everyone assumed it was because of his ability to blend into the shadows and remain unseen until the last moment. Those people had never been on a job with him. The ones who had, like Gavin, knew Drake had an unnatural ability to feel when danger was near.

He'd always reminded her less of a bat than a crow, perched on a branch while he listened to the world around him.

"Stop staring at me." He stopped at a second pub and applied the cart's brake. "Let's deliver another barrel."

By the time Joss rejoined him in the cart, her shirt was stuck to her skin. She knocked on the box. Connie's response was a quick echo.

"Are we going to wander around London all night?" Joss asked, tired of playing the obedient tiger. "Is this your *perfect* plan?"

"We lost our shadow as we made that second drop." Drake never looked at her, never looked back. He dropped his elbows to his knees as the crowd thinned. "This is your last chance, Joss. Go home. Please."

"I promised Connie I'd see her safely through this." And she'd gotten him into this mess. She'd see it through to the end. He wouldn't be left to deal with the consequences alone. "Where are we going?"

"Reading." He straightened and slapped the reins against the horses' broad backs.

"We're going the wrong way."

"I always head west with this shipment. We'll double back at the first turn."

The jingling harness and hoofbeats echoed as they crossed the bridge. Beneath her, Connie swore as her knees banged against her wooden lifeboat. "Do you think we could let her out?"

"In *Reading*," Drake said. "Unless she's in distress, we aren't stopping again."

Past the streetlamps and the lights from houses and pubs, the darkness fell like a great weight that had Joss wishing she hadn't bound her breasts so tightly.

"Are you well?" Drake's question had less of an edge to it.

Once her eyes adjusted, his face became visible in the faint moonlight, though it appeared to hover, bodiless, in a disconcerting way. It reminded her of when he'd come out of the sea, dripping wet and empty-handed. When he'd carried her from the beach as she wailed into his shirt. "I forget how dark it is."

He closed one hand over hers. The leather was supple and warm against her fingers. "I know."

They followed a road she could barely see, and Drake removed his hand to take a firmer hold on the team as they took the route he'd promised. Joss had an irritating urge to slide closer to his large body and steal some of his warmth. "Will your friend be angry you gave away his wine?"

"He's not really a friend." Drake snorted as he made a wide turn to reverse direction. "More likely a few pub owners will get a laugh from having barrels of water delivered to their back door."

Joss looked at the barrels stacked behind them. "Are they all water?"

"The rest are wine, just in case."

Silence fell, allowing the sounds of the night to come in. The wind shifted the trees, making their shadows appear as though they were breathing. An owl screeched, sending shivers down to Joss's fingers. Something crashed through the forest, but it was impossible to tell if it was fleeing or closing in. Joss twisted to check over each shoulder.

"Likely something escaping from the owl," Drake murmured. "If you stay this tense, you'll be exhausted should I need you."

It was impossible to miss his sarcasm. "You know I can be useful."

"Now you sound like Frank *and* look like him."

He was worried about his boys, which was something she understood too well. But she hadn't suggested they help with this escape. "I'm sure they're fine."

"Of course they are. They're wise lads." He chuckled quietly. "Most of the time."

Joss knocked on the box, and Connie's reply rattled over her backside. The clouds slid past overhead, veiling the stars that twinkled so brightly that it seemed possible to touch them. The smell of the forest gave way to the odor of London as they passed north of the city.

"It stinks even out here," she said. "I don't know when I got used to it."

"It didn't take long, but Whitechapel has a way of seeping into you quickly. It took me longer to rid myself of that scent than that of the sea." Just saying it called up the memory of salt on the wind and smoke from driftwood fires. Fresh fish and sun-dried cotton. Wet wood from boats, the tangy bite of pitch. "I miss it."

"I don't. Not most of it, anyway."

Drake dropped his head to stare at his feet. "I missed bluebells until recently. Where did you find that scent?"

"Madeline took me to Paris to round out my education. I found it in a perfumery while we were shopping for lingerie." She'd found a lot of things in Paris. The ability to flirt, the knowledge of color and fabric, and how to lace a dress so it came undone easily. Most importantly, she'd learned that sex could be, should be, enjoyable. And, truthfully, she might have been shopping for books rather than unmentionables. But she liked flustering him.

"Why are you doing this?" he asked. "What is so important that you have to risk everything you used to value?"

"Stratford killed a woman, and the madam at The Peacock dropped her naked body in the river rather than call him out. They should pay for that. Connie should have justice for her friend, and she should be safe to walk the streets of London without fearing her shadow."

"Those are all valid and pretty reasons, but you were in that business long before this secret landed in your lap. This is about getting Mal released, isn't it?"

He made saving her father sound unsavory. "You should be happy. You want me out of the brothel business. This will do that." When Drake stayed quiet, she pressed her point. "Da doesn't need to be in prison—you know that."

"No, I know he doesn't *want* to be in prison. But he *needs* to be there in the worst way. And you know why."

For a storm that happened almost twenty years ago? "Davy's death was an accident, Drake. Nothing Da could've done—"

"He bloody well could have kept us at home like he should have. He didn't need that shipment to feather his nest. He wanted it because someone had told him he couldn't do it. It was a prize he could brag over." Drake drew a deep breath. "I told him it was dangerous. That the route was too long and the storm too close. He risked all of us—even you—because of his greed and his pride."

How could he say that? Her father had done everything to make sure they had food and a solid roof over their heads. He'd kept the sheriff from taking them in and made sure they knew how to read. "He grieved Davy just like the rest of us, and he regretted that decision for—"

"For as long as it took him to find another shipment." Drake glared down at her. "Does he know what you're doing for the sake of his freedom?"

He did, but Joss wasn't going to admit it.

But she didn't have to confess. Drake could see the truth, even in the dark. "And he takes advantage of your *need* to have him out of prison."

What sort of daughter would she be if she didn't do everything she could to win his release? "You would do the same."

"Not for anyone." He turned and looked over his shoulder. "Someone is coming up on us too fast to be friendly." He shoved a pistol into her hands. "Try not to shoot me."

It was a tempting notion.

CHAPTER TWELVE

DRAKE PULLED THE reins and drew the team to a stop. "What are you doing?"

"Not counting on a draft team to outrun two stallions while pulling a heavy load." If he was lucky, the lack of a chase would disarm their attackers.

He knew better to count on that, especially tonight. His luck had turned the moment he let Jocelyn stay at his side. It had been damned near impossible to keep from staring at her backside as she'd struggled with the barrels in town, to treat her like the boy she was pretending to be while she smelled so sweet it made him ache. These two had gotten into range because he'd been too busy arguing, too distracted by his body's response to her, to feel their approach.

The men slowed but didn't dismount. They were too well dressed, too well armed, to be highwaymen. Their uncovered faces chilled Drake's fingers as he tightened his grip on the pistol in his lap. If they didn't expect to be identified, they didn't intend survivors. He tied the reins to the brake, certain to make them tight.

"What are you two delivering this late?" the one nearest Jocelyn asked.

"Wine, bound for Devon," Drake replied, keeping his voice even. Beside him, Jocelyn had a white-knuckled grip on the pistol that was half the length of her forearm.

"Mind if we check?" The second man was moving to the back of the cart before Drake could answer.

The gunshot brought him to his feet and his pistol level in one fluid motion.

The assassin struggled with his horse as he wet his fingers and brought them to his lips. Wine splattered to the ground in a stream, creating the most expensive mud in Berkshire. Moonlight caught his hand as he aimed for a second barrel. It gave Drake a target, and he fired.

The shooter's horse shied away, dumping him to the ground. Drake dropped from the cart and stayed low, using the man's stream of curses to locate him. Behind him, another shot rang out. It was followed by a rough curse. The draft horses stamped and snorted, rocking the cart as they fought the reins and the weight of the load.

"Bill! This boy is a girl!" The last word was wailed.

"Get off me, you bastard," Jocelyn screeched.

Drake turned, which was the only reason his attacker missed skewering his gut. As it was, the blow sliced through his waistcoat and shirt and across his ribs. The brutal sting spasmed his muscles all the way to his fingers, sending his pistol to the ground with a *thud*.

"Shite." He pressed his elbow against the wound and pulled his own knife from its sheath at his back, ignoring the sticky warmth oozing across his skin.

The man, seeing an opening, came forward, slashing again. "Is it the one we're after?" he yelled to his companion.

Drake blocked the blow, slapping the man's arm away. The bite of the blade told him he'd be a mass of stitches on that side of his body, but he'd created an opening of his own.

"I don't know yet," the man said. "She's a right badger, she is."

Drake slashed twice, once forward and once back, in an attack that was as familiar as blinking. The other man stumbled and dropped his weapon so he could hold his cheek together with one hand and cradle his midsection with the other.

Jocelyn gave a yell that would have set the Titans to quaking as the cart lurched forward. Heavy hooves stamped the ground in unison as the horses got their heads.

Drake half ran, half stumbled to the front and grasped the edge to pull himself in. Splinters gouged his palm through his glove, causing almost as much pain as his other wounds. He slammed against the front of the box and barely kept himself level enough to rush at Jocelyn's attacker.

She gave up flailing for the knife in her boot and put her knee in the man's groin, then her boots in his chest. He flew backward and out of sight and landed with a curse they could have heard in Bath. The hapless outlaw leapt to his feet in time to see his friend galloping away. Alone, he lost his nerve and ran for his own horse.

"Are you injured?" Drake wheezed once he was certain they were safe. He stopped halfway to touching Jocelyn. Both his gloves were likely covered in blood.

"None the worse for wear," she said, panting. "You?"

"I'll live." He grasped the reins and pulled the team to a stop, gritting his teeth at the pain flowing through every part of his body. "Let's check on our passenger."

Jocelyn had the lid halfway up when another carriage came barreling from the other direction, its lanterns bright.

"Who now?" Jocelyn asked as she hid Connie once again and stood at Drake's side.

"A friend, I hope." Drake rocked on his feet. "Take the team. I'll make sure."

Jocelyn sat and pulled on the reins, keeping them taut, though she had to press her feet straight out against the cart to do so. Drake positioned himself as best he could between her and the newcomer. "Who goes there?"

"Yarwood," came the reply. "Fletcher?"

Drake sagged in relief as he recognized the voice and the

name—Jasper Warren's man. "Aye."

Jocelyn tied off the reins again and stood. She had her pistol at her side.

Kit Yarwood drew up beside them in a coach only a marquess would drive, though it was likely just a spare. He had the reins in one hand and a pistol in the other. The coal-black team pranced to a stop. The lather on their backs gleamed like sea foam in the moonlight. "I heard shots."

Drake waved a hand toward the men fleeing, draped over their horses in a satisfying way. "We had company. Likely Stratford's men."

"Should we pursue—" Yarwood took stock of the situation— one team cooling from a race, the other pulling a load that would sink a small barge. Even if the cart was empty, they'd never catch anything faster than a tortoise. "Likely not."

"They'll be easy to recognize. I cut one of them from his ear to his smirk. The other one will be holding his bollocks until Christmas." Drake draped an arm over Jocelyn's shoulder and pressed a kiss against the top of her head.

She ducked away and knelt to lift the seat. Connie lay there, wide-eyed, a knife in her trembling hands.

"It's all right. We're safe," Jocelyn said. "Come up out of there and stretch your legs."

She helped the girl to stand, and Connie immediately fell against her shoulder, sobbing. After a few minutes of crying and whispered conversation, she straightened, wiped her fingers beneath her eyes, then smoothed her wrinkled skirts.

Yarwood stepped down from his carriage and over to the cart. "Christopher Yarwood, attaché to the Marquess of Rams-bury, at your service, miss." He offered his hand to help Connie to the ground. "We should be on our way to Wiltshire."

Drake put his hand on Jocelyn's shoulder, intent on leaving for London. She shuddered for an instant before she ducked clear once again. The ghost of a bloody handprint stained her coat.

"Go with them, Jocelyn. Stay with Connie. I'll send for you

both when Stratford is off the field."

For once, she obeyed him and hopped from the wagon without a backward glance to join Connie and Yarwood beside the carriage. A chill settled over Drake, but he refused to think about how lonely he'd be on the trip home and, given the pain in his ribs and his arm, whether he'd make it home at all.

Night settled around them again, quiet except for the cool breeze stirring his hair. Drake tilted his face to the sky and stared at the stars. The Pleiades led him to Taurus; below Taurus was Orion, which would guide them to Highcliffe. Above Taurus was Perseus, who faced off against the great bear that guarded London.

A childhood at sea had made the stars his friends until he had real ones. And when he left those behind, he'd found the tallest steeple in Whitechapel to see the stars and trace his way to the place he wanted to be but would never let himself return.

"Drake?"

The question, combined with a gentle hand on his chest, brought him back to earth. He and Jocelyn were alone on the road. The night had already swallowed the lanterns from Yarwood's carriage.

She'd stayed with him.

Rather than be upset with her, he bent to kiss her. But as he neared her mouth, he saw the bruise forming under her eye. "He hit you."

He would find that man in London and make him wish he'd never been born.

"It's nothing. I've had worse." She swept a hand through his hair, pushing it back from his face. It was likely the only part of his body left unbloodied. "How badly are you injured?"

"It's just a scrape."

"I know what blood smells like." She unbuttoned his waistcoat as she talked.

The fabric fell away, and he grunted as his wound reopened. "It will be fine if you just leave it be."

Jocelyn pulled the knife from her boot and sliced it through a sheet Nicky had used to line Connie's hiding place. "Raise your shirt."

When he failed to obey, she yanked it from his trousers and pushed it up to his chest. Her hot gasp contrasted with the chill on his skin.

"You foolish, foolish man." She pressed the cloth to the cut and then reached around him, her hands sure against his back as she wound the bandage around him again and again. "You were going to send me to Wiltshire and bleed to death on the way back to London."

When she was finished, he was bound so tightly it was difficult to breathe.

"Where else?" Jocelyn demanded.

Unable to find the will to argue, Drake unbuttoned his cuff to reveal the gash on his forearm. "My waistcoat took the brunt of the cut. I'd have hardly bled to death."

"Fine, then." Jocelyn destroyed a pillowcase to make a bandage. "You'd have been weak and the perfect prey for a highwayman, or, worse, those louts would have doubled back to ambush you."

Once she was finished, she opened the carpetbag and pulled out a skirt. Drake was transfixed by watching her remove her boots, undo her falls, and let the trousers drop. "You can't be that worried about me if you're taking time to change."

Drawers had never looked so appealing, especially when she bent to slip into the skirt and the fabric hugged her backside. "We'll gather much less attention if it doesn't look like you're escorting a boy upstairs at an inn." She looked over her shoulder. "Because we *are* stopping so you can rest."

All he could do was nod as she finished transforming from a strapping young lad to a respectable country lady, complete with a shawl over her shoulders. Her hair, caught up with a ribbon, fell over her shoulders and down her back as she put the seat back in place.

"Stop gawking and sit." Jocelyn untied the reins from the brake. "Tell me where I'm going."

He sat close enough that their shoulders touched. When he tilted his head to see the sky, he could feel her breathing. "Follow the twins." He pointed to the two bright stars that formed Gemini. "They'll lead you to Bracknell. I've stayed at the inn there. It's clean, and the food is good."

The rock of the cart was hypnotizing. "I remember the winter you learned to knit," he said. She'd made all of them blankets. His had been too short. He'd had to choose between icy feet or cold shoulders. "I thought we'd have to start stealing sheep."

"It was a long winter that year."

Made longer by Mal's refusal to buy enough coal because he'd deemed the price too high. "The old man bought a racehorse that winter. Do you remember that?"

"The handler said he could run like the wind, and Da believed him." Jocelyn sighed. "He couldn't even beat a breeze."

"Mal should've insisted on seeing him race." Drake's chin dropped to his chest. Every time he blinked, he saw that damned horse as the butcher had led him away. But if he kept them closed long enough, the image of Jocelyn's cotton-covered arse replaced it. In his dream, the fabric was soft against his fingers, and her muscles were firm against his palm. She was warm, and her hands were tangled in his hair as she kissed him.

"Drake?"

He opened his eyes and stared at her hand in his. She was pulling him forward. The inn stood behind her.

"I have a room upstairs, and the groom is going to see to the horses and the cart." She pulled again as though he was a child who needed coaxing. "Come along."

Once out of the wagon, he squared his shoulders. "What did you tell them to explain our state?"

"That we were set upon by highwaymen. No one questioned me. They either have a problem with robberies or they need the coins."

If you paid someone enough, you could buy all the secrecy you needed. He climbed the stairs with leaden feet, pain throbbing through him with every step. The door was barely closed when he began shedding his clothes. A fire warmed the room, which was dominated by a bed piled high with pillows and draped with blankets long enough to cover him from head to toe.

"We need to clean your wounds," Jocelyn said. "Let me—"

"Later." Drake toed off his boots and pushed his trousers to the floor before toppling onto the mattress and pulling the blankets over him. "Come to bed, Jocelyn. It's been a long night."

After a moment, the mattress shifted, and her heels bumped his shin. "Sorry."

Her retreat left him cold despite the blankets and the fire. The only place that didn't ache was the one she'd touched. Drake turned to his uninjured side and slung his arm around her waist. Lace and cotton tickled his fingers. Apparently, she'd included a shift in her travel plan, something he'd not bothered to make for himself. "I hope I don't bleed on you."

Her hand covered his, and she linked their fingers. "It's all right if you do."

CHAPTER THIRTEEN

A LOW MOAN startled Joss awake. Gray predawn light filtered through the curtains. "Dammit. Which of them did it this time?" All the ladies knew customers weren't allowed to stay overnight.

She stepped from bed, reached for her wrapper, and ran into a wall. Blinking, she backed up, stepped, and bumped her nose against the same obstacle. Who had moved her...

The wallpaper was flowered. And the curtains were too lacy, as were the bedclothes. The only familiar things were the clothes draped over the chair.

Memory returned. Her attacker's weight. Connie's tears. Drake's blood and exhaustion. Halfway up the stairs, his heavy arm on her shoulder, she'd been worried she'd never get him to the room.

A muffled gasp drew her attention to the gilt-framed white cotton screen spanning one corner of the room. Joss pushed from the wall, her heart in her throat. What if Stratford's men had tracked them here? She was halfway to the screen, Drake's name on her tongue, before she stopped short. Though she'd slept like the dead, Drake wasn't a quiet fighter.

Had his wound worsened in the night? She should have insisted on cleaning and re-dressing them, but he had practically collapsed onto the bed. If he was back there trying to fix it himself, doing more damage simply by being stubborn, bleeding to death was going to be the least of his concerns. She stepped around the screen, intent on giving him a piece of her mind.

Drake was naked, his back to her with his left hand pressed to the wall. His fingers flexed, and the movement rippled down his long arm and across his broad shoulders. His back shuddered and his hips flexed, all in time to the movement of his right arm. Joss couldn't see his right hand, but years in a brothel had given her a thorough education.

Heat flushed through and urged her forward, made her slide one hand along his right arm to close over his fist, even as the other circled his waist, just below his bandaged ribs. He lost his rhythm, and his fingers fell from beneath hers. When he went to move away, she used her left hand to force him to stillness, so her right could close over his still-stiff shaft.

"Jocelyn, I don't think…"

Drake's words rumbled through his back and across her chest. She could feel an objection building in his muscles, but she didn't know if it was from distaste or modesty. Taking a risk, she slid her hand down his length and dragged it up at a pace that allowed her to feel every twitch. When she reached the crest, she swirled her thumb over the wetness there, spreading it wider.

"Tell me you don't want me to do this, and I'll stop." She whispered the words against his shoulder before she flicked her tongue against his salty skin.

"Christ." He closed his fingers over hers and pumped fast and hard. "Just let me…"

Drake did everything like it was work. At fifteen, he'd worked harder than men twice his age, his focus on little else but the next job, the next shipment, the next moonless night. The few times he'd relaxed and played on the beach, he seemed to have enjoyed it.

He needed more of that.

Joss slid her other hand across his flat stomach, enjoying the play of his muscles as much as the silk of his skin. The bandage hid most of him from her, but she skimmed her fingers over the cloth until his soft chest hair curled around them. She caught his nipple between her fingers, and his muscles seized.

"Let *me*," she whispered.

His hand fell from hers, letting her slow her pace. "We need to keep moving."

"We are moving," she whispered. Her shift tormented her nipples, and the skin between her thighs grew hot and slick.

Drake flexed his hips, driving his length through her hand. She swept her thumb over the velvety crown before sliding her fingers to the base and squeezing.

"What do I do with my hands?" he choked out.

"What do you want to do with them?"

"Throttle you." His laughter ended on a gasp as she stroked the pads of her fingers up the underside of his shaft. "God, Jocelyn." His right hand braced on the wall near his hip, and he widened his stance.

His heart thudded under her left hand and twitched through the fingers of her right. His ragged breaths filled the small space.

Joss rested her forehead between Drake's shoulder blades and drew in a breath scented with vetiver and sex. It filled her lungs, teasing her from the inside out until she could imagine Drake himself was filling her. Her heart thudded against her breastbone and echoed in her ears.

She'd reached the base again, and velvet skin teased her pinkie finger, tempting her to explore. His tight balls filled her palm, and the skin beyond was hot silk against her fingertips.

Drake laced his fingers with her left hand and dragged them down his heaving chest, urging them around his cock. "Please," he ground out.

Joss teased his balls as she fisted his cock. Drake's large body trembled as his feet writhed against the carpet. She pressed an open-mouthed kiss against his shoulder blade, letting his skin scorch her tongue before she scraped her teeth over the spot.

He leapt like she'd shot him and kept moving, pumping

through her hand as he slapped the wall. Head thrown back, neck arched, he spilled over her fingers with guttural shout, followed by another, then a gasp, and finally a sigh.

Joss released him and stepped back on shaky legs, aching with a need she'd have to ignore.

"Wait," Drake whispered as he flattened her palm against his skin.

He reached into the washbasin and squeezed the cloth with one large hand. The water was warm against her fingers as he cleaned them, but every stroke drove her arousal higher. It broke when he lifted them to his lips and kissed her knuckles as he cleaned himself. It was impossible to tell which of them was shaking.

"Thank you," he murmured. "That was... I didn't... It was unbelievable."

Joss's insides were turning to liquid. She gathered her night-dress in a fist near her hip and rucked it up. "Mm-hmm." The air teased her bare skin as she swept her fingers between her thighs.

She put her hand in his back to keep him from turning. She hadn't watched him. She deserved the same courtesy.

Drake faced her anyway. Now instead of staring at his muscled back, she got an eyeful of his hairy chest and flat stomach. The bandages, white against his skin, gave him an added air of danger. And his cock was still at half-mast.

It was too much. Joss dropped to the bench near the basin and braced one foot on the surface and the other on the floor. Closing her eyes so she didn't have to watch Drake watch her, she bit her lip to muffle her cry as she spread her folds and found—

A large hand closed over her shoulder. "Joss. Look at me."

She couldn't. This wasn't something she shared. She didn't want him to see.

A thumb stroked the too-sensitive skin at her collarbone. "Please."

Looking at him meant stopping, and she couldn't stop. Not

now. She was almost there. It wouldn't take much to push her over the edge.

Drake's fingers slid from her elbow to her wrist, stopping there but not stopping her. "Show me how—What to—What you like."

Joss grasped his fingers and slid the middle two inside her, gasping as they drove deep. Grabbing his wrist, she taught him her desperate rhythm and prayed he wouldn't feel the need to repay her for her earlier teasing.

He didn't. After driving deep again, he shifted his fingers and grazed the spot that had her seeing stars. "God, do that again."

"This?" He stroked her until her toes curled.

"Harder." Joss reached between them for the spot she knew would send her flying. She brushed her finger over it once, only to have it nudged aside by a thick thumb.

"Let me," Drake rumbled.

At least, that was what she thought he said. Stars filled the darkness behind her eyelids, fading to black at the corners. Her heartbeat deafened her. Convulsions ripped through her, tightened her like a harp string that sang the end of a song.

She came back to herself in increments. Drake's head was resting on her shoulder, his breath tickling her skin as his hair teased her ear. He was there because she was clinging to him, her teeth scraping his skin.

She leaned back, staring at the mark she'd left near his collarbone. "I bit you."

"Twice." He slid his fingers down her thigh, trailing wetness in their wake. He raised his head and met her gaze, a twinkle in his eye. His lips quirked. "I don't seem to mind it."

Joss tucked a lock of hair behind Drake's ear as he shifted her hem to a more modest length. When he reached for the washbasin, she put a hand on his chest. The rapid, heavy heartbeat nearly undid her.

"I'd better do that myself, or we'll spend all day behind this screen."

He blushed to his hairline and stood, pulling her with him. "Right, then. I'll get dressed and wait for you in the hallway. We can go down for breakfast." The twinkle returned. "I'm famished."

He walked away, giving her a last glimpse of his firm backside and long, strong legs.

She was starving.

DRAKE COULD STILL feel Jocelyn everywhere, and it only heightened his awareness of her on the seat beside him as they made their way back to London.

"Excuse me." He shifted away from her as the cart rocked them against one another.

Waking this morning, for a moment, had been disorienting. Not the room. He was used to waking in new places, to sleeping wherever he could find. True, the room was lacier than he would have liked, but it had been warm and dry.

And he hadn't been alone. That had been the confusing part. At least for his brain. His body had known exactly what to do. He'd come fully awake with his cock so hard he could feel his pulse against the mattress, all while starting at Jocelyn as she slept with her dark hair half hiding her features.

Drake had been grateful she was still asleep, so she couldn't see him appreciate how her shift had molded to her curves and left little to his imagination.

He'd leaned over her, using one hand for balance as he skated the other over her curves. Her softness fascinated him, likely because he never thought of her that way. She'd rarely given him reason to do so.

Her body heat had soaked through her shift and into his palm until thoughts of her skin had tormented him. And, as though she was dreaming of teasing him, she put her bare thigh in his hand.

Her skin was hot, soft, silk covering muscles used to working much harder, and longer, than the ladies of London could imagine. Many were the days when she'd worked at his side until it was too dark to see. But she was thin, and her bones were smaller and finer than his.

It would have been so easy to do anything he wanted with her before she was awake enough to stop him.

That thought had driven him behind the screen, careless of anything but easing the ache that had built during his exploration. Blind and deaf from need, it was little wonder Jocelyn had managed to surprise him.

She always surprised him.

"You are very quiet." She slid closer to him without the help of the cart.

He wanted to kiss her so badly his tongue ached. More than that, he wanted her touch on his skin again. Drake inched away from her. "I'm thinking."

He couldn't *stop* thinking about how it had felt to have a woman's hands on his body.

That was a lie. *Her* hands. Jocelyn's touch had shaped him into a different person. He looked the same on the outside, but under his skin, something had changed.

"Do you want to talk about it?" she asked.

No, he didn't. Because if she learned he'd never touched himself in front of a woman, never had a woman touch him like that… She would likely laugh until they reached London.

It wasn't something he'd planned to avoid. He just hadn't had the opportunity. In Highcliffe, she had been the only girl he knew, and Mal had threatened them all with banishment if they touched her. When he'd arrived in London, he hadn't been able to afford food. A clean brothel was out of the question, and he wasn't going to the ones he could've afforded.

After that, he'd been too busy with the lending circle and his own businesses to give it much thought.

"You think too much," Jocelyn said. "You should feel more."

"Umm-hmm." He was feeling quite enough. Like her tongue on his skin and the way her screams had shivered up his neck. "I'm taking you to Norfolk, to Thetford, until this is over."

She twisted to face him, which put her chin at an even more stubborn angle. "No. You're not. I have things to do."

"What now?" Connie was safely out of London, protected by someone who had more political capital than either of them. For anyone else, that would be the end of it.

Jocelyn wasn't anyone else.

"I have a business to run, in case you've forgotten."

He hadn't been able to forget that since he'd kissed her. It was difficult to reconcile the girl he'd known with the woman she'd become, and he honestly wasn't certain which he liked more.

"Besides that, Stratford has stolen some of Violet's personal possessions. If I can find them, I can tie him to her murder."

Which explained her foray into Parliament. Drake's stomach sank. "You can't mean to break into his home."

"They're pearls, Fletcher. He's not exactly going to wear them around town."

"Taking them from him will only prove *you* took them." She wasn't that daft. "You have no leverage if you have them."

"All I have to do is get them into the proper hands. They'll take it from there."

Proper hands? Who on earth would she know that could put pressure on a peer? He'd only seen her with one man who had any influence. "Spencer? You think Reginald Spencer is the proper person?"

He got his answer when she wouldn't meet his eyes.

"How does that even come up? Do you ask him about murder while you're unlacing your corset?" The question conjured a mental image that darkened on the edges.

"I do not remove my corset for Reginald Spencer," Jocelyn retorted. "We have an understanding."

Spencer wasn't her lover. Drake's relief was short-lived. If she wasn't giving Spencer access to her body, she was giving him something else. "What sort of understanding? Is he blackmailing you?"

"No," she scoffed. "What would he have on me that Society would even care to know?"

She didn't have anything, but some of the more powerful men in London visited the White Rose. They had done so for years. "Does he watch your clients?" There were plenty of places to hide, especially in the dark.

"Ew, no." Jocelyn faced forward. "If you must know, it's pillow talk. Happy men talk to the girls. They tell me. I tell Spencer."

It was a logical path to the most insane scheme he'd ever heard. "Jocelyn. Do you know how many men…how many lives that could ruin? How many enemies that could make you?"

"The White Rose will not be the only place where their lips are loose. Surely to God it's not the only place they're happy. And by the time they learn the truth, I won't be Madam White any longer. No one will know."

Unless her successor wasn't loyal or was frightened half to death. Even if she wasn't Madam White, she'd still be easy to find, even in London. Because she would never leave the city without Mal. She'd given up everything… "You're doing this to get the old man out of prison, aren't you?" They'd reached the outskirts of the city, and Drake had to focus on guiding the team and the lumbering cart through traffic. "Jocelyn, you are playing a dangerous game."

"One you would play if it were someone you loved," she countered. "You know it to be true. How many times were you the last off a ship to ensure we were all safe?"

Every time. But that was different. Those boys had been his responsibility. Jocelyn's father was not her responsibility. He was supposed to be the responsible one.

"I remember the first time you went on a job with me," Drake said as he guided the team around the corner and onto the winding lane that circled the park.

"I was twelve," Jocelyn said.

And he'd been fifteen. That wasn't the point. "You were so determined to be helpful, to keep up, that you nearly fell overboard carrying a crate that was far too heavy for you."

"And I got the damned thing on the skiff anyway. All I had to do was shift the load."

All she'd had to do was not try to prove herself, not do so much so fast.

"Just because you've seen me naked doesn't mean you can tell me what to do," Jocelyn said.

"Someone should," Drake said.

"See me naked?" Jocelyn asked. She'd tightened her grip on seat, either to keep away from him or to keep from jostling, which was worse now that they were on cobbles.

Drake found himself looking for a hole in the road that would shake her loose and send her careening into him. No one else should see her naked. "I've only seen you half-naked. That doesn't count."

Which was a bald-faced lie. It counted in spectacular ways that had him remembering the soft heat of her, the way she clung to him, and the sounds she'd made. Her slick muscles against his fingers had made him think of kissing her. It still made him think of kissing her. Of burying himself inside her until they both lost their minds.

His bandages kept him from getting a deep enough breath, so the tension shivered across his skin until it settled in places that made it difficult to sit.

Charles Street was in view. He thought he could see his roof. *Thank God.* "Promise me you won't go into Stratford's house until I've returned."

He guided the cart into the alley behind the house and then through the back gate. Frank and Harry came outside with Gavin on their heels.

Drake climbed down first, glad to be home and to have solid ground beneath his feet, if only for a few brief moments—and glad to ease the tightness in his trousers. He offered Jocelyn his hand and then gasped as she fell against him. It was as much his wounds as the feel of her. Having her feel his reaction was as embarrassing as it was rude, but he enjoyed watching her eyes widen and her mouth soften. He got the barest glimpse of her tongue.

"You're in no shape to travel on your own," she said. "You should rest."

"Just because you've seen me naked doesn't mean you can tell me what to do," he joked as he tried not to scratch the scabs forming under his bandages.

"Use some sense, Fletcher." Her level gaze, the fingers squeezing his, told him she saw every misery he was trying to hide.

She had always been good at that. Boys who had outgrown their boots had new ones appear. Buttons were repaired. Favorite dishes appeared at random.

"There's no time," he said. "That wine is expected in Thetford." *And I need to warn everyone that I've snared them in a scheme without their knowledge.*

Gavin would never let him forget this.

Still, Drake couldn't be bothered to release the woman who was the source of the disaster. She smelled of the soap at the inn and the outdoors, and her blouse reminded him of the shift she'd slept in. "Promise me, Jocelyn. No scrapes until I return. Don't go near Stratford without me."

"So long as you don't travel on your own. Take Frank. He'll be a better hand than Harry."

Drake looked between the two boys. Frank would handle the team better, and he might be good in a fight, if it came to one. "Frank, be ready to travel in ten minutes. I need to change."

He wanted nothing more than to kiss Jocelyn goodbye. He wanted her to be here when he returned. He wanted to curl up beside her and sleep for days.

"Gav, see Jocelyn home."

CHAPTER FOURTEEN

"WHY NOT CUT Spencer from the middle and go straight to Stratford himself?"

Joss stared at her father from her seat in the center of his cell. Her cloak was open, despite the chill in the air. Condensation trickled from the stone walls, leaving dark trails that matched her umber-colored dress. "What?"

"He could be useful, should he know you held this over his head."

Given the battle she and Drake had survived, Joss was certain Stratford already knew what they held. Though he might not yet be able to put a name with a face. "I am not certain how my lack of anonymity benefits anyone." Not to mention ending up in the Thames. "Or how it brings about any sort of justice."

"The *ton* will never serve justice on their own; you know that. It will be left to shoulders like mine to hold up the system while they look down their noses. She will be just another dead doxy to them, mourned by none but others like her. There will be no reason to act."

Joss hadn't known Violet in life, but now she spent so much time thinking of the girl that her father's words cut. "Then there is a reason for me not to go to him directly. What regard would he have for me, given my line of work?"

"Don't be that way, my girl." He moved closer. "You've

spent your life learning how to make people pay attention."

She forced herself not to recoil. He was her father, after all. But dear God he stank. His hair, his breath, his skin. She had paid the warden for additional toiletry supplies and more bathing privileges, even for chits to do laundry more often. He wasn't pocketing the money, at least not all of it, because new bottles sat on the shelf near the mottled mirror that stood over his wash basin. However, the bottles had looked new during her previous visit as well.

"Da, are you using the things I'm buying you?"

He followed her gaze to the shelf. "Certainly, but there's no real need to use them all the time when I don't see anyone."

Not even when his only child visits, the one who's doing unthinkable things to keep him in tooth powder?

Joss went to the shelf and uncorked a bottle of hair tonic. The fumes made her eyes water. "Gin, Da?"

His neck reddened at his frayed collar. "It helps pass the time."

The bar of soap was little more than a sliver. "Where's your soap?" She looked hard at him.

"I sold it to a guard," he said. "I needed the coin to pay a debt."

How on earth had he found a way to gamble in *prison*? Honestly, that had been the one small bright spot of his spending time at Horsemonger Lane. Trust Da to darken that brightness. "What sort of debt?"

"Penn, two cells down, put a wager on how many pigeons would land on the wall during the hour we were outside."

And Da had lost.

She lifted his tobacco tin and removed the cap. The smell, so strong that it burned her nose, was one she'd learned on her arrival in London.

Forgetting the state of him, she leaned forward to whisper, "Where in the hell did you get opium?" She wasn't paying for a habit he wouldn't be able to break.

"One of the boys on the next block sells it." He glowered up at her, his eyes red-rimmed and bloodshot. His teeth were black at the gum line. "And I don't need a lecture from you."

The words pelted Joss's skin the same as the spittle that flew from his lips. She pulled her cloak from the chair and strode for the door. "Fine. I'm tired of wasting my breath anyway."

But she'd be back here next Saturday, bribing the warden and sitting in that chair to reassure her father she was doing everything she could.

Joss didn't draw a deep breath until she was outside the gate and in her carriage. "To The Peacock, James," she called as she flung her cloak against the opposite seat. Her black veil soon followed. The stench from the prison, from that cell, faded. Joss pulled on a coat that was patterned in autumn leaves, its brightness lightening the umber dress and matching hat.

She shouldn't have lost her temper with her father, but she hadn't slept well. The reason for that had compounded her irritation. One night with Drake, in a bed a day's ride away, had made her sheets that much colder, her room that much quieter. She stared at the ceiling and wondered if he was safe. She touched herself and felt his fingers. She missed lace and a too-soft bed. She even missed that damned dressing screen.

After years of having no one in her life who knew anything but the creation she'd become, it was disconcerting to lose the ability to hide behind that creation. At the same time, she'd missed the girl on the beach, the one who cooked for a crew of hungry boys, who had celebrated the first scrawny potato she'd dug from her rocky, bedraggled garden. Drake gave that girl back to her.

But then she had to don a disguise when she did things like now, as the carriage wound its way through Covent Garden and stopped in front of the Gold Peacock.

"I'll wait here, madam," James said as he held the door. "Sing out if you need me."

"Thank you, James." If that need arose, she'd be dead before he breached the door, but at least he'd know what happened to her. "I won't be long."

Joss couldn't help but compare The Peacock to The Rose. Brick gardens with benches under the trees, as though anyone would sit on them in view of the street. The shutters and door were painted a teal blue that reminded Joss of the sea.

It took too long for the doorman to answer, and his stare was far too assessing. "We're not looking to hire."

She drew her spine straight and pushed past him. "Good, because I'm not looking for work. Please let Madam Price know Madam White is here." She gave him her card. "I'll wait."

After a few moments, Catherine Price came down the stairs at a pace that rivaled the queen. Her silver hair was done simply, and her banyan matched the shutters. She spied Joss, and her eyes widened in her delicately lined face.

"You're much younger than I expected, Jocelyn." She looked to the doorman. "Have someone bring coffee and scones to the conservatory."

A man came down the stairs, still fiddling with his cravat. He tipped his hat, gave a wolfish grin, and left. Otherwise, the house was quiet. The lounge was larger than The Rose's. The bar was in here instead of out front.

"Where is everyone?" Jocelyn asked as they entered the sun-room.

"If they aren't working, they're likely asleep." Madam Price motioned to an overstuffed chair opposite. "Sit, please."

A butler appeared on almost silent feet, placed the tray on the table between them, and retreated. Joss couldn't help but think The Peacock was more of a business than The Rose.

"Madeline finally retired, did she?" Catherine asked as she served the tea. "To Bath?"

"She didn't tell me where she was going," Joss said, adopting the superior air Madeline had taught her to have. It was almost ruined by the bitter coffee. She added sugar until it was almost embarrassing. "And I won't keep you long." Cream was next, pushing the liquid to the cup's rim.

It was difficult to drink politely, but Joss managed. "I've had gentlemen arrive at my door looking for a young lady named Violet. They say she was once here."

Catherine never blinked, but her lips thinned. "She was, though she left several weeks ago."

"I see." Joss kept a careful eye on the other woman, trying to learn the depth of her involvement in this crime. Drake had made her promise not to go near Stratford, not to get in a scrape. Nothing was farther from a scrape than two women talking business while nibbling on scones. "Do you know where she went?"

Catherine sipped her coffee. "Are you trying to steal one of my girls, Jocelyn?"

"No. I don't consider it stealing if you turned her out."

"I didn't turn her out," Catherine snapped. "She left in the middle of the night. I assume she's gone to live with one of her regular clients. She had several."

Joss's stomach flipped. Violet had *one* regular client. "I see."

Catherine refilled her coffee. "However, I'm missing a girl that may have come to you. Tall redhead with a lovely figure. Connie Hall. Has she shown up at The Rose?"

Careful to keep her stare level and her breathing slow, Joss shook her head. "Doesn't ring a bell. I'll keep an eye out for her, though. Shall I send her home if I see her?"

"Please."

Joss placed her cup, half-full of the vile drink, on the table and stood. "Thank you for your time, Catherine."

"My pleasure." The older woman's voice was flat. She didn't stand. Instead, she rang a bell and glanced at the silent butler. "Please show Madam White out."

✣

"THERE'S NOTHING AROUND for miles," Frank said. It was impossible to tell whether he was complaining, impressed, or simply bored. "Is this where you stay when you're working away from London?"

Drake pulled in a deep breath of sweet, cool air. The fields, which during the summer reminded him of the sea, now reminded him of dunes. Hulking hills stood in for cliffs, less jagged but beautiful in their own way. "Yes, when I can."

They crested a rise, and Thetford came into view. Bound by the river on one side and the forest on the other, the village sparkled amongst the autumn foliage. Twin plumes of steam rose skyward, one from the lumber mill and the other from the depot. Using those landmarks, and triangulating with the church steeple, Drake could locate the Galloping Goat the way he located a star. Felton House would be on the other side of the trees, Oakdale Manor would be over the large hill in the distance, and the distillery would be in the valley between them.

"We'll drop the wine at the distillery first, and then make arrangements for staying overnight." He was looking forward to staying at The Goat, with Jennie's good cooking and comfortable beds with soft sheets.

"Like the inn last night?" Frank asked. This time it was easy to hear the dread in the boy's voice.

"Nothing like that," Drake assured him. He'd hated to stop when he did, but he'd been unable to continue. In the middle of the night, cold under rough sheets and thin blankets, his stomach roiling from a greasy stew, he'd vowed to never travel injured again.

Being weak, hungry, and exhausted made for poor travel, and without Frank, he likely would have tumbled from the cart and been left in the mud at the side of the road.

He'd never tell Jocelyn she was right, though. That was a step too far.

Drake took the high road around the valley to avoid the village's narrow streets and market-day bustle.

"I've never seen this many trees in one place in my life." Frank craned his neck to get a view of the horizon. "What's that over there?"

Drake looked toward where the young man was pointing. "The old priory." He tried to recall what Thea had told him about it. "It was one of the last monasteries to be surrendered to King Henry."

"The king who started the church so he could kill his wives?"

Drake barked a laugh at the curt assessment. "Well, technically he started it so he could get a divorce. The killing part came later."

"But he still got away with it because he owned a church." Frank stared into the distance. "Did the people who owned the priory fight to keep it?"

"Well, they were monks, so I'm not sure there was much of a battle." To Drake's eyes, it was little more than piles of weathered stone, which probably made God angrier at him than he already was, but Frank was finally interested in something that wasn't lethal. "We could take a closer look if you'd like, before we return home."

Though he never took his eyes from the road, he knew the boy was staring. He could feel the question press against him. "What is it?"

"You're not leaving me here?"

The words were quick and quiet, and Frank's voice was thick. It took a moment to unravel the question and then to understand the meaning. Of all the things the boy could ask, this wasn't one Drake had prepared for.

"What?" He ignored the road to look at the lad beside him, a boy who suddenly looked impossibly young and fragile. "Why would you think something like that?"

"It's just that... I know you come here for work, and I thought...one of your clients might have asked, or perhaps you might've..." Frank stared at the horizon. "Maybe you wanted me out of the house."

"So you thought I'd offer you a home and then take it away because you scuffle with the others and slouch at the dinner table?" As though he were a poorly considered pet that needed room to run.

"Because I don't really fit, do I?" Frank asked in sharp syllables. "Ed is the smart one. Nicky is the hungry one, and Harry is the charmer. I'm just…just the bully whose father killed his mother and then hanged for it."

As Drake remembered it, this self-styled bully had been receiving a thorough beating when Drake came face to face with the gang. Frank hadn't been able to talk for a week. He also knew from Gavin that Frank had a head for numbers and a gift for languages. "You are not your parents, Frank."

"How can you be so sure?" Frank gave him a sideways glance. His hands were fists on his knees.

Drake recalled that feeling—being angry at the world because he didn't know where he fit, and terrified that where he fit wasn't where he wanted to be. Sometimes it still woke him in the middle of the night and sent him prowling to the library for a distraction, or to the kitchen for a snack.

"Because I am not my parents, and Gavin isn't his." He guided the team around a curve. "You're about to meet an extraordinary group of people who have defied expectations to become whatever they wanted."

"But I—"

"I gave you a place in my home to heal. You decide how long you stay, but I believe that if you'll give yourself a chance, you will exceed even your own expectations." He met the young man's gaze head-on. "Truly."

They were quiet over the next few turns. Stones crunched under the wheels while the wind cracked the rushes together. The wind chilled Drake's ears. He handed the reins to Frank. "Drive for a moment, would you?" He stood his collar up and shoved his hands in his pockets. "So, what do you say about visiting the priory in the morning?"

"If you want." Despite the mumbled reply and the shrug of one shoulder, the boy's eyes sparked as he focused on driving the team.

After a few more miles of rocking over uneven roads, they reached the distillery. Even the horses sighed in relief, nuzzling their noses in the dirt.

"Frank, would you please get the team some hay?" Drake climbed from the seat to the wheel to the ground, thinking hard to make sure his feet hit their marks. He was so tired the world was fuzzy, and he ached to the tips of his hair. "I'll go let them know we've arrived."

He was halfway to the door when Amelia Ferrand swept through, her smile as bright as her blonde curls in the sunshine. "It's about time you arrived. We were considering a search party."

Drake squared his shoulders and braced himself for her exuberant embrace. It was easier to smile after she released him. "We had a detour along the way. Apologies for worrying you."

"Hay's done; do you want me to unload..." Frank whipped off his hat. "My lady."

The young man wasn't much taller than Amelia, and he couldn't help but stare at the split skirt, braces, and linen shirt she wore while working. Still, she was cleaner than the boy, who was doing his best to swipe two days' worth of dust from clothes he'd shoved in a bag in the ten minutes Drake had given him to pack. It called Drake's attention to his own appearance. He normally didn't arrive in this state.

He shouldn't have asked Frank to do it either. He put a hand on the boy's shoulder. "Mrs. Ferrand, may I introduce my ward, Frank Harvey."

Amelia extended her hand in a businesslike handshake. "Welcome, Frank. It's a pleasure to meet you."

The boy nodded as he took her hand. "Thank you, ma'am."

As they separated, Drake flicked his gaze to her hand to ensure her ring was still on her finger. He hated the habit, but it was hard to break. "You shouldn't be wearing that down here. It will fall into the mash, and you'll end up cooking it."

"I tell her the same thing, but you know how she is." Richard Ferrand ambled from the depths of the distillery to stand beside his wife. "Hello, Fletcher."

"Ferrand." Drake shook the hand that was offered. He envied the man's easy confidence and, at the moment, easy stride. Just standing here, Drake's muscles were beginning to harden. "I know exactly how stubborn she can be."

"You two can stop talking about me over my head." Amelia poked her husband in the ribs. "I like wearing the ring. It's still new enough that I'm not tired of looking at it…yet."

Richard kissed her nose. "God help me if you ever do tire of it."

Drake had first come to Thetford when Thea brought him to see the building she wanted to purchase as her inn. The village had become his home away from home as he'd helped her, and then Amelia, succeed.

While he was happy that their success had extended further than their ledgers, times like this made him wonder what he was missing when he left here for London, or Ipswich, or Norwich, or…wherever. It made him feel older than his thirty-four years.

"Darling, this is Frank Harvey, Drake's ward," Amelia said. "Would you please find Ben so the three of you can help unload the wagon and put the wine in the bottling room? And then unhook the team so they can rest for the night. Drake and I need to visit."

Left with no alternative, Drake followed her through the distillery, past the hulking copper stills it had taken four men to install and the mash tub that seemed as large as the bay he'd seen from the window at Highcliffe. "You've been spending too much time with Thea," he joked. "I can't leave if they unhook my team."

"Good, because you shouldn't be leaving until you've rested. You're dead on your feet and you're injured. I don't need Thea's training to feel bandages through your shirt."

"It's nothing." He tugged on his waistcoat and brushed the dust from his trousers.

"Oh, for God's sake. I don't care what you look like, Drake. I care how you *are.*" Amelia pulled a stool across the floor and pushed him onto it. "Tell me about Frank. You told me you had brothers, but you call him a ward." Her grin hitched to one side. "How large is your house in London? I may be overpaying you."

"The boys are brothers, of a sort." He scratched the back of his head. "There are four of them. One of my oldest friends, Gavin, takes care of all of us." It was more than he'd ever said about his family to anyone except Jocelyn. The fact that he was saying this much was probably due to her influence. Though, more likely, he was simply too tired to fend off Amelia's curiosity. "They don't have families of their own," he said.

He could see the questions in her eyes, but he drew the line at Gav's time in prison or how he'd found each boy, or even why he'd been so willing to take four homeless lads and one convict into his home in the first place. "Do you want to review your books while I'm here?"

"No. We were leaving for Felton House when you arrived." She plucked her hat from the table and offered him her hand. "We're discussing the women's college curriculum with Lillian Graves. You and Frank will come with us."

"That will be a heavy load for your horse."

She giggled. "You're funnier when you're tired." They reversed direction, past the stills and through the bottling room. "I'm not riding Molly today. I'm in a cart. A tenant came to the manor offering the last of his firewood for sale. We divided it between the house and the distillery."

They emerged into the sunshine, and Drake shaded his eyes to better see the activity. Frank was rolling the last of the barrels toward them, keeping both hands on the wide middle to steady the wobble. He had a rare smile on his face.

"Come along." Amelia strode into the paddock like someone twice her size. "Let's get you both some good food and soft beds."

CHAPTER FIFTEEN

RICHARD DROVE THE cart, apparently unaffected that his wife chose to ride in the back with her man of business, her legs tucked under her in the middle of bark and splinters. Frank couldn't stop staring, though, thank God, he kept his mouth closed. Every rocking step they took down the road made Drake's eyes droop lower.

He should have stayed in London for a day or two. Jocelyn had been right.

She had been right about several things, including secreting Connie out of London. Given the efforts of their attackers, the young woman likely would have joined her friend in the Thames.

Jocelyn might wind up there as well if he stayed here too long, but he would be of no use to her or anyone else if he were too tired to think. Frank would be a good second in a fight, but he'd be bested on his own.

And it's your responsibility to keep him out of fights altogether.

"…and Harry is the youngest. He and Nicky tried to pick Drake's pocket."

"Together?" Amelia asked.

Drake didn't need to see her to know she was smiling. She delighted in stories about the side of London she never saw.

"Yes, ma'am. They had this scheme that one of them would stop a toff, er, gentleman while he was getting into a cab," Frank said. "Nicky would carry on about a lost dog or their baby sister, or their father, and Harry would lift his purse."

I've never met a lad with lighter fingers.

"Never ladies?" she asked.

"No, ma'am. They had a rule about not stealing from ladies, since their men wouldn't look kindly on them losing their money."

Because Nicky's father had been a nasty drunk who used everyone in the family as a punching bag.

"Why cabs?" Amelia asked.

"Because coaches have footmen and tigers who are paid to protect their masters, and cabs just have a driver who can't climb down too fast. If you can stay clear of his whip, you're safe."

"Remind me to never take a cab," Richard said. "And to keep my purse close to my chest."

"Better to not use a purse at all, sir." Frank sounded very much like a schoolmaster. "Keep them loose in your pocket so we have to fish for them. That's what Drake does."

"Really?" Amelia said.

Really.

"Yes, ma'am. Nicky picked him because he looked like a toff, but Harry found out pretty quick that he wasn't."

Story of my life. Rip a hole in my waistcoat, and you realize how ungentlemanly I am.

"Though I'm pretty sure they didn't mind getting caught. Especially Nicky. He gets regular meals and all the snacks he can reach. Mrs. Harris likes to keep us fed."

"I see. What about you? How did you come to live there?" Amelia's laughter had faded at the thought of hungry children, but her light tone remained. To any casual listener, she might have been talking about her garden.

Drake knew her well enough now to know better. He also knew enough of Frank's history that his senses sprang to life. There was a difference between entertaining Amelia with scrapes and misbegotten adventure and exposing darker parts of the city.

Of this boy.

"My parents both died, ma'am," Frank said. "And none of their families wou—could take me in."

The young man's answer, a combination of honest information and veiled truth, showed a restraint he'd never used before. It was as impressive as his manners. Drake was proud of him.

Why? I'm never there. It's more Gavin's doing, or maybe Ed's.

They made a turn, and the Felton House gate cast a shadow across Drake's eyelids. Over the past two years, the route had become as familiar as any road around Hyde Park. Halfway up, to the left, the dower cottage was tucked under a hill. Thea's mother would be a crow in the garden, all in black while she used tending flowers as a reason to snoop until the lane turned to the left, then nudged to the right, where a grove of trees provided refreshing shade in the summer.

Drake opened his eyes and sat straighter, combed his hands through his hair, and brushed the detritus from his clothes as best he could. All the while, he watched for Frank's reaction when the house came into view.

The hedges came first, sloping up gently from grass level to waist high, when pansies hid their feet. Columnar spruce played sentry, sloping upward in the same way as the hedges—as though they hated to startle you with their appearance. They vanished in the same stages, stopping as the lane arced around a fountain that splashed on all but the coldest of days.

The boy's mouth fell open.

Felton House was buff brick faced with evenly stacked and evenly spaced windows, four chimneys that you could see to count, almost as long as a city block, with a front entrance tall enough to accommodate Richard if he were standing on Drake's shoulders.

It was still surreal that Thea lived here—that Drake knew people who lived like this. Counted them as friends.

He swung over the side of the cart and came face to face with the wet statues glistening under the sunlight as water sluiced around their curves. The cherubs and satyrs he'd expected at the White Rose were here, of all places.

That would make Jocelyn laugh. So would tiny Amelia's take-charge attitude and, though he hated to admit it, Richard's irreverent humor.

The front door opened, and Simon Hawkins barreled toward them, shadowed by an Irish wolfhound that towered over him—though a little less than last month. "*Oncle* Richard, *Tante* Amelia! *Oncle* Drake!"

Frank swung his gaze to him. "You're related to these people?"

Drake feinted to keep the seven-year-old from bashing against his ribs. "No. It's just easier to go along." He'd explain more on the way home.

Oliver and Thea joined the group, holding hands as they did at every opportunity. Drake straightened his spine and squared his shoulders. "Your Grace, may I present my ward, Frank Harvey. Frank, may I present the Duke and Duchess of Rushford, and their son Simon." He ignored the impulse to use Simon's title. He'd already pushed enough in calling Oliver a duke when titles weren't allowed at home.

The duke and duchess rolled their eyes in unison. "It's a pleasure to meet you, Frank," Oliver said. "Welcome to Felton House."

The young man, who had already removed his hat, gave a quick, shaky bow. "Thank you, Your Grace."

"What's a ward?" Simon asked.

Oliver placed a hand on his son's shoulder. "Si, you don't ask—"

Drake ignored the fatherly scolding. He enjoyed Simon's unaffected curiosity and the fact that, in work clothes, the lad didn't look anything like the tiny earl he was. "A ward is like a younger brother, Si."

"Then can I call you Frank?" Simon asked. When Frank nodded, the boy's smile widened. "Would you like to come meet Pinkie?" He walked off, certain of the answer.

"Your horse?" Frank asked as he fell into step, though he shortened his stride so Simon could keep up.

"No. silly. Why would a horse be pink?" Simon said. "Pinkie is my pig, though he's whiter now, and *Oncle* Richard says his bollocks are as large as the clapper on Big Ben."

"Simon," Thea barked, her face red.

"Richard!" Amelia squealed, her eyes sparkling.

"What?" The offending uncle spread his hands wide. "Have you seen them?"

"Have you ever seen the clapper on Big Ben?" Drake asked.

All eyes turned to him. Drake wasn't sure which was funnier, the situation or the looks on their faces. Either way, laughter bubbled through him. It shook his wounds under his bandages, but it felt good just the same. It felt even better when they joined him.

After a moment, Oliver dropped a hand on Drake's shoulder. "It's good to see you, but I'm certain you would rather visit with Thea and Amelia."

"Stay, please," Drake said. He looked into Oliver's eyes, hoping the man could guess why without his asking. He was about to get half-naked with a married woman. Her husband should be in the room when that happened.

"Certainly." Oliver edged closer, wordlessly offering a shoulder if it was needed as they started for the door.

Thea joined them, flanking Drake's other side. "Richard and Amelia, could you excuse us?"

They walked three abreast to Thea's workroom, a stone-walled space that was once part of the pantry.

"Is anything broken?" Thea asked as Oliver closed the door.

Drake sat on the polished wooden table and removed his shirt. "It's naught but a scratch."

Her fingers were warm on his skin. "It's a little more than that, but whoever treated you had common sense."

Jocelyn had treated all the boys at Highcliffe at one time or another, tending everything from splinters and barnacle scrapes to dog bites and knife wounds worse than these. "She's not faint-hearted."

"Ginger would help. Is my supply in your bags?"

Damn. "I haven't had a chance to stop for it, Thea. I'm sorry."

"We'll make do," she mumbled. "I'll mix a poultice for you to wear while you're sleeping, and I'll send you home with a salve to keep on it while the skin finishes knitting." She traced the scab on his wrist. "This one is healing without me. It wasn't as deep."

The salve was cool against his skin, and the leaves tickled. Drake waited patiently, letting the rhythm of it relax him until his eyes were heavy. It was easy to imagine it was Jocelyn's hands on his skin in the dark, that she was the one fussing over him and making sure he was safe.

"Does this have anything to do with the lovely young lady you've been squiring around London?" Thea asked.

Drake came alert and twisted to look at Oliver. "I knew you couldn't keep a secret."

Thea looked between them, but she stopped at her husband, who was grinning in the corner. "You knew?"

"I did," Oliver said as he came to her and kissed her on the cheek. "But I promised I wouldn't say a word about catching him kissing her in Parliament."

"You kissed her *in public.*" Thea's smile now matched her husband's. "Tavie only said you'd come for tea."

Drake snatched his shirt from the table and stood. "I'm going to go rest before dinner."

"You have the room at the front of the house," Thea called after him, still laughing.

AFTER A LONG rest, a good meal, and whatever magic Thea had

worked with his wounds, Drake was better prepared to finish his business. It helped that Oliver's valet had cleaned and pressed his suit. Frank, having spent the afternoon in the barn with Simon, was still getting dressed for dinner.

Drake entered the library and took the whiskey Oliver offered.

"Why is my delivery a barrel short?" Richard asked from his place near the hearth. "Did you get thirsty on your trip?"

Drake sipped his whiskey. It wasn't as good as Amelia's, but it was close. "It got a hole in it."

"Is there some drunken rat stumbling his way through London?"

"No," Drake said as the whiskey warmed him through. "It was a bullet hole." Watching the smile fade from Richard's face was almost as satisfying.

"Someone shot at you and Frank?" Oliver asked. "Nearby?"

"Not me and Frank." Drake sighed. "And not here. In Berkshire."

"Is that where you got into the knife fight?" Oliver asked.

"With the woman you kissed in Parliament?" Richard rested one hip on Oliver's desk.

Because of course Thea told Amelia, and Amelia told Richard. Simon would hear the tale before long. The circle was closing, and Drake was regretting his decision to come here. He should have let Richard's wine turn to vinegar in the coach house.

Except that would harm Amelia's business—and be wasteful.

"I was with her yes, but the part about Parliament isn't as it seems." Richard should understand that better than any of them, given how his relationship with Amelia had begun. "However, it is something that may affect you."

Drake drew a deep breath and told them everything—almost. Jocelyn, Connie, Jasper, Violet, Stratford, Spencer.

"Who is this woman?" Richard asked when the tale had ended, a smile on his face as he looked at Oliver. "Do you know her?"

"I've only seen the top of her head." Oliver smiled over the rim of his glass. "She could be cross-eyed and buck-toothed for all I know."

"She is neither of those," Drake said. "And it's not that way between us. But please do pay attention. Stratford knows I work for you, Oliver, and if he should grow desperate…"

"We'll take precautions, all of us, I promise." Oliver poured them another round of drinks. "But about this young woman who conspires to thwart murderers and gets you to smuggle people in the middle of the night…"

They made Drake sound like the dullest man in England. There had been days when knife fights had been as commonplace as eating dinner.

"Her name is Jocelyn, and I have known her for years. Her father and I worked together." After all, the longer he delayed talking of her, the more everyone would badger him. "She lives in London, but she is not in Society. I doubt that either of you know her."

For so many reasons, he hoped they didn't.

"Is she a client, then?" Oliver asked. "One of Thea's Circle?"

"No." Drake sighed. They were not going to give this up. "She has a house in Marylebone, across from the cricket ground."

Richard made the connection first. "She's at the White Rose? Is this why you punched me?"

Oliver was speechless. Drake would have enjoyed bragging about that to Thea, but he'd have to relay the entire conversation to prove his point. She'd likely be speechless as well.

"She manages The Rose, yes." Drake refused to look away from these men who had become his allies. He might not understand why Jocelyn made the decisions she made, but he would never be ashamed of her.

"Madam White?" Oliver asked. "I've heard she's older than Methuselah."

"The title passes from one to another. Jocelyn is three years younger than me. I've known her since she wasn't much older than Simon." Realizing he was volunteering too much, Drake snapped his jaws shut.

Oliver was quiet for a long time, especially for him, as he considered his drink. Finally, he looked up. "If you trust her, so do I. And I appreciate your efforts to see justice done for this young lady. I will help you as I can."

The taut string between Drake's shoulder blades snapped. "Thank you, Oliver."

"Don't thank me just yet. My influence might not go far if you are caught. Stratford is more popular in Lords, and he is a nasty piece of work. Spencer isn't much better, though his connection with the Crown keeps him mostly honest."

The gong rang, and they all stood. Oliver clapped Drake on the shoulder. "Thank you for coming here to warn us, rather than staying in London with your Miss White."

"Kirk," Drake said. "Her last name is Kirk, and she is not mine."

"If you say so," Oliver said as he walked toward the door. "Dinner is served, gentlemen. Let's not keep the ladies waiting."

"Drake?" Richard said. "A moment, please?"

Drake braced himself for a joke or a ribald tease. Maybe even a lecture on how he'd put the man's new wife in danger even before they'd taken their honeymoon trip. "Yes?"

"I know I'm the last person from whom you'd want advice, but if you find a woman who makes you more yourself…don't think too hard on it." Richard's stare was steady, even if there was a hitch in his smile. "I mean, I could tell you to close your eyes and think of England, but that would ruin all the fun."

The advice, typically given to virgin daughters before their wedding nights, echoed through Drake's skull like the dinner gong. His skin heated and his stomach twisted. How in the bloody hell had Richard learned one of Drake's best kept, most embarrassing secrets? "What?"

"It's not a hard guess. You work like a fiend, and you're too ethical to pursue your clients. Thank God." Richard gulped the remainder of his whiskey. "Besides that, my jaw still creaks when

I yawn." He grinned. "Don't worry. Your secret is safe with me."

"Umm…thank you."

"Amelia would never forgive me if she lost your services because I couldn't resist a tale." Richard walked him from the room. "Just remember…don't close your eyes."

⁓

"MADAM?" HUGH KNOCKED on her door. The name stopped her. He only called her that at night when clients were around. The sun should have eliminated both requirements.

Joss left her ledgers and went to the door. "Hugh? What's amiss?"

"Mr. Macklin is in the parlor. He's asked to speak to you alone."

It must be dire for Macklin to leave his offices in the middle of the day. She knew better than to think Poppy had filched from him while he'd been in her room last night, or any night before that. All the girls knew stealing from clients meant eviction and a warning letter to every reputable brothel in London.

That left disease or pregnancy. Though Sam would have told her if Poppy was ill or had fallen pregnant.

"I'll be down in a moment. Would you please ask Eleanor to deliver tea and cakes?"

"Perhaps something stronger as well?" Hugh asked, the grim set of his mouth signaling that he shared her thoughts.

"Yes. Thank you."

Joss watched him leave before going to her dressing table. The mirror reflected someone resembling the bookkeeper she was rather than the madam everyone expected to see. However, it wasn't business hours, and Mr. Macklin had arrived unannounced. He shouldn't expect decoration and drama all the time.

She made one concession with her hair, smoothing it into a twist before forming loose curls at her temples. A dab of lip rouge and a spritz of perfume were the last of her preparations.

She descended the stairs quicker than usual, but still slow enough to keep from losing her breath. There was a man in the parlor, not a fire in the kitchen. Still, Mr. Macklin had taken time from his business to come here, and she needed to respect that and not dawdle.

"Mr. Macklin? How nice to see you this morning," Joss said as she offered her hand, careful to smile wide enough to hide her worries.

"Madam White." His voice was as cultured as his bow over her hand, which made his confused expression that much more amusing.

"I don't dress in satins during the day," she teased as she sat. "Tea?"

"Yes, thank you." He was still staring. "Forgive me, but you look completely different. Younger, I think."

Her evening wear, from her hair to her shoes, was meant to give the appearance of age and station. Coming down without it was an act of trust that she hoped was not misplaced.

"What a kind thing to say." She delivered his cup, made with two sugars and a splash of cream. "How can I help you, Mr. Macklin?"

He looked around the room, as though expecting the girls to pop up from behind drapes and furniture. "Are the young ladies out?"

"We don't entertain during the day. The girls have other responsibilities when clients are not present."

Like laundry and kitchen chores. The gossip that would arise from seeing one of the ladies up to her elbows in soiled linen or sweating over a stew pot was to be avoided.

"I've come to talk to you about Poppy." He smoothed his collar just above his cravat. "My father has died and has willed his possessions, including his large law practice in Sheffield, to me."

"My condolences," Joss said. It was sincere. She didn't remember losing her mother, but the exact day she'd lost her father to Horsemonger's cells would be one she never forgot. "Do you intend to quit London?"

"I do. I find London disagreeable, with a few exceptions." He tipped his head to indicate a compliment.

Joss imitated his posture to accept it. "We will certainly miss you, Mr. Macklin, and Poppy will be devastated. Would you like me to call her in to say goodbye?"

"No, madam." He dropped his teacup into the saucer and leaned forward. "You misunderstand. I would like to take Poppy with me. As my wife."

It was Jocelyn's turn to blink at him in surprise. The time gave her a chance to see him more clearly. He carried the polish of education. Though his hair was silver at the temples, the rest of it was a rich brown. He was handsome and fit, and his coloring hinted at a man who liked to spend time outdoors. Despite his nerves, he'd not partaken of the whiskey on offer, and the cakes sat untouched. "Has she agreed?"

"I've not asked her yet," he said. "I thought it best to speak to you first. I'm not certain of the legal details of her employment. Is there is a contract to be purchased?"

If he wasn't so sweet about it, she would have been offended. "I don't *own* Poppy, Mr. Macklin. She arrived of her own free will, and she may leave when she wishes. She even has a small savings."

He paused. "I'm not sure I'm comfortable taking it."

It was understandable that he wouldn't want a reminder that other men had paid for his wife's attention, but he took money to defend murderers, for God's sake.

"It is mostly your money, sir," Joss teased. "It can be used as a dowry, but I would hope you would leave it for her to manage and use as she sees fit."

"That would make me feel better, I believe."

His discomfort over the money gave her pause. It was impossible not to find a similarity between his reaction and Drake's questions about the life she'd lived and his dissatisfaction with her choices. "Are you certain you understand the repercussions?"

"No one in Sheffield should know her or anything of her past," he said. "But it wouldn't matter to me if they did." He inhaled so deeply he sank into the sofa cushions. "Do I have your permission to ask for her hand? Poppy says you are the closest thing she has to a parent."

Which was as frightening as it was touching. Joss already knew her answer. As he'd shown more and more interest in Poppy, Joss had discreetly asked after him. He was stable, hardworking, and kind. "If Poppy agrees, I have no objection whatsoever." Joss rose and fought the urge to hurry from the room. "Excuse me while I go find her."

Her pace quickened as she passed the bar and went into the kitchen. "Elsa, where is Poppy?"

"Here, madam." The girl stuck her head around the door to the pantry. "We were just finishing cleaning. Can I help?"

"Mr. Macklin is in the lounge waiting to see you." Joss couldn't keep the grin from her face. She so rarely got to see a happy-ever-after. From the corner of her eye, she saw Elsa shooing everyone else from the kitchen.

"He's early," Poppy said as she reached for her apron. "Something must have happened. Is it acceptable for me to go in this early, dressed like this?"

"He has a question to ask you," Joss said. It was all she could do not to ruin Macklin's surprise.

"He's come to propose, hasn't he?" Poppy's lips trembled. "I won't marry him and watch people laugh behind his back. He deserves—"

"He deserves someone who loves him unconditionally. As do you. And he's quitting London for Sheffield."

Poppy's eyes went wide. "I've never been farther north than Tottenham," she whispered.

"Do you love him?" Joss asked. When Poppy nodded so hard that her tears slid down her face in all directions, Joss squeezed her fingers. "Then be brave and take what you want." She winked. "But wash your face and tidy your hair first. You want him to think it's a surprise."

While Poppy washed up in the sink, Joss found Eleanor in the garden. "Could you please go in the lounge and chaperone Poppy and Mr. Macklin?"

"He's early." Eleanor didn't look up as she dropped a turnip in her basket.

"He's proposing." Joss dropped to her knees next to her maid. "I think, years down the road, they'd rather have you in their stories than me."

"I'm thrilled for her, of course," Eleanor said as she abandoned the turnips and slipped free of her apron. "And I'm happy to help, but I think you're being too hard on yourself, Jocelyn. You've been good to all these girls, even the ones who didn't deserve it." She stood. "The house will be quieter without Poppy, but it won't be as much fun."

From her spot in the garden, with her fingers in the dirt, Joss heard Poppy's squeal of delight and then all the girls' shrieks of celebration—Terrence Macklin would be deaf before his wedding. Hugh popped a bottle of champagne.

Jocelyn had already had her chance to celebrate with Poppy, and she'd have another one at the wedding. Right now, she wanted the girl to remember being surrounded by her friends in her home. She didn't need to have her boss, the woman who represented every obstacle that could have prevented her happiness, near.

Gardening had always been Joss's solace. She turned to it now, looking for meaning in the patterns of roots and the solidness of stones under her fingers. Eventually, she shook the cobwebs from her brain.

She had pursued what she wanted. She was in London. She was wealthy enough to leave gardening to others unless she simply *wanted* to do it. She had money in her pocket, loyal friends, and a viable plan to gain her father's release from prison.

None of that seemed enough now. She wanted what Poppy

had. She wanted a chance with a man who didn't care what she'd done in her past. Every woman dreamed of that when they closed their eyes.

The most ridiculous part was that the man Joss saw was the one man who cared very much about who she was and what she had done—what she was doing. She'd gone to sleep imagining his arms around her and awoken curled around her pillow, cursing its softness and its sweet smell.

Drake would never darken her bedroom door in search of anything but answers he didn't like. She knew that. She also knew that she could catch any one of the dozen men in the parlor tonight simply by opening her fan. She could imagine Drake's hands on her and pretend it was his skin against his fingers.

But that would be a lie. She was a lot of things, but she wasn't a liar.

Not about things that mattered, anyway.

CHAPTER SIXTEEN

YESTERDAY, THE GIRLS had been in high spirits as they celebrated Poppy's engagement. Today, they were celebrating her wedding night—which was spent nowhere near a brothel.

The gentlemen in attendance didn't seem to mind, but Joss's head was throbbing. It worsened when Reginald Spencer walked through the front door. He never visited of his own accord.

Even though all she could see was him on the street corner with Stratford, she put a smile on her face. "Reggie, darling. How lovely to see you."

His cheek touched hers. "And you, my dear. But I have little time."

She took his arm, her headache pushed aside. "Let's go up, then." He might have an agenda, but she had one of her own.

"How is our witness?" he whispered. "Is she safe until it is time to sing?"

If her suspicions were correct, he already knew that she and Drake had been attacked on the way to Reading. Sending him in another direction in search of Connie would simply confirm the direction. "She is."

"Does she have the evidence needed to support her claim?" His elbow tightened, squeezing the blood from her fingertips.

They reached the second floor, where Hugh's chair sat empty. None of the girls had taken clients upstairs yet this evening.

Which was why there should be no noise coming from Poppy's now vacant room. Joss left Spencer waiting, went to the door, and tried the knob. Locked.

No door but hers was ever locked at The Rose.

She banged her fist against heavy oak, vibrating her forearm all the way to her wrist. "Who is in there?"

"Help! No! Get off me!"

The cries were faint, but Joss was certain she heard them. "Hugh," she shouted as she bolted to the stairs. "Hugh! Get up here *now*."

The big man took the stairs in three leaps and followed Joss's direction to the door in the corner. He had to put his shoulder to the wood twice, but he got through.

Beatrice Mills, who should have been in the kitchen doing her homework, scrambled across the bare mattress to the door, her face a mess of tears and her dress ripped from the neck to the waist. It wasn't a dress, Joss realized. It was a maid's uniform.

What the devil was Eleanor's daughter doing upstairs dressed as a maid?

Joss pushed the question aside for later and focused on the man Hugh had cornered. Philip Melton, Viscount Raines, stood there, red-faced with his trousers undone, swaying on his feet. "Call off your dog, Madam White."

"There's only one dog here, Lord Raines. Reggie, give me your coat." She held out her hand.

When the man hesitated, she turned to him. "I will not send that girl downstairs to her mother in this state, and I will not force her to wear her attacker's clothes." She shoved her hand at him. "Give. Me. Your. Coat."

He grudgingly relented, and Joss draped the wool coat over Bea's shoulders before buttoning it to her waist. "What are you doing up here? Where are Lucy and Clara?" She already suspected the answer.

"They wanted to stay downstairs and listen to the party, and I just wanted… I wanted to see up here, madam. I thought, since

Poppy's room was empty now…" Her words were lost in her tears. "And he…he… I'm so-sorry."

Joss put an arm around the girl and led her to the back stairs. "You have nothing to apologize for, other than curiosity, which isn't a bad thing all the time." She'd be having words with Lucy and Clara, who would likely be cowed by what they had allowed to happen. Eleanor would probably send Bea to a convent.

She hugged the girl tightly as Bea's tears threatened her composure. "Listen to your mother more, Beatrice. She knows what she's doing." She opened the door. "Now, go downstairs. We'll talk more tomorrow."

Eleanor was already halfway to them, her pale face splotched with angry red, and her hands were fists. Joss recognized the preparation for battle, but she knew it was futile. The viscount would care nothing for the scolding of a maid.

Joss placed a hand on her friend's shoulder as she kept a steady gaze. "Look after your daughter, Eleanor. Leave the bastard to me."

Once they had descended the stairs, Joss freed the fury she'd muffled in front of the child and entered the room. Reggie was still standing at the door, his eyes wide, as Hugh all but growled every time his prey moved.

"Hugh, toss this rapist out on his privileged arse."

"Now see here." The young man scrambled as Hugh grabbed him by the collar. "My falls—"

"You are lucky you won't be naked as the day your mother first saw you," Joss snarled. "Never darken our door again, or you will lose more than your dignity."

Spencer halted their exit. "Perhaps he is not so much in the wrong, madam. He is quite drunk—perhaps he mistook the young lady's intentions on this floor."

"He's not blind enough to mistake maid's cotton for satin, nor a mob cap for curls." Her maids complained loud and long about their old-fashioned, scratchy uniforms, but it was done for just this reason. She focused her ire on Spencer. "And you do not tell me how to run my business."

Hugh stepped around the too-thin obstacle and kept going, marching the young viscount down the front stairs. His hold was so vicious that the boy's feet barely touched the floor. Joss hoped everyone on the bottom floor saw the pitiful size of Melton's limp cock.

"He didn't rape the girl, you know," Spencer said. "She shouldn't have been up here in the first place."

Was it the entire *ton* who stuck together or just the men? "This is her home."

"What should anyone expect, then, of a girl raised in such a place?"

"That she has the right to her own body and her own mind, and to a place where she is safe." Joss crossed her arms over her chest. "She is the age of your daughter, Reggie. Knowing what you know now, let her dance with him at her next ball. I dare you."

He glowered back. "I don't need to introduce him to my family to get my use out of him. I have invested a great deal in his father's bid for lord high treasurer, and if we had been just a few moments longer, I could have persuaded the man to support my agenda with the queen."

Joss couldn't believe her ears. But then again… "You would trade that girl's virtue and self-worth for another secret to wield?" She wanted to hear him say it, but she knew he never would.

She thought back to all the men who had whispered to her girls, who had then whispered to Joss, who had then whispered to Spencer. They never lost their positions; their scandals were never made public. Yet the next time they visited, the light had dimmed from their eyes. They wore the same expressions as the men on Horsemonger Lane, even though they were free.

Spencer was the only one whose lot seemed to improve. He'd risen through the ranks. His wife was on committees. His daughter had been presented to the queen. His son had a promising career following in his father's footsteps.

He was the warden of a jail full of secrets.

"Some things are more important," he hissed. "Now, do you have the evidence against Stratford? I cannot approach him again without proof."

Joss's brain whirred, looking for something that would frighten him more than her. If he valued power and influence over everything else, perhaps that would work. "He is watching too closely," she said. "There are men outside the house day and night. They follow me. They follow men who leave the house. He is gathering as much information on us as we are on him." She looked into his eyes and told a lie. "I fear we will lose."

His eyes narrowed. "Then how will you get it to me?"

"It will have to be unplanned, and it cannot be here." She made herself touch him. "You have to trust me."

He had no choice. He knew it. She knew it.

Edith led a client up the stairs. Hugh hulked in their wake.

Spencer stepped away. "I'm expected elsewhere, madam," he said in a louder voice. He bent over her hand, his grip painful. "Until next time."

Joss watched him go. The door closed behind him, and the starch dissolved from her shoulders and spine. She felt old and dirty, like a used shoe with holes in the sole that soaked its owner's foot. Sad, broken down, without a mate.

But she still had work to do. She went to the middle of the floor and pulled a chair next to Hugh. "Should I go down?"

"Give it until tomorrow. Eleanor's in a state." He never looked up from his whittling. "She took Bea home and locked the doors. Lucy and Clara are still bawling, and Elsa won't stop telling them how stupid they are. James doesn't know yet. I'll tell him. I'll have to sit on him to keep him from sawing off Raines's tackle." He grinned. "Remind me to never make you angry, though. Bravest thing I've ever seen you do."

"Thank you." She heaved a sigh. "I don't want to go back to the parlor."

He shrugged. "Then don't. I can manage it while James is up

here. Take a night for yourself. You don't do that often enough."

Because she'd never had anywhere she wanted to be. But Drake should be returning soon. She wanted to hear how the trip had gone with Frank. She wanted to make sure they were safe, and that Drake's wounds were healing. She wanted to see him.

Hear him.

Touch him.

She wanted to talk about what she'd learned and how it would affect their plans.

She was tired of sitting still.

"Thank you, Hugh. I think I'll do just that."

Joss climbed the stairs to her room and changed from her satin disguise into a skirt and blouse that were far too respectable for going out at night. She didn't pack a bag, but she did get her reticule and her shawl.

Hugh was waiting for her on the second floor. "Tommy's hailed a cab. I need him here, and I thought you might not want him along." His lips quirked. "Wherever it is you're going."

She kissed the big man's cheek. "Thank you, Hugh. I'll be home in the morning."

Once in the cab, her heart pounding in time with the horses' hooves, Joss had to admit that she might be returning much sooner if she couldn't get into the house. She didn't need to circle the house to know Drake would have removed anything that could be used to climb up—or down, given Harry's last escape from the attic. Dressed like this, she couldn't sneak in anyway. That only left Gavin at the front door.

The cab stopped, leaving Joss no choice but to open the door and climb the steps alone. At least the bellpull saved her the agony of knocking. Everyone sounded brave when they pulled a bell.

Gavin opened the door wearing a pistol on his hip. His sour expression didn't soften. "He's not here."

"I know," Joss said. "But I would like to be here when he arrives."

"That could be days still," the man grumbled.

"You know as well as I do that he won't stay in Norfolk long-er than necessary." Mostly because Drake knew she wouldn't wait forever to break into Stratford's home. "Just like I know that your neighbors will gossip for days if you turn a lady away from your door at night, unaccompanied."

"You aren't a lady."

The words stung more than she'd thought they would. "They don't know that."

Gavin stared at her for a long moment before stepping aside and letting her into the hall. She'd breached the gates.

"Gav?" Harry called down. "Is everything all right?"

"Fine, Harry. Go back to sleep."

She was here to seduce a man who had children in the house, a man who had more principles in one finger than most men had in their entire bodies. A man who would never come to her because everyone would be watching him take her upstairs.

Gavin stood before her with his treelike arms crossed over his chest. "You can wait in the library. Leave the door open and don't pick the lock to the safe."

Joss didn't budge. "You and I both know he doesn't need to see me in a library."

He blinked.

"I know that my father made some poor decisions when it came to you. That he should have done more—anything—to secure your freedom. I'm sorry that he didn't. I am sorry that you suffered, but I didn't hurt you. I don't intend to hurt Drake either. He can send me home if he wishes, but please give me a chance to hear it from him. That's all I'm asking."

No wonder Terrence Macklin kept fiddling with his collar as he'd asked for Poppy's hand. But just like the lawyer, Joss knew what she wanted, and she wasn't going to waver.

"His door's the last on the left. It overlooks the street." Gavin cleared the way. "Don't wake the boys."

"It's good to be home," Frank said as he put hay in the manger and oats in the trough.

Drake passed the brush over the last horse's broad back and patted the giant's flank before leaving the stall and closing the door. "Thank you for your help during this trip, Frank. You made things much easier."

The boy walked next to him as they crossed the mostly dirt garden. "Could I go back with you the next time?"

It was dark, so Drake didn't bother to hide his smile. "As long as it doesn't interfere with your studies, I don't see why not." He looked at Frank, who hadn't bothered to conceal his happiness either. "I'd like the company."

The house was quiet, but the kitchen was still warm as they removed their boots and left them by the door. Scones waited on a plate in the center of the table, and they each took several, chewing as they entered the hall and made the turn for the stairs. "Gav will give us hell about crumbs," Frank said.

"Let him," Drake said. Frank didn't need to know that he'd get up early to make sure the rugs were clean.

At the top of the stairs, Frank stopped on his way to his room. "Thank you for taking me with you. Goodnight."

"Goodnight." Drake watched him vanish into the darkness before turning for his room at the front of the house. Despite the excellent mattresses at Felton House, it had been far too long since he'd slept in his own bed.

There was a fire in the grate, casting long shadows over the carpets but giving him enough light to see the pitcher of water and glass on his bedside table. Drake drained one glass and filled another. It slid down much easier than the first.

A board creaked, a shadow shifted. Drake reached for his knife, prepared to face the intruder. One deep breath.

Bluebells.

He released the hilt of his blade. "Jocelyn?"

"Yes."

"What the devil do you think you're doing skulking about in my bedroom? You know better than to—"

She was wearing his dressing gown, the hem puddled at her bare feet, splashing with every step.

"Gav let me in," she said. "He's probably lying awake waiting for you to start yelling at me."

He'd have to find his voice before he could yell. The lapels of his robe were open almost to the sash at her waist. Her breastbone was bare, and her flat stomach tempted his fingers as much as the curve of her breast.

Don't think too hard.

"I don't want to yell at you." At least, Drake hoped that was what he said. His heart was hammering so loudly that he couldn't hear anything else in the room.

He claimed Jocelyn's mouth, savoring the softness of her lips for a breath before he swept his tongue into her warmth, sliding along her agile tongue and groaning as she drew him deeper.

Her skin was velvet against his fingers, softer than the robe he pushed from her shoulders.

She smiled against his mouth. "I'm so glad."

Drake separated from her long enough to pull his shirt over his head and toss it aside. "You are beautiful."

She truly was. Moonlight cast her curves into shadow as firelight licked her skin. She was thin enough to look delicate, but the muscles under her skin hinted at her strength.

She brushed her fingers over his bandage. "I didn't think. I don't want to hurt you."

"I'll ache worse if we stop now."

He skimmed his fingers up her ribs and was delighted as she giggled and squirmed away. The pleasure doubled as she pulled him in for another drugging kiss that ended on a gasp as he took her breast in his hand.

The weight of it was mesmerizing, the texture tantalizing. The bud under his thumb hardened, and her sigh filled the room. Drake kept circling, though he pulled away to watch her savor the attention—teeth buried in her bottom lip, eyes closed, head thrown back.

He took advantage of the invitation and skated his lips from her jaw to her collarbone, lapping at the salty-sweet taste of her.

"Take me to bed before I melt into the floor." She knotted her fingers in his hair and pulled him back to her mouth. "Please, Drake."

She was easy to lift, and he knew the shadowy room like he knew his own soul. Her presence on his bed changed everything. Drake undid his falls as he watched her watch him, her hair splayed over the sheets, her hands reaching for him. Her feet scraped his calves, helping him rid himself of clothes he no longer cared to own.

"Socks." Jocelyn giggled against his mouth. "You have to take off your socks."

"Who made that stupid rule?" he grumbled as he pushed one off, and then the other. "What if my feet are cold?"

She arched into his touch and coaxed his mouth to follow his fingers. "If you are focused on your feet, I'm doing this wrong."

Drake swirled his tongue over one of her nipples and rolled the other between his fingers, testing which she preferred. She repaid him by dragging her fingers down his spine, making him bow upward so she could taste his neck while her breasts brushed his skin.

Heat radiated from her center, and her hands were sure on his hips. The easiest of movement would join them.

Drake stopped, pulled her hands from his arse, and raised them over her head. "Don't touch me."

She pushed against the mattress, her face a cloud. "If that's—"

Drake put his hand between her breasts and kissed her back into the mattress. He put her hands over her head and skimmed his palms down the undersides of her arms, to her breasts and then her waist. Grasping her thighs, ignoring her silky skin, he pulled her legs away from him. "If you touch me like that, it will be over too soon. I don't want this to end yet, Jocelyn." He stared into her wide eyes. "Please."

She squirmed beneath him, and he worried she would bolt.

"Move the pillows out of my way," she whispered.

He swept them to the floor and was rewarded by her hooking her hands under the headboard and spreading her legs so he had plenty of room to explore. He took advantage, learning her curves first with his hands and then with his mouth, tasting her first with his tongue and then with his teeth.

"I can feel you smiling, you beast," she said as he lifted her leg to lick the bend of one knee while his fingers toyed with the other.

Even the arch of her foot was delicious.

She writhed and panted beneath him. She mewled and arched from the bed, her body begging for his. His sheets were soaked, and his skin was slick when he finally slid two of his fingers into her center and felt her shiver around him.

"God, yes. Please. More." Her fingers wrapped around his shoulder, pulling him forward. "Please."

Drake was as stiff as a new mast, but he kissed her fingers and pushed them back over her head. "I'm not finished yet, Jocelyn."

He returned to her, watching her writhe as he found the spot he remembered, caressed it, rubbed it, watched her breasts flush red as her heels scraped the sheets while she buckled around him.

The room smelled of her musky sweetness, and Drake lifted a finger to his lips to see if she tasted as good. He kept his eyes on her as he propped one arm near her head and leaned over her, careful to stay away from her tantalizing heat.

"Do you remember that day you made us all have tea on the beach before the tide came in, and we had cream tarts topped with blueberries?" He smiled as she nodded. "That's what you taste like."

He kissed her then, a sinful combination of his taste and hers. "I remember those tarts. I took one when I wanted two." Drake swept his tongue along her jaw to her ear. "Now I can have as many as I want."

Her groan rattled against his tongue as he kissed her throat. Her panting breaths put her nipple in reach once again. Her stomach shivered against his teeth. And then he was there, watching her watch him as he closed his mouth over her center and devoured her.

Jocelyn's fingers tangled in his hair as her heels banged against his back. She rolled under him like a ship in the storm, muffling her cries with her free hand so she didn't wake the household.

Or likely the entire street.

When she was limp beneath him, Drake wiped his chin on the sheets and knelt between her thighs. She smiled a bewitching smile, tightened her legs around his waist, and pulled him forward.

It was an overwhelming sensation, sliding inside her and feeling her grip him in welcome. He gave in to the urge to rock forward, to go deeper. When her sheath wrapped him impossibly tighter, he pushed harder.

Jocelyn shook around him, grabbing his hips to beg for more until he was driving into her like a madman. His vision darkened as his muscles tightened. His climax began in his toes and sped upward, spilling from him even as it shivered up his spine until he was buried against her shoulder, shouting her name.

Drake returned to himself in stages, and only long enough to pluck the pillows from the floor and drop one on her side of the bed. He pulled the covers over both of them before shoving a pillow beneath his head.

Jocelyn raised groggy eyes to him as she snuggled against him and ignored the soft pillow for his hard, sweaty chest. Her fingers burrowed into his chest hair as her breath fell into a steady rhythm. Her tangled hair ticked his chin.

Drake loved the dark because it was easier to hide. Usually he was skulking. Now? Now he was gloating as his sated body sank into the mattress. He hadn't fumbled for what to do, and she seemed to be as satisfied as he was. Perhaps she'd never know it had been a new experience for him.

Perhaps, if he was lucky, it could become a regular experience. His eyes drooped closed as a smile curved his lips.

He was known for his luck.

He woke to find Jocelyn using the firelight to find her clothes. Beyond the curtains, lamplight still fought the dark night. One of his first lessons in London was how to distinguish between the glow of gas lamps and dawn.

The sheets were already losing their warmth. "You could stay."

"I shouldn't be here when the boys wake." She sat on the edge of the bed, giving him a chance to distract her from tying her boots. She pushed his hands away. "I am trying to be a good example, Fletcher."

He threw the covers back. "I'll see you—"

"You will see the backs of your eyelids for a few more hours." She pushed him against the pillows and pulled the quilts to his chin. "I know how to hail a cab."

She shouldn't go out the front door alone. The house was still being watched.

"Be sure to—" His yawn stopped his voice.

"Go out the back. I know." She kissed his forehead. "I'll come see you after breakfast. We'll go to Stratford's townhouse from here."

CHAPTER SEVENTEEN

"**I** CAN'T BELIEVE I let you talk me into this," Drake grumbled.

"You're the one who insisted on tagging along," Joss countered. "Go home if you'd prefer."

She would definitely prefer it. Every time she looked at him, she remembered the pleasure in his eyes as he'd enjoyed her body. Being in Mayfair on an autumn day, surrounded by couples out for a stroll, did nothing to help. She would rather be enjoying the rare sunshine and the discretion offered by a parasol instead of being tucked behind a tree, standing in the scant shade offered by bare branches as though they were the ones with something to hide.

He glared down his nose. "If you're not out of there in fifteen minutes, I'll—"

Joss rolled her eyes. "Call the nearest patrolman."

"Try to take this seriously, Jocelyn. It's not a lark."

"Of course it's not." Across from them, Stratford's townhouse looked like every other one in the row. Passersby paid it no notice. But the empty windows and dark front door, stark against the white façade, sent a chill up Joss's spine. "But having the police arrive will cause much less of a scene than your crashing through the front door without good reason."

"Let me do it." He thrust out his hand.

She swept her reticule behind her back and out of reach. "No housekeeper worth her pay will let you in the house, much less leave you unaccompanied. She'll pay you a reward, wish you well, and close the door in your face." She watched his eyes, waiting for common sense to dawn. "You know I'm right."

"But what if—"

"He's in Parliament, Fletcher. He won't be home for hours." But only if she got a start now. She looked up at him and winked. "Do you know your cravat matches your eyes?"

Before he could regain his tongue, Joss stepped out of their hiding spot and into the street, knowing he wouldn't chase her and cause a scene. Traffic was too light for her taste. It was always easier to hide in a crowd.

Her hobnailed boots tapped on the shallow stone stairs, two steps per riser, until she reached the front door. A brass dragon waited there, posed mid-growl, no doubt to deter unwelcome visitors. There was no possibility that he would be more frightening than breaking into a viscount's home—and a murderous viscount, at that.

Her cheap lace gloves stuck to her damp palms. She dried them on her drab brown skirt, taking care to look as though she was just smoothing it out to look presentable. Not that anyone would notice a plainly dressed woman in a homespun shawl and a hat decorated with flowers that had faded last summer after too many walks along the Thames.

Only the man across the street who would accuse her of stalling due to nerves.

Joss raised the knocker, careful to keep her fingers from the dragon's maw, and tapped it. Once, twice, thrice.

The footman who answered was a tall, strapping lad. The buttons on his livery gleamed. His eyes did not. "May I help you?"

"Is the housekeeper available?"

Madeline had insisted that a *ton* accent made the customers more comfortable. A gifted mimic, Joss had picked it up quickly. Unlearning it, adding the Cockney flavor necessary for this disguise, had been a chore.

"If you're looking for work, you'll need to go—"

If he closed the door on her, Drake would never let her forget it. "I have a job. A right fine one. In a hat shop down the way. I've come to return something of his lordship's."

The man offered his palm. "You can leave it with me."

Joss stuck her nose in the air. "I'll do no such thing. This is something I'll only give to a lady."

"Is there a problem, Ronald?" The woman who approached reminded Joss of a weasel, so thin that her belt was the only hint of where her waist would be. The high collar on her blouse would have sent Joss into a scratching fit, but this woman wore it with grace. Likely because the fabric and lace didn't touch her skin.

"This woman insists on seeing you, Mrs. Grumby."

The housekeeper's smile was as thin as she was, but her eyes were warmer than the footman's. "How can I help?"

"I'm Abigail Kirkwood, missus. I believe this may be Viscount Stratford's." Joss produced the snuffbox from her reticule. It took everything she had to let Mrs. Grumby pluck it from her palm. This was her least scandalous plan to gain access to this house. If it failed…

"Indeed it is. He's been searching everywhere for it. Wherever did you find it?"

"My beau, Hugh, and I were walking past Kensington Palace a few weeks back. Hugh likes to think we'll see the young queen, which I think is right foolish. But you never know, do you? Anyway, he was gabbing on when I saw this bright blue trinket on the edge of the cobbles near the drain, blinking up at me from a pile of litter."

"And you knew it was his lordship's?" The woman cast a wary glance toward her.

"Not at first. Though I reckoned it had to belong to a lord or a fine gentleman." The last phrase soured on Joss's tongue, threatening her accent and her smile. "I will admit I opened it and saw the initials on the top, which got me to thinking about which gentleman it could be, but I didn't dare take it into Parliament and hand it to a page or a valet." She focused all her distaste on Ronald. "You never know who might filch something that pretty. I wouldn't even let Hugh touch it." She drew a breath. "I thought I'd have to visit every gentleman in town to ask them, but then I recognized the church on the top, next to the river. My gran lived in Stratford, and I've walked past Holy Trinity many times."

"How astute." Mrs. Grumby reached into her pocket. "Let me pay you for your—"

"Oh no, missus. I couldn't possibly take money for something that wasn't mine to begin with." Joss drew her shawl tight against her shoulders. Her shiver was the most genuine thing about her costume. "But might you spare a hot cup of tea?"

The housekeeper's gaze swept from Joss's faded hat to her scuffed boots and back again before she nodded. Her smile softened. "That's certainly a small reward, but come into the hall. I'll fetch you a cup from the kitchen."

Joss took a seat on a tufted bench as far from the door as she could manage, and sat with her back straight and her reticule in her lap. All under the watchful eye of the dratted footman. How on in the hell was she supposed to snoop with a liveried guard dog on her heels?

But then a giggling maid walked past carrying a feather duster as large as her head. Her skirt was a respectable length, her lace apron was starched so that it looked as though it would snap at a touch, and her lace cap looked more like a crown than servant's gear. But the glance she gave Ronald was anything but respectable.

The footman glanced at Joss, winked, and followed the girl into the library, closing the door behind them.

Blast. The cheeky couple had taken over her primary target.

Joss hurried upstairs, careful to keep on the carpet to muffle her steps. Gambling that Stratford's rooms would be to the back of the house rather than facing the street, she went to those rooms first, opening the doors just enough to see the contents and closing them without a sound. The third door she opened revealed her goal.

She slipped inside and leaned against the closed door as she took in the spartan decor. Stratford's lack of sentimentality would make it easier to search, but the coldness of it stole Joss's breath.

This isn't a lark, Jocelyn.

She quickly ruled out searching anywhere the necklace and diary might be found by the staff. Stratford wouldn't want questions, even unasked ones. That ruled out the wardrobe, his dressing table, and his desk. Joss went to every painting and tapestry, lifting a corner from the wall and peering behind, searching for a safe or a vault—even a hole in woodwork.

Nothing.

That only left the bed. Gulping back a swell of bile, Joss went to that end of the room and stood at the foot of an imposing bedstead. He wouldn't put the pearls under a pillow, and he wouldn't risk someone turning the mattress and finding them. That meant—

A shout from the first floor was followed by a scream and then a wail. Steps thudded against the stairs.

Joss strode to the nightstand and opened the drawer. Nothing.

"You foolish boy," Mrs. Grumby shouted. "How many times have I told you to keep your brain out of your trousers?" The farthest door slammed open. "Mary's a good hand. I'm tempted to fire you instead of her. I will if you've let that woman up here to thieve." The door closed like a clap of thunder.

"Perhaps she just grew tired of waiting and left," Ronald said, sounding much less cocksure than when she'd arrived. The middle room door cracked open.

"You'd best hope so." Mrs. Grumby's words were muffled.

Joss dropped to her knees and looked under the bed, searching for a hiding place. It likely wouldn't help. The housekeeper was doing a thorough search.

As her eyes grew accustomed to the shadows, she spied a

maroon velvet box in the floor, just within reach if a man was lying in bed and thinking of inappropriate things.

Joss snapped open the lid, plucked the pearls from their silk bedding, and replaced the box exactly as she'd found it. Then she made for her only escape route, the double doors opposite the bed, sure to click them closed in her wake.

The patio was small, but the concrete rails were spaced widely enough to slip through. Joss slid the pearls over her head before doing just that and dangling from the side. The stone and plaster were thick and cold against her fingers, and her lace gloves were slick. She wouldn't be able to hold on long, and she shouldn't anyway. They'd soon expand the search into the garden.

Shoulders screaming, Joss glanced backward. There was another patio below her, surrounded by an equally sturdy railing and enforced with planters. If she landed wrong, she'd be crippled—or worse.

Holding her breath, she swung forward as much as she dared before pushing backward and letting go. Her heart went into her throat as she fell, circling her arms as the boys had taught her to do when cliff diving.

Her landing jarred her knees and palms into the lawn, and her breath left her in a *whoosh*. The ground-floor patio was too close for comfort, but she'd missed it. Now she just had to avoid capture.

Gathering her thoughts, she bolted for the hedge that separated the viscount from his neighbor. Branches snared her hair and clothes, but Joss fought through them and came out intact on the other side.

Straightening her posture, Joss smoothed her hair under her hat and eased her grip on her reticule. Then she dusted her skirt and draped her shawl over the rip in the arm of her blouse. Calm and serene, like she was in a park rather than running for her life, she walked past the carriage house and through the back gate, out into the lane. No one looked twice at her or the grass stains on her gloves. If the flowers were askew on her hat, they assumed she'd meant it that way.

It was a good walk to the end of the row and around to where she'd begun. She was breathless when she made the turn, just as Ronald and Mrs. Grumby came out the front door. Drake was prowling the lane of trees where she'd left him. He spied her and strode to her side.

Joss led him away from Mayfair, listening for shouts and thundering footsteps but hearing only carriages and the wind.

They'd gone two blocks before Drake pulled her to a halt. "What the hell happened to you? You look as though you've been in a tree."

"Not a tree." Her voice, with its *ton* inflection restored, sounded more like hers, but it was difficult to breathe. Joss put her hand to her chest and brushed the pearls, which were cold and lifeless. She wrenched them over her head, but they tangled in her hat, trapping her. "Get these off me."

"Stand still or you'll break them."

His nearness, his fingers in her hair, and the scent of him surrounding her calmed her in a way that had alarm bells clanging in her already tired brain. They grew louder as she dropped her forehead against his shoulder, and he pulled her close enough to hear his heart thundering in his chest.

She'd have to think about it later. She'd had enough disconcerting things happen this morning.

"I COULDN'T GET the diary."

At least, that was what Drake thought Jocelyn said. Between his coat muffling her words and the blood rushing through his ears, he couldn't be sure. "We'll figure it out later."

She was missing some of the flowers in her hat, and the wire stems were in danger of taking out his eye, but Drake didn't dare let her go. He drew his first full breath since she'd disappeared into the bowels of Stratford's townhouse.

He'd already decided to call for a patrolman after his next turn when he'd seen her waiting at the end of the block as though they were going to tea. All the way to her, he'd gathered steam for the tongue-lashing he'd rehearsed as he'd paced. It dissipated the moment he'd seen her scratched and stained.

Drake shoved the pearls into his coat pocket before hailing a cab. He gave the driver the address of their next destination before opening the door with his free hand. "Let's get you off your feet. Your knees are likely bruised."

Jocelyn pulled herself up the steps, her lack of grace hinting she was in pain. "It wouldn't be the first time."

There were all sorts of reasons a woman in her profession would be on her knees. All of them brought heat to his ears that leached down his neck and made it difficult to swallow. He sat beside her, closest to the door in case they passed Stratford's townhouse.

Drake dared not look at her for fear that she could read his thoughts, and he didn't close his eyes because it gave his imagination free rein to paint those images in the dark. It was bad enough he'd woke this morning craving her hands on his body.

"Gardening will do that." Jocelyn bumped her shoulder against his.

Drake snapped his gaze to her face and saw the smile he could hear. She was too busy unpinning her hat to notice as he swept in. Grasping her chin between his finger and thumb, he pulled her face to his and kissed her.

He'd meant it to be just once, but her skin was soft, her bones were delicate, and her wide, dark eyes were staring at him. He lowered his head and claimed her mouth again, reveling in the taste of her as he swept his tongue past her lips. The sinful sweetness of it was compounded by her response. There was no parrying for mastery as he explored her mouth and tempted her tongue to play with his.

Jocelyn's soft cotton blouse did little to hide her warmth, but her corset kept the rest of her body locked away. The need to feel her, ever-present in the past week, built to a higher pitch. Drake slid his fingers against her neck and curved them to her shoulder. Her collarbone flexed against his thumb and then his palm. The nape of her neck was warm silk.

Unable to resist the pull of her, Drake trailed his mouth from her lips to her jaw before skimming his tongue down the side of her throat to lap at the hollow at its base. She tasted salty and sweet, and her pulse throbbed against his lips as her fingers tangled in his hair.

"Drake." She sighed his name like he was a cup of hot tea. He didn't need to see her face to know the dreamy look from last night had returned as she slid her hand under his coat.

The bottom button of his waistcoat slid free, and then, with aching slowness, the second one. Jocelyn's hand traveled up his body, leaving butterflies in its wake, softening parts of him while hardening others. He returned to her mouth, driving inside her.

His eager body strained against his clothing as though it had a mind of its own. The thought of her hands on him again darkened his vision at the edges.

The rough cobbles jarred them together, forcing him to choose between releasing Jocelyn or damaging her tongue.

"We're entering a dangerous part of town," he whispered as he traced the shell of her ear. "We need our wits about us."

He did, especially. He needed to stop thinking of her naked against silk sheets while he tried to figure out how best to please her.

The only distraction he could find was counting the ways to destroy a corset.

CHAPTER EIGHTEEN

A s Jocelyn rebuttoned her blouse and straightened her shawl, Drake retrieved her hat from the floor. It was crushed beyond repair.

She ran her fingers along the deep dent his knee had made in the crown and up to the ragged shards of straw before plucking at the bare wire that had served as stems for silk flowers. Then, staring out the window, she tossed it to a group of young girls playing along the pavement. The last glimpse Drake had of them, they were all waving wildly as the first tried it on.

He remembered being one of those children, celebrating what others cast aside or skulking about for what he could steal. For so many years he'd thought it normal to be amongst people who weren't related, to be too tired to eat before going to bed. "I was their age when I first saw England."

Her hand covered his. "Where had you been before?"

"Everywhere and nowhere." Wherever the sea had taken them. He'd learned to count at the quartermaster's elbow, and he'd memorized maps in the captain's cabin as he mopped the floor and emptied the chamber pot out the windows at the rear of the ship, where it wouldn't spray up to douse the crew on deck. The ship's doctor had been tasked with teaching him to read. "When Mal found me in Highcliffe, I was just glad to have a home that didn't leak. Though it was odd not to be rocked to sleep."

The cab stopped at the mouth of a narrow alley. "Guv?"

Drake opened the door and stepped down. Though the lane was wide enough, there was no room to turn around. It would be hell if the cab was ambushed. He offered Jocelyn his hand. "This is where we leave him."

She'd rid herself of her soiled gloves, and her fingers were warm against his. Even in the shadows of the slum, she was lovely, though a nasty scratch ran atop her cheekbone. Drake traced it, careful not to reopen the wound. She'd been scarred again on his watch. If there was a way to make Stratford pay for this—

"It's nothing." She curved her fingers around his and lifted it away. "Cosmetics will cover it without issue."

"I have a friend in Norfolk who's an herbalist. She sent me home with a salve that will keep it from scarring. I'll bring it by."

He offered the driver his pay plus a hefty tip. The man touched the brim of his hat, but his frown stayed in place.

"I won't be able to wait, sir."

"I wouldn't expect you to. I just appreciate your bringing us this far. We'll be fine on our own from here." He had a pistol tucked under his coat. He was certain Jocelyn had something in the reticule she'd carried in a death grip since they had left Mayfair.

Except when he'd been kissing her.

Jocelyn watched the cab leave. "Are you sure of that?"

"He wouldn't have waited anyway, and there are always cabs *leaving* Whitechapel." He took her hand and looped it through his elbow, careful to cover the rip in her blouse. "Now, where was I?"

"Telling me about your lady friend in Norfolk."

Maybe it was thinking of Thetford that made him smile, but more likely it was the barb in her tone. Did he dare think she was jealous? "Ah yes. You'd like her. She's a lively redhead, far too cunning for her own good. She owns an inn there. She even proposed to me once." He tilted his head to hers. "You've met her husband briefly at Lords."

Jocelyn's lips quirked. "A few kisses have made you incorrigible, Fletcher."

"Is that what you call it?" He laughed and danced away from her suspiciously heavy reticule. There was definitely a pistol in there.

They rounded a corner into a lane of shops that had likely once been bright and new. The third on the left at least had a freshly painted sign.

Jocelyn dragged him to a stop. "A pawnbroker? We're not pawning these. We agreed—"

"Of course we're not pawning them, but Bob has forgotten more about jewelry than most men know." He tugged her forward and to the door, which opened with a cheery jingle that was wholly out of place in Whitechapel.

Bao "Bob" Shan had been stooped at an angle for as long as Drake had known him, thanks to a fall from a mizzenmast in a storm. The ropes saved his life but mangled his spine. *"Lóng, wǒ de péngyǒu! Hěn gāoxìng jiàn dào nǐ!"* the old man said, his smile wide.

Bob had always been glad to see him, even when he'd arrived late in the night, starving and filthy after a miserable week on his own after fleeing Highcliffe.

Drake bowed and took the man's offered hand, which was still strong. *"Bào lǎoyézi wǎnshàng hǎo."* A proper Chinese greeting was the first phrase Bob had taught him aboard ship. It was one of the few he remembered.

"Please do not worry after me. You're busy making a go of it, I'm sure." Bob cast an eye up at Jocelyn. "Finally found a girl who could stomach you?"

"Only just." Jocelyn dropped a curtsy. "Jocelyn Kirk, sir."

"No sir, here. Just Bob." He turned and limped toward the curtain that divided the store from his home. "I was sitting down to tea. Come through."

While the front of the shop was cluttered with other people's items, Bob's rooms were those of a sailor who had never had much of his own. A bottle of Eamon Brewer's finest whiskey sat on the table in front of a lone glass. Bob went past the table and returned with two more in hand, so clean they reflected the lamplight.

"What have you brought me?" Bob asked, a gleam in his eye.

"Can I not simply visit an old friend?"

"You *can,*" Bob said. "But you have the look of a dragon with treasure."

Drake preferred *dragon* to *bat.* He pulled the long string of heavy pearls from his coat pocket. "What can you tell me about these?"

Whiskey forgotten, Bob replaced his glasses with a loupe and bent over the piece, running them through his fingers one at a time.

While he worked, Jocelyn carried her drink to the far wall, where framed sketches flanked the doorframe. Drake joined her and pointed to a large, three-masted vessel. "That's the ship where Bob and I met."

"Ah, the *Sister Fletcher*!" Bob said without looking up. "She was a fine vessel. I cried when she was sent to the bottom."

"Fletcher?" Jocelyn's bright, curious gaze was tangible. "Is there a connection?"

There was, but not the one she was making. Drake sipped his whiskey. This would reveal more of his life than anyone, save those like Bob, knew. "I took my name from the ship."

He knew she wouldn't laugh, but he saw the curiosity he'd expected flash deep in her eyes.

"I was younger than Harry when someone brought me to the docks and found a captain who needed a boy who could work hard."

If Drake had to guess, given his observation of children, he was likely the same age as Simon Hawkins, so six or seven. His deliverer could have been his mother. She might have been an aunt, or a neighbor who was tired of feeding a stray.

"Where?"

He didn't remember. He didn't want to. "It wasn't England, I don't think. It doesn't matter."

"She didn't even tell us his name," Bob said from the table, his voice muffled as he continued to examination of the pearls. "For the first voyage, we just called him *boy*. I think we were all worried about getting attached if he lost his footing and went overboard."

"Which I didn't." Drake pointed his drink at his oldest friend.

"I couldn't get a word out of him until we were in port, and he saw a silly boy whining about a birthday gift." Bob looked at him. "He wanted to know what a birthday was."

Drake refused to look at Jocelyn, to see the pity he could feel. "You told me my Chinese zodiac."

After the old man had to guess at the year, given his size. Drake had chosen that day on the docks as his birthday. For him, it was the day he began.

"*Lóng*." Bob grinned. "Dragon. Luckiest fellow I've ever met." Bob patted the table. "Come see what I've learned about your pearls."

Drake held Jocelyn's chair for her before sitting by her side. She was too quiet for his liking. He wanted to know what was in her head, having learned that the Drake she'd always known was once a country-less, nameless—and motherless—child.

"Where did you find these?" Bob focused on Jocelyn. "I'm assuming you found them."

"I stole them, sir. From someone who stole them before me. I hope to return them to the original owner's family."

"A goat if I ever saw one." Bob sipped his whiskey. "Your pearls are lovely and well made, the knots and silk are fine and strong, and the cameo is custom work, likely a silhouette of its owner. Dirty hands have left their marks, but it should clean up nicely." He turned the strand so that the clasp was between his fingers, gleaming gold in the light. "The key to ownership is here.

There is a coat of arms embossed in the gold. I recognize it."

It was homework all good pawnbrokers did. Knowing past ownership could raise the price or give another option for a sale—or a ransom. "Who?" Drake asked.

"Viscount Burnley, a distant cousin to the Duke of Manchester. I understand the family is searching for a daughter who disappeared into London. Do you know her whereabouts?"

Drake lifted the pearls from the older man's gnarled hands. "She was left in the Thames, Bob. These are the keys to bringing her murderer to justice."

"Then I have never seen you." The old man stood and led them to the door. "But I do have the ginger you ordered. The box is under the workbench."

As Drake finished his business, Jocelyn browsed the books until she found one she wanted. She opened her reticule in search of coins. It tipped, revealing a heavy silver revolver. She dropped the payment, plus a little more, into Bob's palm, and went back to reading.

"Quite the prize," Bob whispered.

Drake's eyes never left her, tall and straight as she found a passage that made her smile. "I know."

THEY EXITED BOB'S shop, and Joss handed the pearls to Drake. They vanished into his breast pocket.

"How do you think a viscount's daughter ended up in a brothel?" she asked, though she already knew the answer.

Young ladies of the *ton* could be compromised and caught, compromised and abandoned, or widowed and left penniless. There were rumors that some had been kidnapped and sold, or simply kidnapped and kept.

Madeline had cautioned Joss to never take on a girl who didn't come to the door on her own. Surely Madam Price at The

Peacock had the same rule.

The thrill of success zinged under Joss's skin, and it was all she could do not to bolt for the nearest cab. Spencer would have to set her father free if she solved the murder of a viscount's daughter.

Drake was quiet beside her, ramrod straight as he listened for what was under the sounds in Whitechapel. She adjusted her pace to his and stayed quiet until the streets, and the people, were cleaner.

He blinked at her. "My apologies. What were you asking?"

Try as she might, she couldn't imagine this composed, contained man as a boy who had chosen his own name. Her questions about someone else could wait. She wanted to know more about Drake. "Thank you for introducing me to Bob. I like him."

"He likes you, too." He looked over his shoulder. "I worry about him there alone."

"Why doesn't he live with all of you on Charles Street?"

"I asked him to, but he doesn't want to leave his home." He glanced behind them again. "It's difficult to imagine that place as a home."

But it had been. "You lived with him after you left Highcliffe?" she asked.

He nodded. "In his attic. I did odd jobs for the merchants on his street until I was hired as a groom for those stables." He pointed to the building, freshly painted with a haystack as tall as its roof. "I moved there, to a room in the loft. If I kept my clothes on the east wall, they would get soaked when it rained."

He flagged down a cab and helped her inside. "I worked nights so I could spend my days as a messenger. I bartered that service for accounting lessons. I know where all the best bins are near Parliament, where the lords toss the newspapers on their way inside. Since they have breakfast at home, there's no food in the garbage. I read the financial pages and asked questions."

The images he painted of a boy on his own broke Joss's heart, but the effort he'd put into going straight made her proud. "So this is the third time you've reinvented yourself?"

"Fourth." He watched London pass by the windows. "The boys were the beginning of this stage. Five years ago, I told Ed he'd be welcome to live in my house so long as he followed the rules. I'd just started working for Thea, so I had enough money to help someone. Ed was a safe wager. He wants to be a doctor. Did I tell you that?"

He hadn't. "What about the other boys?"

"Taking Frank to Thetford opened his eyes to some possibilities." He grinned. "Did I thank you for that?"

"We've been a little busy," she teased.

His blush was endearing. "We have been, haven't we?" He threaded his fingers through hers. "You've learned a lot about me today."

Joss had a feeling she had only scratched the surface. "Very few men in this town can say they built themselves from scratch. Fewer of those have had success built on more than money. Do your clients know the truth?"

"Tavie does. It was only fair, since she was my first client. And Thea insisted I tell her everything bad, so she knows back to Highcliffe but no farther. Her past made her wary." His smile was indulgent. "But Amelia doesn't care to know. She's this odd combination of a *ton* lady who just assumes everything will work out and a stevedore who puts her back into it for results."

The coach stopped in front of The Rose. Across the street, the cricket pitch was full of players. Joss thanked her lucky stars that they'd arrived in time. As the coach left, she searched the small crowd and found who she was looking for. "Is that Nicky?"

She already knew the answer to this question, too. Nicky was the first of Drake's boys she'd recognized. She'd watched him for months, always alone as he took in the game from the sidelines. His legs were barely long enough for his feet to touch the ground, but his braces already strained over his back and shoulders.

"It is." Drake walked her inside her gate and turned back

toward the street. "I'll be back in a moment."

Joss sat on the bench she'd always used to keep an eye on Nicky from a distance. The girls never crossed the street to the cricket grounds, where families watched the matches. It would be too much like streetwalking, and a streetwalker talking to a ten-year-old would draw all the wrong kinds of attention.

Now she watched Drake sit beside him. The man followed the boy's finger as he explained the game. He admired Nicky's cricket bat, which Joss had sent Tommy across the street to deliver with some ludicrous story of trying to find its owner, but since no one claimed it, did he want it? Because Tommy didn't play cricket.

That last bit had been the only true part in the whole charade.

As Drake and Nicky spoke now, the man's shoulders softened. His back curved as he rested his elbows on his knees. Joss's ears itched to hear their conversation, but she couldn't help but compare Drake's approach to her father's. Da had talked, but he rarely listened. Drake listened with his whole body, all the time. She had no doubt that, when Drake stood to come back to her, Nicky knew he was important to the adult in his life.

Drake tucked her hand into his elbow as they walked to the front door. "He wants to play cricket."

"That's excellent."

"I know nothing about cricket." He ushered her through the entry hall and to the stairs. It was too early for anyone to be in the lounge. "Except it's impossible to tell who's batting and who's fielding, how the score is calculated, and what the actual rules are."

They made the turn to climb to the third floor. "So you'll learn," she said. "Maybe Bob has a book."

"Trust me to be the only man to learn the national game in a Whitechapel pawn shop," he grumbled as he walked through her bedroom door. "What do I owe you?"

Joss's brain stuttered to a stop as ice formed in her veins. "What?"

If he thought that being in her room meant payment for her company, she'd toss him out the window headfirst.

"For the bat, Jocelyn. You could have just told me he spent his afternoons here. I would have taken care of it."

"I bought him the bat before I knew you were in his life. It was a gift." Hoping to soften her next words, hoping he would hear what she was suddenly embarrassed to say, she took both his hands in hers, knitting their fingers together. "In this room, you and I don't talk of money. Ever."

Understanding flickered through his eyes, quickly followed by a more primal emotion that sent gooseflesh across her skin in waves.

"Am I a cad if I want you right now?" He lowered his mouth to hers.

Joss was still shaking her head when he caught her bottom lip between his teeth and nibbled until her tongue was thick from need and her body ached for his touch.

She reached for her buttons, but Drake stilled her. "You cheated me out of this last night."

Joss relented, but solely because giving in also let her unwrap the layers that would expose him to her.

It became a race that ended in a tie. They stood before each other, she in her corset and stockings, he bare-chested with his trousers loose at the waist. The heat in his gaze held her captive as he reached between her breasts to open the first hook. Then the second.

Joss tangled her fingers in his silky hair and pulled him down for a kiss, twining her tongue with his in a wordless plea for haste. The man simply grinned against her mouth and kept tormenting her.

So she shoved her hand into his trousers and grasped his shaft, stroking her thumb from root to tip, where she circled the velvety skin until he was shaking.

The damned corset tumbled to the floor, which should have made it easier for her to breathe. Her sigh came out as a groan when he cradled her breast and stroked her nipple in the same tormenting circle.

Joss broke the standoff by dropping to her knees, pulling him free of his clothing, and taking him into her mouth. It took two wet strokes before the tip tickled the back of her throat and his head thudded against the door. His hips pumped forward as though they had a mind of their own.

"Christ, Jocelyn."

Blood rushed through her ears. She stroked upward to catch her breath and then swept back down, again and again, while Drake's whispered curses filled the room and his heels tapped the floor.

His balls tightened in her hand, and Joss looked up the length of Drake's glorious body to find him staring at her.

And then she was airborne, pulled to his mouth while her legs circled his waist. His flesh teased hers as he strode to the bed, dropped her onto the mattress, and slid inside her in a thrust so deep it sent the bed sideways. Joss hooked one of her ankles over his shoulder, letting him go so deep she screamed.

The unlit candlestick toppled to the floor.

Drake's muscles flowed beneath his skin, telegraphing each movement before it happened, doubling her anticipation. He pressed a kiss to her ankle and then scraped his teeth over the bone.

Her book tumbled after the candlestick, and her release left her wailing.

Drake caught her limp leg in the crook of his arm, held her open, and thrust forward again.

Joss lost focus as he seated himself deep inside her, every short thrust striking her center in such a way that sparks shot to her fingers and toes. He leaned over her, his arms shaking as he gasped her name and poured himself into her.

He collapsed, pinning her under his sweaty body. His heart thudded against his ribs and into hers. When he went to move, she raked her fingers over his sweaty skin, trying to keep him close.

But he was stronger. "I'm crushing you." He pulled her with him so they could lie in a panting pile in the middle of her bed that was now at an angle across the floor. "Is it always like that?"

The flip answer that all the girls said was on the tip of Joss's tongue, but something about Drake's voice gave her pause. She studied his face and listened to what he wasn't saying.

A blush crept up his neck to his ears, and then his hairline. The man who had just literally shifted her world caught his bottom lip between his teeth and raised his eyebrows.

Something popped in Joss's brain and chest at the same time. "No, sweetheart. It isn't." She pushed herself to one elbow and faced him. "How does that... Why didn't you..." She gave up on finding the right words. "What?"

Drake's crooked grin and laughing gaze were rare, but when they happened, it was sunshine after a storm. "Apparently, I've been too busy for cricket *and* sex."

"No one is that busy," she teased softly.

"I tried once." He flicked his gaze to her and then back to the painting opposite them on the wall. "After Tavie hired me, and I had a few crowns to spare. I visited The Peacock."

"I will not be jealous about that." She nudged him in the ribs.

"The young woman who took me upstairs was beautiful, and she said all the right things. It was something I *wanted* to do." He pulled in a deep breath. "But I couldn't get over the idea that she didn't want to, that she was being paid to spend time with me. It was a business transaction, and I don't believe intimacy is about business."

Joss wasn't sure if she should be touched by his romantic nature or hurt that he'd just insulted her trade.

In the end, it didn't matter. She wasn't staying in London, and he was more important to her than money.

He pushed to the top of the bed and propped himself against the pillows before pulling her into his arms. "I don't know how to play, Jocelyn."

"Then we'll go watch a few matches so you can learn."

He sighed. "No. I don't know how to *play*. Not at anything."

"Yes, you do. We played all the time at Highcliffe."

"Maybe at first."

She could ignore a lot of things, but this was not one of them. "We played *all* the time."

"You and the boys did," he said. "I played until I was thirteen, then it was work."

"Tag," she said.

"Escape," he shot back.

"Hide and seek."

He rolled his eyes. "Evasion."

She pulled out her favorite. "We did that play on the beach."

"Where everyone learned to use disguises." He winked at her. "You picked that up quite well."

Damn. "What about picking berries?"

"Lookout training." Drake put a finger up to interrupt her. "Including the bird calls." His kiss was soft and sweet, but there was a sad flavor to it. "You needed to know how to take care of yourselves, and Mal wasn't doing it. It was easier if it seemed like a game."

Joss tossed her gaze around her room, hoping she had a game—*any* game—to make him smile. All she had was chess, and he played chess all day.

Left with nothing else, she danced her fingers up his ribs. He squirmed away, chuckling. He didn't go far. "What are you doing?"

She stroked his calf with her toes. "Teaching you to play."

CHAPTER NINETEEN

I T WAS AN ordinary night at The Rose, though the crowd was larger than normal due to a party hosted by the most persistent matchmaker in London. Every avowed bachelor had cried off with illness—either their own or a member of their family's. The thought of The Rose as a convalescent home would have been amusing if Joss's head wasn't pounding from the cacophony of singing, laughter, and shouting over cards.

The dragon lurking under the roof didn't help matters. Joss strolled from the parlor to the bar, where Drake was perched on a stool facing the door. A half-full glass of gin rested near his elbow, ignored. He was a storm cloud in the middle of the oasis she'd learned to create for *ton* men eager for entertainment.

"Do try not to glower so," she whispered. "You're making a hash of my liquor sales, not to mention the way the men scurry in and out of the parlor."

"I won't sit so that I can't see who's approaching. How am I supposed to protect you if—"

"I pay two men, one much larger than you, to tend the door." She put a hand on his shoulder, enjoying the solid feel of him but wondering how he would look in anything but black. "Go sit with Imogen in the parlor, Fletcher." His frown did not abate. "She's been nattering about her hat shop so much that the other girls are beginning to avoid her. She's eager for help with every detail, especially the budget."

The war on his face was plain, but talking business won out over sitting idle. "You'll be careful?"

She handed him his drink. When the smell didn't remind her of fir trees, she brought it closer to her nose. Only he would drink water at a bar. "I'm going to choose not to be insulted by your belief that I can't protect myself in my own house."

His fingers brushed over her knuckles as he took the glass. "In return, I'll ignore your belief that Imogen's hat shop would distract me from keeping you safe."

The wish to kiss him overwhelmed her. It was a feeling she battled every evening before she went to sleep in an empty bed and one that returned the moment she opened her eyes, smiling against her pillow. She spent far too much time wondering if he'd spend the night if she broke all her own rules and asked him.

"I've seen the gleam in your eye when you speak of money, you dragon." She pushed his shoulder. "Go talk to Imogen and try not to tempt any of the other girls into respectability."

He sauntered away, holding his glass like it was the gin he'd sold her rather than water from the pump in the kitchen.

"I like him much better than Spencer for you," Hugh said from behind her. "He's much more honorable."

It wouldn't take much to be more honorable than the duplicitous Spencer, which was another problem she'd have to face. Later. "I don't know that he's for me, Hugh."

"You might need to tell him that, because he looks at you as though he'd keep you all to himself."

She'd found herself wishing today that Drake's lovemaking was more than a response to the danger they were in. His intensity was an aphrodisiac no one could bottle, and to be the subject of it was a heady thing.

But there were more things than danger between them. "That remains to be seen."

Hugh leaned closer. "I don't think it would be such a bad thing, Joss. I don't know why you agreed to be Madam White in the first place."

Because my father needed me to be.

"What working girl, in our trade or otherwise, wouldn't want a promotion?" She bumped her elbow against Hugh's. "Especially one that involves the third-floor bedroom, where I don't have to listen to Edith moan in her sleep."

Hugh scratched the back of his head as his ears reddened. "About that…"

Joss's mouth fell open in a way a lady's shouldn't, at least not in public. Stoic, sensible Hugh and *Edith*? The giggliest girl in the house? "How long?"

"Since the summer." He held her gaze. "I know the rules about men past hours, but we figured if I didn't pay her, it didn't matter." Now that he was talking about it, his words were coming out in a flood. "I'm always gone well before daylight so the other girls don't figure it out. Though Edith is weary of their teasing her about her dreams."

Joss would put a stop to that right away. "But Hugh, how do you sit up there with her…" She couldn't even say it. The thought of Drake tupping Imogen had made Joss physically ill, and that was when he'd done naught but kiss her.

"James and I switch places sometimes. And, well, it's her job." Though Hugh said the words, he wouldn't look her in the eye.

Edith needed a new job. "I'll find something—"

"Madam White?"

The voice was an icy finger down her spine. She'd only heard it that day in Parliament, but it had appeared in her nightmares ever since. Especially for the past week. Joss forced a smile before she turned and faced Viscount Stratford.

Drake would scold her for years if he learned she hadn't watched the door.

His insistence on protecting her at Parliament had robbed her of a view of the viscount. Now she got her first full view. He had likely been handsome in his youth, but now he could best be described as fashionable or, less charitably, striking. High forehead, narrow eyes, and thin lips gave him a cruel countenance. His blond hair was going gray at the roots.

One morning, years ago, Joss had come across a sea snake on the beach. They'd stayed opposite one another for several long moments, sizing each other up and determining the threat. Now she was in a brothel in London, facing a snake of a different stripe.

"Viscount Stratford." She bobbed a curtsy and hoped her fingers didn't tremble when he took her hand. "It's an honor to have you join us instead of spending the evening at The Peacock."

If it was telling tales to know where he spent his evenings, she could blame it on Madam Price, who name-dropped about her visitors at every opportunity.

"Connie, my favorite girl, left Madam Price. I thought she might have come here, given The Rose's reputation."

He suspected Connie was here because Joss had foolishly trusted the wrong man. Rather than watching her surroundings and carefully choosing her partners, she'd focused on the prize.

She'd forgotten the first lesson Drake had taught her.

"Thank you for the compliment, your lordship, but we haven't added anyone to our house in the last year, at least." She hovered between him and the door, ready to open it the moment he made to leave.

"Perhaps another, then. If she's moved on, I might as well find a new favorite." He walked to the parlor and hovered near the threshold, surveying the room.

Joss joined him, now thankful for the crowd. "All the girls are currently paired with clients, your lordship." She caught herself before she pulled his arm. It would never do for him to think she didn't want him here. She had to act as though he were any other peer. "If you would like to wait at the bar…?"

Of course he wouldn't. No peer would want to be seen as waiting in line. He'd look his fill and leave.

"What about the redheaded lass tending to the card game?"

Maisie was sitting on the arm of a chair occupied by a young earl who considered her his lucky charm. "That's Maisie, your lordship. The earl will want her at his side as long as he's winning."

This time Joss did take his arm. "I am sorry we couldn't help you with your favorite." *Do not suggest she left London. Don't put that thought in his evil brain.* "It would have been a feather in my cap to steal the next master of the ceremonies from The Peacock."

"You follow Parliament?" he asked.

She looked into his narrowed eyes and realized her mistake. "It is in the best interest of my staff and my clients to stay current on events, and if gossip is to be believed, you're surely about to be named master."

At that moment, a hearty laugh rolled from the room, startling as much for its unaffectedness as for the man doing the laughing. Joss had heard it years ago, though it had been rare even then.

Imogen had made Drake laugh at the worst possible time.

Stratford looked over his shoulder and spied the two of them on a settee. His arm tensed under Joss's hand. "Madam White, we should continue our conversation upstairs."

"Your lordship, I could not possibly leave the—"

"You have something that belongs to me," he hissed, close enough his breath stirred her hair. "We will either go to your room to discuss its return, or I will see this house razed."

She would be fine under her own roof. Hugh would follow her up after ten minutes. Drake would likely be on his heels. All she had to do was stall for ten minutes and then make as much noise as possible.

By the time they reached her room, her arm was throbbing under his grasp. Joss closed the door and resisted rubbing the tender flesh. "Viscount Stratford, I do not—"

"Where is she?" he demanded. "Bring her to me at once."

His polite mask had fallen. His pale skin was marred by red blotches, and his lips were tight against his teeth. This was likely the last face poor Violet had seen.

Joss made her steps slow as she went to the table where her supply of personal liquor sat. "You can search this house from attic to larder and from the front gate to the carriage house. There is no one hiding here." She kept her back to him so he didn't see her fingers tremble on the glass or the flick of her thumb as she opened the poison ring that had been Madeline's last gift.

The sleeping powder dissolved in the glass as Joss poured a second drink. Saying a quick prayer, she gambled. Keeping the drugged whiskey for herself, she took a small sip as she offered Stratford the unpolluted one.

He avoided it. "I'll take yours, if you please."

"As you wish." Joss gave him what he'd asked for and placed the perfectly good drink on the table.

"Is Rushford's man a steady client here?" Stratford took the seat blocking the door. Joss took the other, hoping to put him at ease.

For six more minutes.

"Rushford's man?" She didn't need to act confused. It was difficult to think of Drake belonging to anyone. "Do you mean Mr. Fletcher?" She kept her smile even though the viscount did nothing but lift an eyebrow. "He visits Imogen regularly."

Joss ran her tongue across her lips, chasing away the bitter taste the words left, while she listened to the mantel clock tick the seconds away. Joss had set the ten-minute rule with Hugh early on because she didn't want him overhearing her conversations with Spencer. She didn't want anyone questioning her machinations or her motives, and she didn't want to explain her father's circumstances.

"He was at Parliament the day Cust and I addressed Lords." Stratford's words slowed, spurring hope that the sleeping powder was working. "He was outside my rooms there with a woman, but not a blonde like the chit downstairs. Her hair looked more like yours."

Ten minutes was a foolish waste of time. Joss stood. "I'm sure there are endless brunettes in London who would find Mr.—"

Stratford moved swiftly, and his hands around her throat stopped her breath.

"Where are my pearls?" he snarled.

They weren't his pearls any more than they were hers. They belonged to Violet. Joss shook her head as she clawed his hands. "What pearls?" she choked out.

His grip never abated. "Come now, Madam White. Do you really want to die protecting another whore's baubles?"

She didn't want to die at all. Her pulse thundered so hard that her vision pulsed with each beat. She pounded her fists on Stratford's forearms, trying to loosen his grip. All she could do was shake her head.

"Whatever you're trying to accomplish, it won't work." His words were growing mushy, if she was hearing correctly. "My family buys and sells people like you with the queen's blessing."

Through her graying vision, Joss watched his eyelids droop. He stumbled against her, and they toppled her table, sending the decanter and glass tumbling to the floor. The whiskey would likely stain the rug.

Focus, girl. Your foolish rule will see you dead if you don't get free.

Joss pried one finger from her throat and managed a quick breath before he latched on again, this time with both hands.

"You'll just be another dead whore."

His clumsy lunge sent her crashing into her dressing table. Flailing for a weapon, she grasped a useless figurine. It would do no damage, but it might cause a racket. Gathering all her strength, she fought for position and hurled the porcelain doll at the door. It shattered in an unimpressive display.

Stratford's drug-induced clumsiness trapped her between him and her wardrobe, giving him leverage as he fell against her. She had no choice but to follow him to the ground. She should have put actual poison in that damned ring.

Blood rushed through her ears, filling them like seawater. She was drowning again. This time in her own room in a fancy dress—alone.

You're going to die because of recklessness and pride.

Joss's head hit the floor as her world faded to black.

She might have gotten a breath.

She might have heard a crash.

Someone might have shouted her name.

Then again…

CHAPTER TWENTY

THERE COULD HAVE been an army in Jocelyn's room.

Stratford could have had a gun leveled at the door.

She could have been sitting, drinking tea, in her dressing gown.

But instead…

She was on the floor, purple-faced, and more still than Drake had ever seen her.

Porcelain crunched under his boots as he raced to her. The Aubusson rug padded his knees as he dropped to the floor.

"Jocelyn?" He put his hand on her chest and cursed the layers that hid her from him. "Breathe, you stubborn woman."

Her cheek was still warm when he slapped her. Her eyes fluttered open and then went wide under her tear-spiked lashes. "Ow."

That one word, as scratchy as coral against his toes, sent her hand to her throat and a shuddering breath into his lungs.

She came to life, wriggling and kicking for freedom, but he tightened his hold. "You're fine, love. You're…"

The words did nothing to calm her. What did was Hugh's presence at his shoulder.

"I think this is what's frightening her." The other man pulled the viscount from Joss's lap and left him sprawled across the floor, his mouth hanging open. He looked like a dead fish.

"Did she kill him?" Imogen whispered from the door.

They all watched and waited for movement. Drake half hoped there wouldn't be any. Things would be so much easier if Stratford simply disappeared.

A loud snore split the silence.

So much for easy.

Drake sprang into action. "Imogen, pack a bag for Madam White, please. All simple clothes. Be quick about it. We're leaving as soon as I can carry her downstairs. Hugh, send for Dr. Goddard and direct him to my home on Charles Street. Number 12, end of the row."

"I can—" Jocelyn sounded like she'd swallowed burlap and gravel.

"You can't." Drake put a palm over her mouth, loosely but enough to beg her to be quiet. "Not this time."

Her face reddened, making the bruises on her neck turn a garish, near-black shade of purple. Drake considered all the ways he could make Stratford vanish.

"He will come to and be back here, looking for you. Or he'll go looking for me at Charles Street. If we run, now, we look like two scoundrels who gambled and lost. He'll think he's come out the winner." He looked into her eyes, praying she'd see sense. "Let him think that for a moment, Jocelyn. Not forever. Just for now."

Hugh took her hand. "We'll be fine without you, Joss. We'll put the word out that you've gone to Bath to visit Madeline. No one will think twice about bothering us." He chuckled. "The curiosity might help business. You never know."

She cast her eyes at their sleeping prisoner.

"I'd like to put him in the Thames." Hugh half snorted a laugh. "It would prob'ly spew him out again. But don't you worry. He'll be safe and none the wiser." He clapped Drake on the shoulder. "I'll send Harry for the doc and then hail a cab. Give me five minutes and head for the back gate."

Once he was gone, Jocelyn shoved Drake aside and pushed

herself to her feet, only to collapse against his chest like a sail with snapped rigging. He swept her into his arms. Imogen closed the door to the wardrobe and snapped the bag closed.

"Get us out of here," Drake said.

The girl led them down the back stairs, holding a lantern high so he could see where his feet landed, but with Jocelyn in his arms, it didn't matter. He had to feel his way down the narrow passage and out into the night. Hugh was waiting beside the cab, the door already open. "Keep her safe."

Drake had barely closed the door when they lurched forward. His head bounced against the squabs, and he lost his hold on Jocelyn. Rather than escaping, she looked past him, out the back window, at the lone lantern in the lane.

He'd done the same when he left Highcliffe. Standing on the edge of the woods, he'd stared long and hard at the candle burning in a window and at the sea beyond, debating if what was ahead was worth losing his home.

"This is the right thing to do," he whispered now, as he had then.

By the end of the lane, she'd moved from his lap. When they made the turn around the cricket pitch, she changed seats so she could face him. Drake stretched his legs to their full length, blocking the door. Jocelyn crossed her arms over her chest and dropped her chin in a sulk.

Which was fine. He couldn't see her bruises that way, and if she didn't talk, he didn't have to hear his failure in every gravelly syllable.

The carriage rocked to a stop at Charles Street, where there was a light in every window. Drake stepped down, Jocelyn's bag in one hand, and offered her his empty one. It was a shock to feel her fingers curve around his, but it was brief. The moment her foot touched the ground, she was racing ahead of him for the door. Whether it was to escape danger or him, he wasn't sure. Her hair had come loose in places, brushing one shoulder and the opposite scapula while one stubborn braid clung to her crown.

The lamplight set her red dress ablaze, making her a rose in a rock garden.

Or a warning beacon.

Dr. Goddard was waiting in the hall, speaking with Ed. Both turned when Jocelyn entered. Both sets of eyes went wide.

"Holy hell," the doctor breathed. "What happened?"

Drake flicked his gaze to Ed. There was a lot the boy didn't need to know, but there wasn't a lot of time. "She had a violent client."

Harry came thumping down the stairs, only to stop halfway. His mouth dropped open. "Madam White?" Nicky and Frank stopped behind him.

Jocelyn stepped behind Drake, and it dawned on him that she was injured and vulnerable, alone in a room of men. He turned and kept his eyes on hers. Her pale skin and smeared cosmetics made a garish sight. "You're safe here."

Only she could tell him he was ignorant using just a glare. To emphasize it, she swept a hand from her head to her waist. Vanity, not fear—never fear—had sent her scurrying.

Drake chuckled. "They've seen worse." He took her hand and brought her forward. "Dr. Goddard, you can take Jocelyn into the sitting room. Please keep away from the windows."

He waited until they were out of the hall and behind a closed door. "Ed and Frank. Watch the doors. No one enters, no one leaves. Harry and Nicky, go upstairs and watch the street. Sing out if you see someone who shouldn't be there."

He left Gavin on the stairs. "Make sure she doesn't make a run for it while I pack a bag."

Drake checked his watch as he walked. Parliament had been in session today. If Stratford had come straight to The Rose, then it had been almost an hour since adjournment. If they hurried, Oliver would still be in town. He was scheduled to travel tonight.

"Harry, come in here," he shouted. To hell with the neighbors.

The lad appeared at the bedroom door. "Yes, sir?"

Drake scrawled a note on the first piece of paper he could find, waved it in the air to dry the ink, and then folded it. "Take this to the Duke of Rushford in Mayfair, number 25 Park Street." He gave the boy cab fare. "Take a cab there and back. Pay him to wait while you get a reply, and get a good look at the driver. Be sure—"

"I know, I know," Harry grumbled. "Make sure they don't switch him on me." He pulled his cap over his eyes and bolted for the stairs.

It took moments for Drake to prepare for travel, thanks to his frequent trips to Thetford, Ipswich, and parts in between. Besides that, a few white shirts would last for weeks if he was near a laundry. Waistcoats and socks were snatched blindly and stuffed into the bag. They didn't have time for his vanity. God only knew how long Stratford would be asleep.

Drake returned downstairs and dodged Gavin on the last riser, which was made more difficult by the dim light. They'd put out most of the candles on the bottom floor. The stairs flickered ominously in the firelight.

The drawing room door opened, and Goddard stepped into the hall alone. Drake joined him, leaning forward to open the door so he could watch Jocelyn on the sofa. She appeared to be asleep, but looks could be deceiving. *Her* looks especially.

"How is she?"

"There should be no permanent damage, though the bruises will be ugly for some time," Goddard said in a low tone. "The more she rests her voice, the quicker it will heal. If you had licorice root for tea, it would benefit her."

"I know a first-rate herbalist. She'll have something for the bruising as well." Drake could do that much, at least.

Jocelyn had positioned herself so she faced the door, even if her eyes were closed. He'd wager she had the fire poker hidden under the blanket covering her to her shoulders. He'd also wager she'd like to use it on him.

"She's resting." Goddard produced a packet of powders from

his pocket. "If she has trouble sleeping, give her one of these. Limit her diet to warm drinks and soft foods until her voice returns. I've told her that, but…"

"She's stubborn." Drake reached into his pocket for payment, blindly thrusting coins at the man. "Thank you, Sam."

Goddard sorted through them and returned half. "I suppose I haven't seen you."

"If you don't mind." Drake motioned to Gavin. "It's also best if Gavin shows you the back way from the house."

As soon as the doctor was out of sight, Drake went to the library. Keeping the door open so he could hear any fight for freedom, he unlocked the safe and scraped half the funds into the bag before rearranging his clothes to hide the sum.

Gavin put a tea tray beside it. Drake dumped a packet of sleeping powder into the pot. Jocelyn would forgive him for this eventually.

Perhaps.

"She and I are headed east," he said. "I'd take you all, but—"

"We'd slow you down," Gavin said.

"You'd make us noticeable, and I'd make you a target. If I'm gone, they'll leave you alone." At least, he hoped they would. Everything in him protested leaving Gavin and the boys to face the mess he'd dragged them into. "If they don't—"

"We're not stupid," Frank said from the door. "We'll stick to our story and stick together." He slouched against the frame. "As far as we know, you've eloped to Scotland with the queen."

"Leave the queen out of this." Drake put his journals in his bag. If the house was searched, he didn't want to leave a trail straight to his clients. "And don't slouch." He looked at the young man. "Make sure Ed comes straight home. No walks through the park. You two are responsible for Nicky and Harry. Never go—"

"We'll go everywhere in pairs, like marching onto the ark," Frank said.

"Good man." Drake stared hard at the boy. "But you need to go back upstairs and help Nicky keep watch."

"I told you something like this would happen if you got involved with the old man again," Gavin said once they were alone.

Drake opened his mouth to argue. He was not involved with Malcolm Kirk. This was about bringing a murderer to justice—someone who had now put his hands on Jocelyn with malicious intent. But Stratford would never have done that if Jocelyn hadn't stolen from him, and she never would have stolen from him if she hadn't been scheming for her father's release. "I know."

"That's what you said when you first saw her, and what you said a fortnight ago. That's what you always say. Yet here we are—"

"In a safe, dry house. In a part of the city where the cabs aren't afraid to travel in the daylight. Where there's plenty of food, and we came by it honestly." Drake pulled in a deep breath as he worked not to roar at one of his oldest friends. "Where we could stay and cluck our tongues over the stories of prostitutes pulled from the Thames and how no one can catch their killers."

After a long moment, Gavin nodded. "I never thought I'd say this, but Frank's right. We're not stupid, and we can manage ourselves. You watch your back." He looked across the hall. "From all sides." He clapped Drake on the shoulder. "Come home in one piece."

"I intend to."

Drake strode to the drawing room, and Jocelyn's eyes flew open as he entered. Before the anger set in, he saw a glimmer of pain.

"Tea?" He didn't bother to wait for her answer. The warmth of the liquid soothed him without drinking it. The honeyed scent didn't smell the least bit medicinal. She sat upright, and he lifted the poker from her hand.

Jocelyn's lips moved, but all that came out was a squeak. She sipped the tea, cleared her throat, and put her hand over her mouth. It did little to block her ragged scream. He sat beside her and filled her cup when it was empty. He stopped at three. She was nodding off before she'd finished it.

Drake left her long enough to fetch the basin Goddard had used. The water was still warm through the porcelain. Using the napkin from the tea service, he cleaned her face. If she didn't want to see the boys looking a fright, she'd definitely want to be presentable for a duke.

The house was quiet and dark. The fire popped and the clock ticked. Ed's yawn echoed through the entry hall. Gavin did the dishes in the kitchen. Outside, no rattling tack signaled a carriage approaching. No footsteps thudded on the pavement, no shouts. Jocelyn's deep, even breaths soaked through his coat and into his skin.

He pulled the pins from her hair and used his fingers to unravel the tangles as best he could. The strands were like sea foam against his fingers, and the scent of bluebells filled the room. Unable to resist, he pressed a kiss to her forehead. He might have imagined that she breathed easier. He didn't imagine the way her fingers clung to his. Keeping hold of that hand, he leaned back to survey his work.

She had the appearance of a young girl who'd fallen asleep playing dress-up. Except for the bruises.

Their rescue had yet to arrive. Oliver might have already left for Thetford. He was always in a rush to return home. But Harry should have been back by now, regardless. Drake's stomach soured. If he'd sent that child into danger, he was no better than Malcolm Kirk.

The back door opened with a *thud*. Voices grew louder. Drake lifted the fireplace poker from the sofa and stood between Jocelyn and the door.

Harry came into the room first, followed by Oliver dressed in the working clothes he preferred. He took in the scene, his eyes widening when they fell on the drugged, bruised woman. "I assume I'm your escape plan."

✑

JOSS WOKE IN a room that wasn't hers. She knew it from the dark paneling and the placement of the windows. Despite the canopy bed she'd wanted since she was a child, it was a very masculine room.

Had Stratford kidnapped her? Was she miles from London? Where was Drake? Was he…

Panic shot through her, ricocheting with every question. She pushed herself upright in bed and sagged with relief when she saw Drake slung across the sofa in the corner of the room. The coverlet had slid from his chest, though it still covered his legs.

"Drake."

Another jolt went through her when her voice came out in a strained whisper. It worsened when she touched her neck and found bandages instead of skin.

"Mama put a poultice on it."

The explanation came from a thin boy with wild, dark curls who was peeking around the door. A large dog loomed over him, his tongue lolling in a grin.

"I'm Simon." The boy looked to Drake as he tiptoed into the room. "I'm not supposed to wake you, but you're already awake." The dog followed him. "This is Brownie. He just looks scary 'cause he's big. He won't hurt you."

"Hello," Joss whispered, wincing.

"Mama says you aren't supposed to talk so you'll get better faster and *Oncle* Drake won't worry so much."

Joss looked between the large, sleeping man and the tiny boy. There was a slight resemblance, but Drake didn't have a family. He'd said so himself.

Unless he'd been lying.

"Simon." One of the most handsome men Joss had ever seen poked his head around the door. "You're not supposed to—" He blinked, and a blush spread under his skin. "My apologies for interrupting your rest, Miss Kirk."

She recognized that voice from Parliament. Holy God, she was in a duke's home in a shift like some shipwrecked waif.

"I didn't wake her, Papa. She was already looking around."

"Well, that clearly makes it all better, doesn't it?" The duke rolled his eyes. "Miss Kirk, if you would like to join us for breakfast, you'd be welcome."

Drake didn't move from the sofa. If it wasn't for his snoring, she'd worry he had died.

"He'll be a while. He didn't sleep for two days while we traveled."

"Two days?" Joss asked.

"Three, actually. You've been here a day already."

She remembered nothing. Not the trip, not the bandaging. Nothing past Sam's examination at Drake's home on Charles Street.

And Drake giving her tea.

Anger flooded through her as she guessed the reason. "He drugged me."

"Which is why Thea thought it fair to do the same to him before he dropped from exhaustion." Oliver motioned for Simon to follow him. "We'll wait for you in the hallway. There's a wrap at the foot of the bed."

Joss stood, testing her shaky legs before she reached for the robe and tied it around her waist. She was slower than she liked, but stopping the hungry tremble in her stomach would probably go far in relieving her wobbly knees.

She looked over her shoulder at the man still sprawled across the sofa, oblivious to everything going on around him. With a sigh, she went to him and lifted the coverlet from the floor so she could arrange it over his large body. He hated being cold. She brushed his hair away from his forehead. Deep shadows were smudged under his eyes, so dark it was difficult to see where his lashes rested. She wanted to beat him about the shoulders and hold him close at the same time.

The duke was waiting in the hall as he'd promised. He offered his arm to help steady her as they descended the stairs. Simon and his giant dog went ahead of them.

"Thank you, Your Grace." Joss was alarmed every time she spoke. Her voice sounded nothing like her. Not even after she'd swallowed enough seawater to sink a galleon.

"Oliver, please." He smiled at her. "May I call you Jocelyn?"

She nodded.

"Thank you." He stepped slowly, making sure she could keep pace. "Now, for what you probably wish to know but can't ask—I helped Drake get you out of London to Norfolk, which is where you are now. In Thetford, at our country home—Felton House. Drake is a family friend and our man of business. I believe you've met my wife's Aunt Tavie."

Ah, right. The fog in Joss's brain was lifting. Tavie had mentioned her niece the duchess, but they'd never hinted that Drake was a relation. She pointed at the boy in front of them. "Drake's. Nephew?"

Dear God, she sounded like a wounded bird.

"No. It's just easier."

"Papa wouldn't let me call him *Oncle* Drake until he helped save me when I was stolen, and Mama and I fell in the river."

That sounded very much like Drake.

"And then Papa and Mama got married, and I got an *Oncle* Drake, and then a baby sister named Carys. Then *Oncle* Richard came to live with us, and now I have a *Tante* Amelia." He reached the bottom of the stairs and grinned up at her. "And a *Tante* Jocelyn."

Oliver's laughter shook all way the up his arm and into hers. "That about sums it up."

The lump in her throat had nothing to do with her injured throat. It might have been panic. Possibly laudanum or hunger. It couldn't be tears.

She expected the du—Oliver to lead her into the dining room. Instead, he walked her slowly toward the kitchen, reaching in front of her to push open the door. "We have a guest for breakfast, *Pepinilla.*"

A tall redhead, her curls caught back in a tie, turned. Her

patchwork robe hinted at a story that would take hours to tell. The baby on her hip reached for Oliver.

"Take your daughter, *Mono*. She wants nothing to do with me."

They switched positions, the duchess coming to Joss's side while her husband plopped their daughter on his shoulders and walked to the stove for coffee while the baby held handfuls of his hair.

"It's nice to meet you, Jocelyn. I'm Thea." She held out a chair. "Come sit. I've got a pot of licorice tea on the stove, and honey to sweeten it." She pulled the teapot from the hearth as she spoke. "How are your bandages? Do they itch?"

Joss hadn't noticed, but now all she wanted to do was scratch. She nodded.

"We've been changing them once a day, so we can check again this morning after breakfast." Thea paused. "If you'd prefer to see the doctor, I can arrange it, but Drake said you had a thorough exam before you left London, and, frankly, Dr. Anderson is a bit of a busybody, and his methods aren't modern."

"Says the woman who makes people wear leaves," Oliver teased. He danced out of his wife's reach, and the baby squealed with glee.

It was bedlam, but it was the sweetest bedlam Joss had ever seen.

"Leaves are fine," she whispered.

Thea patted her hand and winked. "Drink your tea. I'm afraid breakfast will be disgusting because it needs to be thin enough to get past the swelling. But it will keep your stomach from growling."

The baby finally spotted her, grinned, and reached. Her pudgy feet bounced against her father's chest.

"Carys wants to see you." Oliver swung her down and went to hand her over.

"Oliver, you can't just hand someone a baby." Despite the words, Thea's smile at her husband was wide and lovely.

"She's irresistible." Oliver winked at Joss. Twenty years ago he would have fit in with the boys at Highcliffe. "Would you like to hold her?"

The little girl's squeal, her rosy cheeks and pudgy arms and legs, made it impossible to refuse. Joss settled the baby on her lap.

They explored each other. Carys was fascinated by Joss's robe and her hair, even the bandages circling her neck. For her part, Joss loved watching the child consider the world around her. Her tiny fingers touched everything and tried to put it in her mouth. Her eyes telegraphed every tiny question, every thought, every frustration.

"She likes to play hide the Simon," the boy said from over Joss's shoulder. "Watch."

Using Joss as a wall, Simon poked his head from every angle, each time with a new goofy face. Brownie got involved too, bouncing in every direction, huffing in encouragement, his giant tail sweeping everything in its path aside. Joss and Thea had to hold their tea up in the air to avoid spillage. Everyone was laughing, even Joss. It didn't hurt as badly as she'd expected.

"Jocelyn!" The bellow soaked through the ceiling.

"He lives," Oliver drawled. He went to the kitchen door and propped it open. "In the kitchen," he shouted.

"If Hazel heard you yelling like that, she'd take after you with a wooden spoon," Thea said.

"Then it's a good thing she finally married Fred and doesn't come to work until luncheon." Oliver kept the door open for Drake. "Coffee?"

Drake's hair was still a mess, and his collar was open at the throat. No waistcoat, and his shirt sleeves rolled to his elbows. He looked as wild as his eyes, which finally settled on Joss. "Why aren't you resting?"

"It's not like she's working a saw at the mill," Thea said.

It's not like I haven't been drugged for three days. Joss looked up at him and, unable to talk, stuck out her tongue.

Thea put a plate of eggs and bacon in front of Drake. "Eat

before you stick your foot further into your mouth." She took Carys from Joss's lap and put a cup of gruel in front of her. "I've done the best I could with it."

Maybe it was Thea's efforts, or maybe it was that Joss hadn't eaten in three days, but the porridge, which was the consistency of cream soup, was delicious. So much so that Joss went to the stove for a second helping.

Oliver and Simon left for school, and Thea took the baby upstairs to the nursery. That left Joss and Drake alone in the cavernous kitchen. He toyed with his coffee mug, twirling the handle clockwise five times, then counterclockwise five.

"I never thought I'd miss your yelling at me," he whispered. "I know you're angry about my bringing you here."

"Kidnapping me," Joss rasped. It helped if she put her hand against her neck, at least until she touched a tender spot. The laudanum hadn't dulled her memory of how close she'd come to dying at Stratford's hands. "Thank you."

He kissed her like she was fragile. "Just a few days, I promise. Let Thea make you better. I can show you the village and where Imogen's hat shop will be."

Joss nodded. She would do anything to erase the haunted look in his eyes.

Almost.

CHAPTER TWENTY-ONE

"WHAT WAS DRAKE like as a young man?" Amelia asked, giggling over her tea. "I have difficulty seeing him in anything but a waistcoat."

"Same, I'm afraid," Thea said as she bounced Carys on her knees and imitated her daughter's surprised expression.

Joss took a sip of warm tea that was mostly honey, but there was a bite of whiskey as it slipped down her throat. "He was just as bossy." Sip. "Just as quiet." Sip. "So when he spoke, everyone listened." The last word broke in the middle, and she took another small sip to soothe her throat.

The ladies were patient as she rested her voice. Over the last three days, Thea and Amelia had been her constant companions, at least as much as their schedules allowed. When they were working, usually with Drake as they discussed their plans for the university, she'd been left to wander the house or the estate as she wished.

She wasn't sure which was her favorite—touring Thetford on Drake's arm while he showed her the businesses he'd begun and planned to begin, or curling up in the library under the protective gaze of the family butler.

Even today, as storm clouds rolled in, it was lovely to be with friends and near a fire.

"So he was always this poised," Amelia grumbled. "I was

rather hoping he was a mess of a boy. Seems a waste otherwise."

He'd always been careful with his things and the people around him. It came from having so little, but Joss didn't think it was her place to tell that story. "He grew like a weed in a garden. I let the hem out on his trousers until they were nothing but frayed edges, and they were still too short." She smiled at the memory. "And when he lost his temper, everyone ran for cover."

After Davy's death, he'd thundered for days, raging at times, silent at others, except for the way he banged through the house, refusing even the most basic help. Some of her pots, now gathering dust in her kitchen overlooking the sea, still had dents in them.

When she'd finally screwed up her courage to confront him, he'd already vanished.

"I still can't believe he introduced you to Tavie before us," Amelia said.

"I can." Thea laughed. "He's never been able to tell her no about anything except investments."

Joss liked how these women were themselves with her, how they held nothing back, how they'd risen to the challenges their passions demanded. She wanted to be as honest with them, though the consequences might be dire. "He worried you would think differently of him."

She hated how her injury made it necessary to keep her sentences short. It made everything a blunt confession. But now she had their attention.

"My business is less savory than yours."

"What could be less savory than a distillery?" Amelia asked.

Joss stayed quiet and let them fill in the answer. One glance at Thea told her the duchess already knew. Of course she would. Drake would have told them who was under their roof. Though she was surprised he hadn't combusted from embarrassment.

Amelia, however, had a comical transformation as her mouth fell open and then curved into a shocked smile. "You can't be a…a…"

"Madam," Joss said. "I manage the White Rose."

"Across from the cricket grounds." Amelia giggled. "We used to wonder why so many of the young men would leave for cricket and not take their bats." Her humor faded when she looked to Thea. "You already knew, didn't you?"

"Oliver told me."

"Well, if Oliver knows, then Richard does, though it probably killed Drake to tell him." Amelia's gaze flew to Joss. "I didn't mean that the way it sounded. It's just that Drake is so…stiff, and Richard isn't at all."

Thea and Joss choked on their tea before sputtering in laughter. Again, it took Amelia a moment to realize what she said. She clapped her hand over her mouth, but her eyes danced with glee.

"What's so funny in here?" Richard asked as he came into the room in his work clothes, his wild hair a match for his nephew's.

Amelia took one look at her husband and howled with laughter, which served to start Thea and Joss into peals that continued until they were wiping tears from their eyes.

Drake followed Oliver into the room, his smile widening as he strode to her side. His warm gaze danced over her.

Of all the things Joss enjoyed about Thetford, seeing him every day was near the top of the list. Without his waistcoat and black coat, his hair tangled by the wind, he was a combination of the boy she'd known and the man she loved.

She couldn't name when it had happened, but as he approached her and her heart thudded in time with his steps, she knew it was true.

Oliver kissed Thea. Richard kissed Amelia. Joss knew Drake wouldn't kiss her. Public displays embarrassed him. But his feathery touch on her jaw, the way his thumb swept across her chin, was almost as good. He touched her the same way every night, smoothing so much salve over her neck that it was amazing she didn't slip from the pillow as she slept—though she preferred his chest to any pillow. They lay awake every night, his fingers stroking her spine as he told her of his plans. She fell asleep to his voice rumbling through her as he talked about shipyards, rail lines, and freight companies.

There was also a canal boat in there somewhere, though she might have dreamed that one.

Joss loved sleeping next to him, loved having his voice lull her to sleep. But every touch, every glance, made her long for him to treat her more like a grown woman and less like a wounded bird.

"We come bearing news," Oliver said as he took his daughter in his arms. "Cust has been appointed master of the ceremonies."

Stratford had lost. Thank God.

"We received an invitation from the Yorkes today. They are hosting a party in his honor." Thea heaved a sigh. "I suppose this is one of those ducal responsibilities we can't escape."

"Victoria Yorke?" Joss smiled when Thea nodded. "We met at Parliament."

"That must have been an eventful day." Richard chuckled.

Drake took her hand.

One alarm bell clanged through the relief of Cust's success. Stratford would fade into anonymity. He'd be just another peer with a bad temper and regrettable tendencies. What he'd done to Violet would be forgotten.

"We have to confront him now," Joss said.

"Jocelyn—" Drake's hold tightened.

She pulled free of him. "You know I'm right." When he didn't agree, she looked to Oliver and Thea. "Tell him I'm right."

"Drake—" Thea began.

"Absolutely not." Drake's words were as solid as his jaw.

Richard leaned forward, his elbows on his knees. "You would agree were it anyone else, Fletcher."

"The party is a perfect forum," Joss said. "He'll have to attend to save face."

"Jasper will have received an invitation," Richard added. He looked to Amelia. "Your rakish cousin is hiding the witness in Ramsbury."

Drake rose from his chair and paced the room.

"If Jasper is coming, Kit won't be far behind," Amelia said. "He'll be doing what Jasper can't."

"He needs to look into Madam Price at The Peacock." Joss ticked that item from her list.

"The prime minister will be there, as will the Duke of Manchester, so that will give us an advantage," Oliver said. "The Burnleys will attend with the duke."

The poor family wasn't even aware they should be in mourning.

Across the room, Drake prowled from wall to wall, head down, pinching the bridge of his nose.

"Well, if everyone else is going, I'm going," Amelia decreed. "I'm tired of being the last to know anything. Father has been wanting Richard to serve as his proxy, and this is the perfect event to begin."

Oliver turned to his wife. "Can you wrangle an invitation for Drake and Jocelyn?"

"If we can call on her in London, I may be able to do it myself." Joss perched on the edge of her chair. "That way, if things turn ugly, you aren't—"

"Stop talking, Jocelyn!"

Drake's command cracked through the room like thunder when lightning struck too close. His eyes were coals in his grim face and his white knuckles were stark against his black trousers.

The dreadful silence in the room was broken when Carys began to whimper.

Joss wanted to screech at him, but all her thoughts tumbled together in a pile that re-sorted itself with every turn. What finally fell out was that, even though he deserved a tongue-lashing, she would not embarrass him in front of his friends.

Instead, she set her teacup on the table with quiet precision. Ignoring her burning throat, she dipped her head to her hosts. "If you'll excuse me."

Despite the tears building in her eyes, she refused to bolt from the room like a scolded schoolgirl. She didn't even slam the door.

She was halfway up the stairs when the door flew open behind her. She didn't need to see Drake to know it was him. Every sense was attuned to him.

"Jocelyn, I'm—"

She spun to face him and raised one finger in a demand for *his* silence. She didn't care to hear his excuses right now, and she couldn't scream at him. Her throat was on fire, though she'd never confess that to him.

That was the only reason a tear slipped down her cheek. It had to be. Maybe if she didn't wipe it away, he wouldn't see it.

HE'D MADE HER cry.

That one tear had made Drake feel more of an arse than any of Amelia's harmless glowers or Oliver's pitying glances and the way Richard had patted his shoulder as he'd taken Amelia home. Even Thea's tongue-lashing for the last half-hour paled in comparison.

He plodded up the stairs to their room, trying to focus on not spilling the latest in an endless line of soup. At least now Jocelyn could have bread if she soaked it in the broth first.

She rarely cried. She'd moaned in pain while she slept beside him, but she never wept. Not even her reflection and the bruises that formed a garish three-strand necklace had made her cry.

Even in Highcliffe, when he'd mishandled the crate and sliced her chin open, she'd simply pushed him down in the wet sand before stomping off to the house. He'd only seen her in tears that dreadful night they lost Davy. She'd thrown all her fresh vegetables at him when she learned that he'd buried the boy without telling her.

Drake would have gutted himself before he let her see what was left of their friend.

He'd half expected her to throw something at him this afternoon. Hours of silence and seclusion were worse than if she'd shot him.

The bedroom door wasn't locked, which didn't surprise him. She was stubborn and determined, but she was never childish.

She hadn't had the opportunity to be.

Drake set the tray on the table they used for more meals than was likely polite. He couldn't help it. He preferred having her to himself. "Dinner."

His voice sounded too loud in the quiet room.

Jocelyn rose from her favorite chair near the hearth, her latest book in her hand. She placed it on the table like it was a bar of gold before lifting the cover from her plate. "Oh, look. Soup."

"At least it's a puree this time. It's a bit thicker."

Without a word, she stirred her spoon through the mush and lifted it to him like a weapon. Her arched brow issued a silent dare.

Drake took the mouthful in a gulp. Watching her eyes widen as they did during sex was the only reward for his bravery. The lukewarm gruel had carrots and peas in it, but he couldn't tell which was what. "Yum," he said through a grimace that ended in a cough and then a laugh. She joined him in a scratchy giggle that bit at his flesh like a living thing.

Drake sliced a piece of his steak, bisecting it again and again until his fork couldn't spear it. Instead, he pinched it between his thumb and forefinger and offered it to her. "Chew carefully," he warned. "If you choke, Thea will yell at me more than she already has."

Jocelyn took his fingers into her mouth, gently scraping her teeth against his skin, licking him clean.

Drake's body sprang to life the same as if she'd wrapped her hand around his shaft and pulled. His hair was likely standing on end. "Jocelyn."

"Stop treating me like I'm broken," she commanded in a raspy whisper that cracked in the middle.

He dropped his forehead to hers. She smelled of cloves and lavender, the herbs in the salve Thea had made to help her heal. He missed bluebells. "Every time your voice does that, I see you on the floor." He hoped she never wore purple again.

"Then look at me now." Jocelyn lifted him away until her eyes came into focus. Then her lips. The swell of her breast tempted his fingers.

She tasted like a sweet store—licorice, horehound, and honey. Warm and wild, she sighed as he delved deeper in search of the flavors he'd missed for days. As soft as her skin was, he knew her hair would twine around his fingers until he—

Her gasp sent him backward. "I'm sorry."

With a growl, Jocelyn pushed him off balance and onto the mattress. Before he could get a breath, she'd pushed her dress from her shoulders. He blinked, and her corset fell away. Her shift vanished in a breath. Drake couldn't look away as she crawled up his body to kiss him like a wild creature and opened his trousers as though the buttons didn't exist.

Days of depriving himself of her body had him ready for her after an embarrassingly short number of strokes. He arched from the bed to push his clothes out of the way, and when he fell back to earth, she came when him, sliding down his shaft with a ruthless precision that stole his breath.

Drake's eyes rolled back in his head. When he refocused, he didn't see her bruises. He saw where her body met his and the creamy softness of her belly. He pushed her hands from her breasts, and her soft flesh filled his fingers while her nipples teased his palms. With her head thrown back, her hair tickled his thighs every time she claimed him. Seeing her muscles play under her skin had his climax sizzling through his body to pool low in his gut.

Jocelyn stopped riding him into oblivion. The shallow circle of her hips contrasted with her nails teasing the very spot where his tension had gathered. Her smile was sin itself.

"Witch." Drake grabbed her hips and pulled her down on

him, again and again until her breasts bounced in time with her curls, and his name was a litany whispered into the canopy above them.

His release ripped through him and into her, and her gasp echoed his as he watched their moisture combine. Raising his eyes to hers, he dragged a finger between them to the place she'd shown him the first time he touched her.

Her eyes slammed shut while she shivered around him, impossibly tighter, writhing to get closer.

"Look at me, Jocelyn." He didn't relent. "Please."

She did, and Drake kept the pressure and the rhythm, using her wetness to break her apart again and again. Her hungry gaze lost its focus as she put a hand on his chest for balance. He didn't stop when she tried to push him away because, despite the protest, her body still pursued his. Her sweaty skin sparkled in the firelight until she was soft around him, and her forehead rested on his chest.

Drake eased her to her side and took a moment to knead her trembling thighs and calves. She stretched into the attention like a satisfied housecat.

"I'll be back in a moment." He kissed her ear before he pushed against the mattress.

His trousers tied his ankles together, and his shirt tail tickled his bare arse.

"Whoops," Jocelyn croaked. "Serves you right for making me scream like that in someone else's house."

Her smile dazzled him to the point that he almost crawled back to her. "Me? I believe you're the one who climbed on top of me like I was a horse at Ascot." He wrestled free of his trousers before pulling his shirt over his head. Both were draped over a chair to dry before he fetched the basin and a cloth. He carried both back to the bed. "Maybe they'll think we were fighting."

Watching her laugh was his second favorite thing to do.

"I doubt that." The last word ended with a moan when he wiped the cool cloth over her back, from her neck to her hips and back again.

He did too, but he'd worry over it later. Drake nudged her shoulder, and she rolled over, confounding him with how he was supposed to bathe her without getting distracted. "They like you."

"I like them." Jocelyn yawned. "Drake?"

"Hmm?" He trailed the cloth over the curve over her hip.

"I'm hungry."

He traded the basin for his dinner plate and cut a cube of cold potato into tiny pieces that he pushed in her direction "If people knew how decadent eating naked is, they'd never have dining rooms." He popped a full-sized bite into his mouth.

"Or they'd be full every night." She draped the coverlet over their hips. Raindrops tapped the window. "It would certainly make the Season more interesting."

Drake chewed a bite of steak to buy some thinking time. Going to London was the only thing to do. Stratford had to pay for what he'd done. Jocelyn had to be the bait, because she wouldn't put anyone else in danger, and because the man didn't believe she could hurt him. The marks on her neck proved that.

The Viscount of Stratford was in for a rude surprise.

"You won't be alone with him again," Drake said. "We'll confront him at the party together. Jasper's man, Yarwood, has been looking into matters. It won't just be our word."

She nodded. "The diary?"

"I'll get it. I don't want you near the man." He caught her hand and held it until she looked at him. "I mean it, Jocelyn."

"I'd prefer that as well." She squeezed his fingers. "Thank you." The words grated like a bow against the rocks.

If the *ton* didn't punish Stratford for Violet's death, Drake would have his own revenge.

Lightning struck in a heavy, thick bolt that pulsed before receding. The shadows had hardly faded when thunder shook the windows. Rain lashed the glass in waves, sending a shiver up Drake's spine. Jocelyn's fingers, still joined with his, trembled.

"That came from nowhere," she whispered.

Drake moved the plate to keep from spilling food onto the bedclothes and then drew her against him so they could brave the storm together. "No, it didn't."

He loved the feel of her in his arms, the way her hair fell over her shoulders to tease his forearms. He loved the way she leaned against him and tucked her head against his neck so he could feel her breathe.

He loved *her*.

"The stars weren't as bright last night." He'd learned that from Bob years ago—you didn't need clouds to see rain. "If you can't see the North Star in all her glory, there's a storm brewing. You have a day to prepare, more or less."

Drake tugged a lock of her hair to ensure she stayed awake. "The clouds today looked like the sea when the tide rolls in, and the air smelled wild and cold like it came from somewhere else."

"And the sea went black," Jocelyn mumbled.

He didn't need to tell her they were miles from the sea. She wasn't daft. She, like him every time a storm raged, was years away.

"I told Mal it was dangerous, that it was going to blow like the devil." He dragged the coverlet over them like a cloak and slid his hands across her warm skin. "That Jimmy and El and I had talked it over and we weren't going to drown for shoes we wouldn't even get to wear, and that he'd never be able to sell because he couldn't risk taking them to London."

Drake pulled in a deep breath. He'd never told her this story, but she needed to know how to look out for herself. "He told me that if I was going to whine over a little rain, he'd send you and Davy." Because Davy's ego was three sizes larger than a man twice his age, and because Jocelyn never told her father no. "He knew I wouldn't let you two go alone."

"It rained so hard I couldn't see," she said.

The theft had been simple because the crew had gone to quarters to wait out the storm. The crates had been light until they were a pile that shifted with every wave. There hadn't been enough room for all of them to sit, so Drake had put Jocelyn in the middle of the crates and ordered her not to get crushed. He'd put Davy on the bow as a lookout, and Drake had taken aft so he could steer. They'd almost made it to the cove when a wave swamped them. The boat had rocked like a cradle and dumped all of them into the churning sea.

Drake had dragged Jocelyn out of the undertow by her hair and then dove in search of Davy until his lungs were ready to burst. He'd found him five days later, three coves away, covered in sand and crabs.

"He never gave a damn about us, Jocelyn. It was always what we could do, what we could *get*."

"I can't believe that."

Not *I don't*, simply *I can't*. Because he was her father. Children were supposed to believe the best of their parents.

"I know," he whispered against her hair.

The rain punctuated the silence that stretched between them.

"It wasn't always bad," she finally said. "Because if it was, you wouldn't have a home full of boys just like you."

She was right. Highcliffe had been the start of many things. Friends his own age, being able to go to school when they hadn't been hiding from the Navy or constables. Mal had taught him things that had kept him safe in London and given him the confidence to fight for what he wanted. Not all of it had been bad.

But if he brought the old man into his home, he'd look at those boys and know in an instant that Ed was great at a con, and Frank had a head start on being a master thief. That Nicky matched Gavin in fisticuffs, and that Harry could pinch the rings from your fingers while looking you in the eye.

Because those had been the first things Drake had seen, too.

Malcolm Kirk wasn't his father. He didn't have to trust him.

"I can't have him around the boys, Jocelyn."

"I know." Those two words were an insurmountable chasm.

When they returned to London, after Stratford was unmasked, their paths would diverge. Drake would have to let her go.

Jocelyn's kiss was soft and sad, and her lips lingered until he crawled under the sheets with her and pushed her into the mattress. He spent the rest of the night memorizing her curves and swallowing her sighs, closing his eyes as she did the same.

Building new memories for the next time a stormy night kept him awake. Alone.

CHAPTER TWENTY-TWO

AFTER A WEEK in Thetford, London was too crowded, too smoky, and too impersonal. Joss had been loath to leave the quiet of her garden, where she could focus on living things. Trimming back her roses gave her a reason to take cuttings that she could pack for the trip home.

Though she wondered how they would fare in Highcliffe's stingy soil.

The garden was where she'd been when Alfie ran from the house, eyes wide, to tell her two *ladies* were in the parlor.

That was how she'd ended up in the Duchess of Rushford's carriage, with Tavie at her side and Thea opposite them, on their way to call on Viscountess Burnley.

"Victoria Yorke's note arrived today. She's looking forward to seeing you at the party," Thea said. "You made quite an impression on her at Parliament."

Just thinking of that day made Joss ache. It was the first time Drake had touched her.

Two days ago had likely been the last. He'd ushered her into The Rose, pressed a kiss against her forehead, and left for a meeting with Jasper Warren. *I want to see what he's learned since we last met.* He'd left as though he'd be back in time for supper.

She'd known better. How on earth was she supposed to go to a party on his arm, knowing every step with him was leading to goodbye?

"Are you certain this is wise?" Being in Thea's company at her home was one thing; having the woman introduce her to the *ton* was altogether different.

"It's too late to lose your nerve." Tavie patted her hand. "Charlotte Burnley is a lovely woman. Very gracious."

Would she still be that way when the tart in her drawing room told her that her daughter was dead?

"And she'll know from those bruises that you are…different."

Because no man would leave a *ton* girl with bruises people could see. Jocelyn put her hand to the high collar on her most respectable day dress. She looked more like a governess than a madam. "They're fading." They'd gone from purple to a putrid shade of green. "And not as painful. The salve Thea made for me is miraculous."

"It helps that Drake keeps you greased like a pig for market day." Thea chuckled. "How is he?"

Every night, Jocelyn looked in the mirror as she stroked the clove- and lavender-scented cream against her skin and wished her hands were Drake's. "Preparing for the party in his own way."

"Which means he's working." Tavie sighed. "He's done that far too much, but then he's never had a reason not to."

"He's always preferred to be busy," Joss murmured as she looked out the window. Mayfair houses stretched in an unending row of white. She would not tell these women that her prisoner father had come between her and the best man she knew. That she was leaving him to make sure Da could live the rest of his life under her watchful eye.

She liked them too much to lose their friendship. And she didn't want to arrive at the Burnleys' door in tears.

The carriage stopped, and the footman came down the stairs to meet them. He helped Tavie descend to the street. Joss reached for Drake's hand and came up with empty air.

"I can't do this," she whispered. "I can't go in there."

Thea grasped both her shoulders and gave her a gentle shake. "You can do *anything*, Jocelyn." Tears sparkled in her eyes. "This woman deserves to hear her daughter's fate somewhere other than a ballroom."

Joss made herself nod. Thea was right.

"If you need a hand, you have mine." The duchess released her only to prove that point. "I will be beside you all the time."

Charlotte Burnley greeted them at the door, beginning with Tavie, whom she kissed on the cheek. "Octavia. It's so good to see you. I hated missing Lady Short's tea, but my head was pounding."

She was a small, plump woman in a lovely, deep pink day dress that likely matched the roses in her cheeks when they were there. Which they weren't. It could easily be attributed to a headache.

Charlotte greeted Thea with a curtsy. "Your Grace, it's a pleasure to see you again."

"Thank you, Lady Burnley, but I do wish you'd call me Thea. My aunt speaks so highly of you that it is my hope we can be better friends."

"Only if you call me Charlotte. Lady Burnley always reminds me of Harold's mother, who is still terrifying."

"Charlotte, then." Thea turned to Joss. "May I present Jocelyn Kirk, a family friend we're visiting while in London?"

Joss said the right things, did the right things, all while assessing their hostess. Her smile was too bright, her eyes too dull, and her dress gaped at the arms as though it had been made for a larger woman. Standing in the bright entry hall in her own most respectable day dress—a yellow lawn print that would never catch any man's attention—Joss knew the look of a woman who was about to fall apart.

You didn't need to wear black to grieve.

In the drawing room, Joss had her first glimpse of the girl who had set her on this path. Violet—dark hair, deep brown eyes that twinkled with mischief, and a sweet smile—stared down from a painting given pride of place in the room. The cameo rested a respectable distance from her breasts. "What a lovely girl."

"That is Violet, our daughter. She is…out for the afternoon."

As Joss sat on the thinly padded, mahogany-trimmed sofa, she wondered how many times Charlotte had used that explanation to dodge questions about her daughter.

They had made a plan. Tavie was to break the ice, and Thea was to pave the way for Joss to ask questions. But as the older women nattered on, Joss couldn't stop staring at the portrait. No *ton* family would keep a portrait of their disgraced daughter, whom they'd cast into the street, on display in their public rooms.

But there was something else she couldn't name, nagging her by skipping along the edge of her mind.

"What is it?" Thea asked in a whisper only a vicar's daughter could manage.

"I'm missing something. I can feel it," Joss replied, using a whisper she had learned while sneaking through piers and warehouses in the middle of the night. "What do you see?"

"She's very striking, even in that dress."

That was it. The dress. Thanks to years of outfitting young women to tempt men, Joss now recognized last year's gowns without effort. The sleeves were longer, the neckline higher. Society mamas had used taffeta to both hide and highlight their daughter's breasts. Shawls had never been a match for ball gowns, but there was Violet, clinging to one like a marooned sailor.

Joss recognized a disguise when she saw one. Her mouth went dry. She recognized Violet's because she herself had been wearing it for a week.

"Bruises."

She didn't realize she'd spoken aloud until Charlotte looked her way. The concern in her eyes made Jocelyn jealous of a dead girl whom everyone missed but no one had really known.

"Forgive me, Lady Burnley," Jocelyn said.

"No, dear." Charlotte touched her own neck. "I'm sorry, but I couldn't help but notice the bruise here. It must have been painful."

Joss nodded, fighting back the lie that would shelter this woman from the ugliest parts of London.

"Would you prefer honey in your tea?"

The mere mention of it turned Joss's stomach. She'd had enough honey to last a lifetime. "No, ma'am, but thank you for your kindness."

"Violet bruises easily as well—the slightest thing raises a welt on her skin. She's forever bumping into furniture or stumbling, and young men can be so careless when they dance." Charlotte looked up at the portrait. "She had one the day of her last sitting. Claude, the artist, was kind enough to hide it. He usually prefers a much more honest approach to his art."

For the briefest of moments, Jocelyn wondered if Viscount Burnley had beaten his daughter. He wouldn't be the first gentleman to do it. One look at the portrait told a different story. A girl with that smile was not mistreated.

"I don't know where she is, Octavia." Charlotte's whimper galvanized Thea even as it paralyzed Joss. Somehow, in all her planning, she hadn't expected tears. Parents never cried.

Did they?

Charlotte had collapsed onto Thea's shoulder. "We woke one morning last spring, and she was just…gone. She left a note saying not to worry, that she'd be fine. We thought maybe she'd eloped with someone from the dance the night before." She looked between Tavie and Thea, and took the handkerchief Tavie offered. "Several young men had paid attention to her at supper, to the point that she wouldn't have been able to eat if Viscount Stratford hadn't shooed them away. He and Harold were at school together, and he's always been so kind to Violet."

Thea kept her arm around the weeping woman's shoulder as she looked at Joss. "And you haven't heard from her since then?"

Charlotte buried her face in her hands and shook her head.

Joss let the scenario she'd built collapse to the ground so she could rebuild it. She'd supposed that Violet had been punished by her family for an indiscretion, as Imogen had been.

That was wrong.

Connie had supposed that Violet was a sweet, common girl who had no other way of making a living because that's what Connie was.

That was wrong.

Everyone had assumed that Stratford had visited The Peacock and been charmed by a lovely face. That he'd protected Violet from the ills of a life she'd been forced into either by mistake or by fate.

That was wrong.

She never harbored fantasies of being a viscountess, Connie had said. Joss looked up into Violet's painted eyes. Claude, whoever he was, had managed to capture the glint of a secret in them. This was a girl who had every romantic notion, every well-meant intention, of being Viscount Stratford's second wife.

She had been so, so wrong.

The bastard had tricked her into leaving her home, paving the way to The Peacock, where Catherine Price put her in a gilded cage right under her parents' noses. They had searched every-where but the brothels because their daughter would *never* go there.

If Violet regretted her decision, she would have thought it was too late to go home—that her parents wouldn't forgive her. So she'd made friends with women she'd have never met otherwise and watched the world from her window.

Until one fateful night, when someone left her cage open, and she'd flown into the parlor. Where men could see her. Where they could recognize her.

Where they could *help* her.

Heart in her throat, stomach in her shoes, Joss knelt on the floor in front of Charlotte and took her limp, wet fingers. "Lady Burnley, I need you to listen to me very carefully…"

BY THE END of the story, all four of them were drained. Joss took solace in Charlotte's peaceful, resolved expression.

"You say he has her diary?" the lady asked.

"I believe so." Joss sat on the floor, her knees under her. The circle of these women, the chance to finally do something, was intoxicating. Besides that, she lacked the strength to stand. "Could you tell me where you purchased it? If possible, we will need a copy."

"They are bespoke. We have them shipped from Scotland." Charlotte's eyes widened as she leapt to her feet, almost crushing Joss's fingers beneath her shoe. "Wait!" She hurried to her desk and pulled the bottom drawer so hard that it landed at her feet. "I almost forgot…"

She returned with a journal bound in the softest leather Joss had ever held. The front cover was branded with violets, and a V was stitched into the spine, surrounded by vines and flowers so that it looked like the beginning of a chapter in the Bible that sat displayed in Highcliffe's chapel.

"She wrote so often that we began buying two or three at a time."

Joss's breath caught as hope formed. "Do you have the old ones?" It doubled when Charlotte nodded. Violet likely wrote *everything* down.

The clock chimed three. "We should go," Tavie said. "Will you be all right on your own?"

"I will. Harold will be home—" Charlotte stopped. "What do I tell Harold?"

"Whatever you would like," Thea said. "You needn't bear this alone."

"I think I'd like to, just for a little while." After a moment, Charlotte nodded. "If he knows we are to be in mourning, he won't let me go to the party, and I must be there. Plus, if he confronts… I will not say his name again." She drew in a long, deep breath. "I will not give Harold the opportunity to ruin your plans."

They walked to the door and said their goodbyes. Charlotte kept Joss's hand as she kissed her cheek. "Thank you, Jocelyn."

Joss nodded, unable to speak for the lump in her throat. It persisted as she climbed into the carriage and as they rounded the corner. The people in the street didn't hold her attention. Thea and Tavie's conversation was nothing but the roar of the ocean, like when she held a shell to her ear.

Stratford had all but kidnapped Violet, abused her, debased her, and killed her. Madam Price had helped him in exchange for money. Lord Spencer was willing to look the other way for power—a quest Joss had treated like a game, gathering secrets to keep her father in hair tonic and tooth powder while she waited for something that would secure his release.

Violet had died alone in a brothel. When they'd pulled her from the Thames, her bruises had likely matched the ones under Joss's collar.

And Joss was going to use her to get her father out of prison. She hadn't bothered to ask any questions. All she'd seen was the path to freedom, built on a dead girl's hopes.

He never gave a damn about us, Jocelyn. It was always what we could do, what we could get.

The tears came without warning, and the tightness in her chest demanded release. Joss dropped her forehead to the window and sobbed, deep, racking cries that couldn't be hushed or muffled, no matter how hard she tried.

THE STREET WAS dark, but the moon washed the front of Stratford's townhouse an eerie white. It made the windows as fathomless as the sea. Drake stood across the street, blending in with the shadows, biding his time. On nights like this, he felt like the bat Gav teased him of being.

He stepped back as a cab passed, its lanterns casting wide circles in the freshly swept street. Darkness reclaimed the house, then the trees. Drake lifted his collar against the damp cold of the night.

The gas lamps could be avoided with ease. He'd done it plenty of times, most recently an hour ago, when he'd left Charles Street and taken a route to Mayfair that had left even him dizzy. He was wagering his life that he'd lost the hulking shadow that had followed him since he walked away from Jocelyn.

It was for the best. He told himself that every day. On the hour. Sometimes on the half-hour. No matter their goals, he wouldn't risk her being attacked again. She was strong, yes, but she wasn't as invincible as she pretended to be.

Neither was he.

Leaves rustled behind him, too uniform to be the breeze. Drake eased his hand to his knife. Its cold hilt was a welcome bite, like shaking hands with an old friend.

A blackbird chirped behind him, its song halting and rusty like a gate that hadn't been used enough. His shoulders relaxed. "You're out of practice."

"You shouldn't have assumed it was me," Jocelyn whispered. She took another step, dragging leaves in her wake. "Damned cloak."

"Safe assumption." He kept his eyes on the house. "Blackbirds don't sing at night. You never listen to me."

Because she wasn't supposed to be here at all.

"Yet it's the only song you taught me."

Despite the task in front of him, Drake smiled. He'd tried for months and finally surrendered to the fact that Jocelyn, for all her other talents, was tone-deaf. He turned to watch her reaction as he teased her. He ached to see her laugh. "It's because you can't…"

She was in trousers. Growing up, she'd worn them so often that she'd considered a skirt a disguise. Drake had never thought twice about it—about her. It was different now. Those had been castoffs. These were made for her, clinging to her legs from her waist to the tops of her dark boots.

Now he ached for something else. "I may need the name of your tailor."

"I couldn't very well be a lookout in a gown." The air between them crackled as she stepped closer on silent feet, nothing catching the light but her lovely face. "You must be freezing."

He couldn't feel his elbows, but his gloves kept his fingers warm. They were all that mattered right now.

"The coat gets in my way." She might, as well. "You shouldn't—"

"You cannot do everything yourself," she said. "I knew you wouldn't risk Gavin or one of the boys." She lifted the diary into the moonlight. "Besides. You'll need this."

"Thank you." Drake slipped the empty book into his waistcoat. Thea had told him about their visit with Lady Burnley and what they'd learned. What it had done to Jocelyn. "Are you well?"

"Yes. Did you talk to Ramsbury?"

Drake suspected Jocelyn was lying, but now was not the time to confront her. "He's sending Yarwood to the Burnley household tomorrow."

While everyone else would be visible at Lords, Kit would be reading the tale of Violet's life in her own words.

The street cleared.

Without any announcement, Drake stepped out of the shadows, knowing Jocelyn would follow. He avoided the gas lamps without worrying she wouldn't. He had taught her to do this, after all.

As they neared the house, she pointed to a window on the bottom floor. Stratford's library was on the same side of the first floor as his was on Charles Street. Maybe that was a sign of good fortune.

Maybe all houses in London were the same.

Jocelyn stayed behind him as he skirted the house to the side window. It was latched, but the frame was loose. It wasn't what he'd have expected by looking at the façade, but it was another stroke of good luck. If this one was in disrepair…

He crouched low and followed the wall to the corner, stopping only for a moment to check the garden. Darkness and quiet greeted him. The terrace, cast in shadow by the one above it, was the perfect entry point.

Jocelyn pulled him to a halt and pointed overhead. "Bedroom."

Perhaps not perfect, then, but quick. Drake swung his leg over the railing and assessed the door. Simple latch, heavy drapes, cavernous space beyond. Given the layout of the house so far, it was either a ballroom or a dining room. Likely dining.

He pulled his knife from its sheath, slid it under the latch, and flicked upward. The doors swung open with barely a whisper.

He looked over his shoulder to Jocelyn and pointed to her feet in a silent command he knew she'd obey. She might be rebellious and stubborn, but she knew how to do her job.

The darkness of the house was different from outside. Drake locked the door behind him and stood until shapes grew recognizable. Chairs first, then the table. Sideboards were next. The door was a cavernous mouth on the other side of the room.

No time to dawdle.

Drake's toes were icy in the soft boots necessary for work such as this. He used his lack of a coat to explain the chill down his spine. It was not a thrill. He would not be excited about breaking into a home, no matter the reason.

A quick peek through the door cleared the way into the hall, past the stairs, and to the library. Holding his breath, he put his ear to the door. Nothing. He entered and eased the door closed in his wake, breathing only when the latch closed with a *snick*.

Pulling a candle stub and a match from his pocket, he went to work. Though, after creeping about, the light was almost too bright, even shaded by his gloved hand.

If this task had meant searching for a book in the Chitesters' mishmash of a library at Oakdale, Drake would have walked away. But he'd gambled that Stratford wasn't much of a reader or a collector. He'd been wrong. There were enough books here to make this task impossible for one person.

However, Drake was familiar with Stratford's habits, thanks to Jocelyn's earlier visit. He'd kept the pearls near him but hidden. He'd likely do the same with the diary.

Drake stepped to the desk and sat in the chair, sweeping the candle over the pristine surface. No diary, but he really didn't expect it to be there. It would be on a shelf, low enough to be in view.

Yowl. Snarl. Bang. Clatter.

Drake snuffed the candle and wedged himself into the nearest shadow, masking his face as best he could with his glove.

"Damned cats. I've told you not to feed them." It was a younger male voice, likely the randy footman. "If they wake the old man, there'll be hell to pay."

"He came home pickled to the gills," an older woman replied, too close for comfort. "He won't be waking until tomorrow afternoon."

The door opened just enough to show a sliver of light. "Come see what I found in the library. It might be worth a bob or two."

Drake's heart thudded in his ears, and he drew in a deep breath, then another. Each exhale heated his glove until the leather was damp against his nose and his hearing returned. Breaking windows in an escape hadn't been fun even at a younger age.

"I think we've reached our limit of what we can blame on the sneaky chit, mum." The lad was closer now, too. Though he sounded young, his shadow loomed large. Drake hoped it was a trick of the light. "He's already asked me about them pearls until I wished I *had* stolen them."

"Those pearls." The woman sighed. "You're correct, though.

I'd rather stay out of his way." She closed the door, sending the room back to the comforting darkness. "Let's go back to sleep."

Drake's heart told him to hurry, but his head counseled patience. It had never served him wrong. After a few minutes, he lit the candle and returned to his chair.

His stomach soured as he closed his eyes and pretended to be Stratford, at his desk, admiring his keepsakes. Writing his notes and doing his business with a reminder of his crime nearby. Drake acted as though he was writing and stopped. The inkpot and quills were on the other side of the desk.

The viscount was left-handed.

Drake reversed hands, looked to the right, and raised the candle. Violet's initial glowed like a signal fire.

He drew the book from the shelf with one hand and placed the decoy with the other. The leather was icy, even through his shirt, as he put out his candle. While it cooled, he pulled a piece of sturdy string from his pocket.

Simple and quiet is always best. Malcolm had taught Drake this trick years ago, and it had always served him well.

Open the latch. Tie the string. Open the window. Climb out. Close the window. Pull the string to close the latch. Loosen the knot. Keep pulling. Like he was never there.

He plucked a pebble from the dirt and tossed it at Jocelyn's shadow. She was to him in half a breath, her eyes bright in the moonlight. "I felt sure you were caught."

"Who, me?" He wanted to kiss her so badly his teeth ached. "Let's fetch your cloak. It's freezing out here."

CHAPTER TWENTY-THREE

"T HE DUKE AND Duchess of Rushford, the Marquess of Ramsbury and Miss Constance Hall, Mr. and Mrs. Richard Ferrand, Mr. Drake Fletcher, and Miss Jocelyn Kirk."

Joss passed the butler and took her place in the receiving line, surveying the crowd all the while. She had chosen a dress in a shade that reminded her of a foggy sea with a neckline so demure it was almost unfashionable. She'd never worn it at The Rose. Her hair was done up so that her curls added to her height, and jeweled hairpins caught the light whenever she turned. The style exposed her neck, and she'd covered her fading bruises with cosmetics and a ribbon that matched her dress. She looked like every other lady in the room.

Her nerves clattered under her skin. Her real name, her true face, her new friends… This was the first time in years she hadn't entered a room in a disguise.

Heads turned. More than a few men's eyes widened.

Drake covered her hand with his, warming her through her satin gloves. It was uncomfortable because her palms were already sweaty. Her wish that he'd never release her made it worse.

"You are lovely," he whispered. "But is that ribbon comfortable, especially with the brooch on it?"

Joss lifted her fingers to the white stone surrounded by a

delicate gold filigree frame. It had arrived at The Rose a few days earlier, and she'd been stunned by the simple beauty of it. Then she'd lifted it into the light and seen the carving.

A dragon and a goat curled together and surrounded by roses.

"It was a gift from Bob." She opened her fan for no other reason than she needed something to do with her hand. She would not hide from these people. She had no reason to be embarrassed about her behavior. Especially tonight. "I feel braver wearing it."

Every time she swallowed, she felt Stratford's fingers around her neck.

They had reached the guest of honor and their hosts. It took a good while for Oliver's gaze to fall on them. "Sir Edward, Lady Cust, may I present my brother-in-law, Mr. Richard Ferrand, and his wife Amelia, the daughter of Baron Kilverstone. Richard carries the baron's proxy, as business keeps Augustus near home this season." He winked at Joss in a show of support so quick it might have been missed. "My man of business, Mr. Drake Fletcher, and Miss Jocelyn Kirk, a friend of the family."

Sir Edward Cust reached them and took Drake's hand. His military past was easy to read in the way he carried himself, but in that same comparison, Drake could have been a captain himself. Straight back, wide shoulders, strong jaw. His ivory waistcoat made his chest seem broader—or maybe that was because Joss knew how it felt beneath her hands.

Just as she knew how difficult it was for him to give an easy smile to Sir Edward while his back was to a crowd.

Drake Fletcher was no longer the boy who lurked around corners and skulked in the shadows. Here in this ballroom, with the tails of his coat stopping just above his knees, it was easy to imagine him as a proud dragon.

But not a lucky one. He'd worked hard for what he had, and he wasn't ready to stop yet. But he was risking it all for her, a stubborn, common goat who ran a brothel.

She offered a hand to Sir Edward and curtsied with the same

level of deference every other lady in the room had used. "Congratulations on your victory, sir."

"Thank you, Miss Kirk." Despite the man's stern posture, there was a twinkle in his eye. "I understand you are a friend of my family as well."

Victoria Yorke greeted her with a warm smile and her free hand. Her other was tucked in the arm of her husband. "Miss Kirk! I am so glad you found a way to attend. I would have sent an invitation, but I realized I did not know where to reach you."

Behind them, a man barked a cough. It was a poor disguise for laughter.

Victoria didn't bat an eye. Either she was a skilled actress or a kind soul. "So it was a happy coincidence that you are acquainted with the duke and duchess." She looked at the tall, attractive man at her side. "Steffan, may I present Miss Kirk. We met in the balcony at Parliament the day of Father's speech at Lords."

"The Duke and Duchess of Manchester, Viscount and Viscountess Burnley, Lord John Russell, and Lady Russell," the butler boomed. "Major Christopher Yarwood and Miss Fiona Allen."

Joss's pulse quickened and her mouth went dry. Everyone who needed to be in the room had arrived. The time was near.

But it wasn't here yet. She doubled her focus on the couple in front of her.

She had never been so happy not to recognize a man. Steffan Yorke had never darkened the door of The Rose. It didn't mean he hadn't visited The Peacock or maybe had a mistress in an apartment somewhere. However, given the way he smiled at his wife, Joss doubted it. "Mr. and Mrs. Yorke, may I present Mr. Drake Fletcher."

As the gentlemen became acquainted, Victoria leaned closer to Joss. "Everyone is staring. You'll likely have a full dance card, should Mr. Fletcher release your hand."

The dance card would have been amusing, but she liked Drake's hand on hers, though it would have been cooler if he wasn't clutching it so hard. It would also be lovely to consider Victoria Yorke a friend, but Joss knew any friendship needed to be honest.

"They are likely wondering if I'm the same woman they've done business with across town."

Under any other circumstance, with any other person, it would have been comical to watch Victoria's eyes grow saucer wide as realization dawned. Joss braced herself for the inevitable cut.

"How intriguing." Victoria took her arm and led her away from the men. Joss released Drake's hand. It would cause less of a scene if they weren't dragged out as a group.

But Victoria stopped near the edge of the dance floor in full view of the company. "Which house do you run?"

"The White Rose," Joss replied in the same low tone. "Though I can assure you that your husband—"

Victoria waved away the explanation. "We've not been married long enough for him to grow bored, and I can promise you I intend to ensure that never happens. For either of us. I believe Lady Tinsdale's husband is a client, however."

He was. He was also an obnoxious blowhard whose pillow talk had proved profitable. "I'm sorry if the lady—"

"She's not the least bit upset about it." Victoria plucked two glasses of punch from a passing tray and delivered one to Joss. "But she says she'd object if he went anywhere else. The Rose's reputation for discretion and the…health of its ladies is impeccable."

For the first time this evening, Joss felt less of an impostor as she took a sip of punch so laced with rum that it made her eyes water. "Forgive me, Mrs. Yorke, but this was not the reaction I expected."

"Victoria, please. You likely have dealt with Society matrons who choose to ignore the seedier side of the Marriage Mart. Some of us younger ladies have lost far too many friends who have been preyed upon by lordlings and then betrayed by their families."

Joss looked around the room, imagining it not as a party but as an evening in her parlor. Most of the men behaved themselves, but there were those who stood too close or waited for a chaperone's turned head before urging a young lady outside. Then there were the mamas who saw their daughters near the veranda doors and willfully turned their heads.

"My friend Lady Violet, the daughter of Viscount Burnley, left our first Season abruptly, and there were rumors that she…was in your part of town. I would hope that she found a house like yours."

"She did not," Joss answered. "I wish she had."

"You speak in the past tense." Victoria's Society smile faltered. "The rumors are true, then? Father and Steffan seem to think I'd be better served only hearing the best of people, but…"

"I find I'm most surprised by happy news." Joss saw Oliver approaching. Thea was behind him on Drake's arm. Their smiles had taken on a grim sharpness. "Forgive me, Victoria."

She retrieved the pearls from her reticule and clasped them around her neck. The cold weight of the cameo lay against her skin. The combination of the necklace and the brooch at her neck likely made her look more a strumpet than if she'd entered the room in her corset and stockings. But she wasn't meant to fade into the fashionable crowd.

"Those are Violet's." Victoria placed a hand at the base of her throat. "How did you—"

"Please trust me," Joss whispered as Oliver reached them.

Oliver nodded a greeting to Victoria before offering his arm to Joss. "I believe it's time, Jocelyn."

He led her onto the floor, but Joss couldn't stop staring at Drake. He was straight as an arrow, his face a stern mask.

"He'll lead Thea onto the floor in a moment," Oliver whispered. "We thought it best that you be with me when Stratford sees you." He pulled her into position as the music began. "There's little time. He's here to save face, and he'll leave as soon as it's polite to do so."

One turn about the floor was enough to draw his gaze. It helped that, at Oliver's prompting, she faced his party as they passed, baiting him with a glimpse of the stones. Joss was vaguely aware of Jasper and Connie on the floor, and the same with Richard and Amelia. But she could feel Drake's presence so keenly that it was easy to pretend he was holding her.

Another turn and Stratford's stare branded her, but the sting was mitigated by Viscountess Burnley's pale face and the tears dampening her cheeks. Despite all that, she nodded in solidarity.

The music came to an end with Joss in the center of the floor, under the chandelier. She was still curtsying to Oliver when Stratford snatched her arm and hauled her to her feet.

"Your Grace, are you aware you are dancing with a common whore and a scheming thief? I would check my pockets were I you."

Oliver stood his ground and squared his shoulders. Thea came to his side. "Those are serious accusations, Viscount Stratford. What proof have you?"

"Proof?" Stratford all but screeched. He swept his free hand across the crowd. "Any number of men can identify her as the madam of the White Rose. She does not hide her identity." His grip on her arm ground her bones together.

"No, she doesn't." Oliver's voice was level, but the flush under his skin made his eyes that much brighter. "In our acquaintance, I've never considered Jocelyn common, nor have I known her to lie. However, I do have trouble believing her a thief."

"I have taken nothing from the viscount," Joss said, struggling to keep her voice calm and strong. His touch was unbearable, and everyone was staring. This had been far easier to *plan* than it was to *do*.

"You lying witch." Stratford raised his hand high above his shoulder, telegraphing his strike.

Drake came from behind him and stopped the swing. "That is

quite enough."

"How dare you touch me," Stratford thundered. "You two are in league. You may have fooled everyone else in London, but I see you for—"

"Here now."

The words were fatherly, but the voice was not. The stunned crowd parted, allowing Lord John Russell, the Duke of Manchester, and Viscount Burnley to join them under the chandelier.

"Release her." Drake's words were a low growl. "Or I will break your arm."

Stratford obeyed so quickly that Joss would have tumbled to the floor had it not been for Jasper and Richard, who kept her upright. She caught her breath before acknowledging the prime minister, the duke, and Violet's father, whose eyes never left the necklace.

"Lord Russell, this…woman has come into my house and stolen my possessions," Stratford sputtered. "And dares to show her face, flaunting her thievery."

The prime minister looked her up and down, frowning. "I see nothing that would belong to you, Stratford."

"Those." A bony finger pointed to Jocelyn's chest. "Those pearls are *mine*. I purchased them from—"

"Liar!" Connie stepped forward, flanked by Jasper and Kit Yarwood. "Those belonged to Violet. You took them from her after you killed her."

A gasp went through the crowd like a rising tide. Drake's hold moored Joss to him.

The prime minister turned his gaze to Connie. "What proof have you of this?"

"We worked together at The Peacock, your lordship." Connie's voice was quiet, but firm. She never wavered. "Violet wore them—"

"The word of another common who—"

"Please watch your language in my home." Victoria Yorke walked onto the dance floor on the arm of her husband. She turned to the men. "Prime Minister, I can add my voice to this young lady's. I was present the first time Viscount Burnley's daughter wore these pearls. Perhaps he can better identify them."

The older man lifted his hand toward Joss. "May I?"

Joss fumbled with the clasp. She couldn't wait to be rid of the blasted things.

Drake's fingers brushed hers aside. "Allow me." His whisper brushed her skin, and his fingers were equally gentle. He swept the necklace away from her and offered it to Burnley. "Your lordship."

Burnley directed his attention to the clasp, holding it to the light and turning it until the coat of arms was thrown into relief. Tears came to his eyes. They flowed freely when he held the cameo.

Joss glanced to Stratford, who had shrunk two sizes. He reminded her of a crab in a trap.

"We gave these to my daughter for her first Season. The cameo was made in her image, and the clasp bears my coat of arms."

The Duke of Manchester stepped forward and put his hand on his cousin's shoulder. He rubbed a large pearl between the fingers on his other hand. "These belonged to my grandmother, John. I would recognize the strand in the dark." He looked from it to Joss, from her to Connie. And then to Stratford. "You say this man murdered her?"

"I do, Your Grace," Connie declared.

"There is no proof," Stratford shouted. He looked past his accusers to the crowd. "These people seek to ruin me as sport."

"Lord Russell," Burnley said. "We have been searching for Violet for months. She quit our home in April and has not been seen or heard from since. The last sighting was indeed at the Gold Peacock. A young man came to the house and said she had asked for rescue. By the time I arrived, she had vanished again."

"But we have no way of proving anything past that," the prime minister said.

"Perhaps this will help, sir." Drake pulled the diary from his coat. "Before Viscount Stratford objects that it is stolen. It is. Twice. I liberated it from his library, but I believe it was Violet's before that."

Burnley ran his thumb over the book's spine, tracing his daughter's initial in a continuous loop. "It was a birthday gift, Lord John. She wrote it in every day." He turned to Stratford. "How were these items found in your home?"

Stratford reminded Joss of a fish that had been stranded on the sand after a storm. "Burnley, Prime Minister, you cannot believe these thieves and scoundrels. There is nothing to prove these accusations."

Jasper entered the tightening circle. "Prime Minister, Major Yarwood has investigated the matter at my request. Perhaps we could take this to another room and review his report in more detail."

So they could explain in private how Violet had died and found herself in a watery grave. How she was buried anonymously in a potter's field just outside the churchyard in the parish farthest from polite society. As though it wouldn't all come out in Stratford's trial.

"Yarwood is a good and honest Welshman, sir," Steffan Yorke offered. "I've never met a better soldier."

After a moment, Lord Russell nodded. "Just so." He bowed to Victoria. "We've taken far too much of Edward's celebration, Victoria." He nodded to Manchester and then to Oliver. "After you, Your Graces."

They left the room, Kit Yarwood keeping a close watch on Stratford. The viscountess clutched Joss's hand as she walked past. "Thank you."

Richard and Amelia gathered Fiona Allen with them, so she wasn't left unescorted. Drake led Joss into step behind them.

Spencer snatched Joss's arm as the crowd closed behind her. His hard glare matched his bruising hold. "Do you realize what you've done?"

She'd helped ensure a murderer would be held accountable, that a death was repaid, and that a family could have horrible answers to all their questions. The Burnleys could finally grieve.

But her father would not gain his release. Spencer likely wouldn't have secured it anyway.

She pulled free of his grasp. "I do."

THERE WAS A bright line at the horizon when the carriage stopped at The Rose's gate. Dawn wasn't far, and it promised to be a lovely day—as though Mother Nature had decided to reward them for a hellish night.

Joss's limp skirt weighed twice as much as when she'd left, and her curls drooped in sympathy. Next to her, Connie's red-rimmed eyes were stark in her pale face. She had cried away all her cosmetics hours earlier as she'd sat with the Burnleys and told them about the last months of their daughter's life. In the end, the family hadn't been given much privacy. Investigators had been as thick as sand fleas.

Joss and Drake had been questioned separately, but between sessions, he'd stayed at her side. Even now, he was across from her, his long legs stretched so their shoes could touch if they wished it.

James must have been waiting at the window, because he ran through the garden to reach the door and help Connie down. Drake climbed down next and gave Jocelyn his hand. She clung to it like a lifeline.

She stopped halfway, under the protection of the trees. If he walked her to the door, she'd make a fool of herself and beg him to stay. Which he couldn't do.

They had done what they promised. They had brought down a viscount and brought answers to the Burnleys. Violet had been avenged. But in the process, Joss had become the face and the voice of the biggest scandal in London.

Drake's business, his clients, and his friends did not need that exposure. They had done enough.

"Jocelyn." He traced his fingers over her face, as light as feathers and as soft as sea foam.

She loved everything about him, even the inky shadows under his eyes and the grim line of his mouth. She cradled his strong jaw in her hand as she memorized the feel of him.

This man, this *good* and *decent* man, did not need to be whispered about every time he walked into a room. He was doing the right thing, protecting his family from her father.

Sometimes the right thing to do wasn't easy.

Unshed tears blurred her vision. She didn't dare speak for fear of blubbering. If she wept, he'd stay until she was calm. It would only prolong the pain of losing her heart.

Joss dropped her hand, turned her feet, and walked toward The Rose, all while feeling Drake's eyes on her. She didn't dare turn back. She closed the door between them and held her tears until the jangling harness and the hoofbeats faded to nothing.

CHAPTER TWENTY-FOUR

D RAKE STOOD AT the top of the stairs and listened to the boys whisper over breakfast. At least, the time told him it *should* be breakfast. There had been no stampede down the stairs, no plate-threatening dash to the sideboard, no fights over the best apple or the largest scone. For three days, they'd lived like ghosts in their own home.

All because he'd faded away. The life had drained from him the moment Jocelyn vanished under the trees that shaded The Rose's front garden.

Since then, he'd slept in fits and starts, the sheets tangled around his knees or ankles and his arms around the pillow she'd ignored. When thoughts of her drove him from bed, he ate the stale, cold food Gavin had left at the door. Cold potatoes and the financial pages had kept him from going mad in the middle of the night.

Gavin stopped at the foot of the stairs. "Are you rejoining us?"

Drake forced himself to take a step. It was time to move forward. "Yes."

"I'll ask Trudy to air your room and change your linens." Gavin held out his hand. "That dressing gown needs to go in the wash as well."

"No."

"You've worn it for three days. The scent is gone, Drake."

He knew that. It wasn't the smell of her on the fabric that kept him in a robe he'd only purchased because a newspaper ad said all fashionable gentlemen wore them at home. The satin reminded him of Jocelyn's skin against his in the dark. Her arms went around him whenever he tied the sash. "Tomorrow."

"You'll say that tomorrow as well." Gav sighed. "I'll bring you the correspondence that's piled up."

"You're not my butler, remember?" Drake teased as he lifted the still-folded newspaper from the table near the door. That had been Gavin's biggest concern when they moved into the house. *People will think I'm your servant.*

"You'll start reading and miss breakfast altogether," Gavin said. "You need a full, *hot* meal." He walked toward the library. "Besides, the boys have missed you."

Those same boys fell to silence as Drake entered the room and went to the sideboard. The smell of food made his stomach churn, and he knew it would taste like straw. Still, he filled his plate and poured a cup of coffee that wasn't necessary for him to stay awake.

"Are you feeling better?"

The voice was so small, Drake had to turn to make sure it had come from Harry, the boy who had ended up on the street after his mother was taken by pneumonia.

"I'm much better, thank you." His skin was all that was holding him together, but he made himself smile as he took the letters from Gavin. "What have I missed?"

The letters were from men he'd never thought he'd know. Manchester, Cust, Burnley, Yorke. All of them had spoken to either Oliver or Jasper, sometimes both. All wanted a meeting to discuss business, either his or theirs.

Drake put them aside to listen to tales of anatomy books, history lectures, or cricket matches. Harry walked on his hands for the length of the room without falling over and risking his neck. Gavin took a seat at the table with a plate piled so high it made Drake's stomach ache.

Just like aboard ship or in Highcliffe, he'd chosen these young men to be with him through this next chapter. He'd given them a home for as long as they wanted. However, this time they were the ones who would decide when that page turned. Jocelyn's involvement in his life, her encouragement of Ed's love life, and nudging Drake to travel with Frank and learn cricket for Nicky, the softness she inspired with Harry, had given Drake a real family. One he didn't want to lose.

A lull in the conversation gave him a chance to pose a question. "I've been thinking over the past few days." He swallowed the lie. They didn't need to know the idea had just come to him. "What if we became a proper family?"

Gavin stopped chewing.

"What would you all say to taking Fletcher as your last name?" Drake met each wide stare, suddenly terrified they'd reject him, too. "You don't have to, you understand? You'll still have a home and anything you need from me."

"We can do that?" Nicky asked in a whisper. "Just call ourselves something else?"

Drake shrugged. "I did." He put his elbow on the table and his chin in his hand. "Which is a story for another day. Right now, all in favor…" He raised his free hand over his head.

Four hands shot up without hesitation. He should have asked them this months ago.

"Are we getting a mother, too?" Harry waggled his eyebrows over his wide grin. He'd never hidden his admiration of Jocelyn.

The thought of her in this house, at this table, almost made Drake regret everything he'd done this morning, and it wasn't even eight o'clock.

"Ow! I was just asking."

"Frank, don't hit your brother," Gavin said, his smile wide. Apparently, he approved of the new arrangement as well.

"Not even if he's being mean?" Frank asked.

"How is asking about a mother being mean? All families have

a mother."

"Ours doesn't." Ed's flat statement wasn't loud, but it echoed through Drake's brain like a dinner gong.

The idea of Jocelyn haunted him. It likely always would. He already dreaded walking in the park without her, of visiting Tavie and hearing her sigh over his lost chances, of having to explain to everyone in Thetford why he wouldn't pursue her and make her change her mind.

He didn't like her decision, but he understood it. After working for the past decade to help women pursue their own path, he had to let Jocelyn choose her own way. She deserved that respect.

"Besides, she'd be our sister instead of our mother," Nicky said. "Wouldn't she?"

"Another good question." Drake refocused his attention on the boys. "I'm rather tired of being a guardian." He winked at Harry. "I certainly don't want to be called a master. So brother or father?" He hoped putting his choice first would sway their votes.

"Brother." Ed raised his hand. The others joined him.

Thank God.

Drake had time for one last question before they left for school. "How would everyone feel about leaving London?"

Frank's hand shot up. Nicky's was next. Ed had turned to stone.

"Ed, it's close enough to Cambridge that we could visit often, but if your heart is set on Oxford, we'll make it happen." Drake glanced at the pile of letters waiting near his elbow. Surely there was an Oxford man in there.

"You'll have a home here if you want it," Gavin said.

Harry's eyes widened. "You're not coming with us."

"Village life isn't for me." Gavin looked at each of them. "But I think it would suit all of you down to the ground. When you come back with Drake to visit, you'll have a room."

Drake relished Gavin's growing confidence that he'd be able to stay here. Not too long ago, the man had spent most of his day looking over his shoulder.

"I will have to come back to London frequently," Drake warned the boys. "The nature of my clients means I make most of our money in town. So you'll be on your own." He'd have to find a patient, likely half-deaf, housekeeper.

"Did you see in the paper that they've opened more of the rail line into Norfolk?" Frank asked. "It should save us a day of travel, maybe more."

Us. Drake liked the word as much as he liked the glint in the young man's eye. "That settles it, then." He slapped his hand on the table. "Meeting adjourned, Fletcher family. Everyone to school, and I'll get back to work."

They came to life, all happy chatter as they gathered their books and talked of plans. Once they were out the door, silence stretched between Drake and Gavin.

"That was a surprise," Gavin began.

"You don't mind?"

He shook his head. "It will be good for you to be away from here, and the fresh air can't be bad for them."

"If you change your mind, you're welcome to join us." Drake wasn't certain if he could handle the four of them on his own. "They might run me ragged in a week."

"Probably so." Gavin chuckled. "But London fits me better." He inhaled. "I might rent out the rooms, if you don't mind."

Drake shook his head. He was going to miss Gav every day. "Find some young men who need a respectable address and a discreet landlord." He clapped his friend on the shoulder. "Just leave my room for me when I'm in town." He stood, taking his coffee in one hand and his correspondence in the other. "I'd better get to work."

He'd put an entire country between himself and Jocelyn. He'd keep himself busy with raising his new brothers and building a business amongst his friends. It would help.

Eventually.

Something had to.

JOSS'S FATHER GREETED her with a smile, waving the newspaper at Cecil, who was standing guard for their visit. "Did you see what my girl did? Brought a viscount to his knees in front of the whole *ton,* just to get her da out of prison."

At least he'd washed before she'd arrived, and his clothes were clean. His teeth were still foul, and his eyes were pink rather than white.

Joss perched on the edge of her usual chair, not bothering to remove her cloak. It gave her a level of protection she would likely need.

Her father's release was a brick in her reticule, signed by the prime minister himself. This was a test Da had to pass.

"I'm happy that you're proud of me," she said as he danced around the room, putting all his baubles and tins in a wooden box. "It was the right thing to do."

"And your business?" he asked. "Still good?"

She'd been worried that the publicity would drive away her patrons, but the opposite had happened. The men had arrived at the door with a smile and a deep bow for the woman who counted the prime minister, the master of the ceremonies, two dukes, a marquess, and at least one viscount among her friends. Not to mention she had the best whiskey in town. "I've been so busy I've lost track of the days."

She hadn't seen Drake in fifteen days, ten hours, and twenty-four minutes.

All the girls from The Peacock had arrived on her doorstep, hoping for a job. She'd only been able to hire three, replacing Imogen, Poppy, and Edith, but she'd found the others fine houses in other cities. Though she'd kept them out of Sheffield and the whole of Norfolk.

Connie was considering her offer to be the next Madam White, and Edith had moved to the kitchen to train with Elsa.

Hugh had given up whittling in favor of tasting everything that came from the oven, no matter how badly it was burned.

"Good, because I've been thinking. Penn is getting out in a few months, and he'll need a place to stay while he sets up shop, and then Grimsby around the corner should be out soon. He's a good man to have on the door."

"I have a doorman, and I don't need an opium peddler."

His eyes narrowed. "We'll see how things go. Because I've been thinking… If you could collect enough secrets to send that viscount to prison, imagine how much money we could make if we kept those secrets for ourselves."

Jocelyn's heart plummeted, taking her stomach with it. "You want me to keep running the brothel? I thought we were going back to the coast."

He waved her words away like pesky flies. "The ocean is always there. Ships are always sailing, but this… Joss, girl. You have a bird in the hand. It would be a shame to toss away a king's ransom." He leaned forward. "Penn swears he'll have clients around the block once he gets up and going. Those gents won't know what hit them once their heads are wreathed with smoke."

Livelihood over lives.

"No." She stood so fast the chair toppled backward. Cecil shifted to attention behind her. "That's just the thing, Da. Spencer wasn't happy to lose his chance to blackmail Viscount Stratford. He's backed out of our deal."

Spencer had been the one person in the plot to escape unscathed. She'd helped him bank enough secrets to save his hide. It was something she'd have to learn to live with.

As her father realized he'd have to stay in prison, Joss stepped out of reach and closer to the door, careful to keep the reticule in view. If she hid it now, he'd know she was lying.

The keys jangled in the lock.

"You gave me up for a chit you didn't even *know?*" His eyes blazed for a moment, then two. His gaze flicked to Cecil, and he drew a deep breath. "Well then, I'm sure you have enough dirt on Spencer to get him to change his mind."

"No." Joss hated that the word shook so badly. More than that, she loathed that she wasn't used to saying it. "I won't drag his wife and children through the mud. Not for anyone."

"You bitch," her father sneered as he lunged for her. Cecil yanked her through the door and slammed it shut, leaving the madman she'd once worshipped grasping at empty air.

She turned to leave but thought better of it. She had one last question, though she already suspected the answer. "The night Davy died, the night I almost drowned, did you know that storm was coming?"

"What has that cur Fletcher been telling you?"

The truth. He always tells me the truth. "I'm not talking about him, Da. I'm talking about you and me. Did you know that storm was coming in?"

His jaw had the same stubborn angle she saw in the mirror every morning. Her heart was breaking into pieces, but she would have the truth from his own lips before she left this place forever.

"What was I supposed to do? That ship was sailing the next day, and there was a fortune to be made on its cargo if we could get it."

So he'd sent three children into a wild sea with a boat that was too small. He hadn't cared what would happen to any of them. Not even to her.

The world had lost Davy. It had almost lost Drake. Her father needed to pay for that.

"Goodbye, Da."

His curses echoed from the brick walls as Cecil hurried her away, his hand firm on her back. Tears in her eyes, Joss almost ran to the gate. Cecil pulled her up short.

"Are you well, madam?"

Not yet, but she would be eventually. "Yes, Cecil. Thank you. For everything."

He opened the gate and gave her a boyish smile. "Jane's

agreed to marry me," he said. "We hope you'll come to the wedding."

"You have my best wishes, lad." She kissed his baby-smooth cheek. "But I'm getting the hell out of London, and I hope you do the same."

Once she was free of the prison, Joss removed her veil and threw it into the street, where it was promptly run over by a dairy wagon. She thought about doing the same with the cloak until she saw a mother carrying a child and flanked by her two sons. She clung to the arm of the eldest. His coat was new, as were his siblings'. Her coat, though, had seen far too many winters.

Joss remembered being in London with little to eat and less money than worries.

"Excuse me, ma'am." Joss approached her. "I no longer need this, and I was wondering if you would take it with my good wishes?"

"We don't take charity, miss," the older boy said. "I can get my mother whatever she needs."

He was barely old enough to wear trousers. "I'm sure you can, and I meant no insult. Perhaps…" Joss looked around for an idea. "If you found it on that bench and took it home, that's not charity, is it?"

After the briefest of thoughts, the boy grinned. "No, miss, it isn't."

Joss offered her card to their mother. "If you'd like honest work, we need a maid, and there's a young lady who could watch your daughter while you work. Come see me by the end of the week."

She wouldn't be there after that.

Joss dropped the cloak on the bench and climbed into the carriage.

The woman walked by, and her youngest swept the garment over his shoulder.

"Don't let it drag in the dirt, Davy," his brother scolded.

"All right, Charlie." Davy lifted the fabric higher so that it fluttered in the wind like a sail. "Let's go home."

"On to Whitechapel, madam?" Tommy asked from the box.

"Yes, please."

She had one last thing to do.

CHAPTER TWENTY-FIVE

HE TWO-STORY HOUSE with a wide gray portico was surrounded by patchy snow and flanked by narrow cypress trees that looked more like poles. Graveled paths led to outbuildings that served as gateways to fields bisected by stone walls and hedgerows.

"You said it was a farmhouse," Jocelyn scolded Thea from the safety of the coach. For some reason, she'd expected Drake to settle in a ramshackle pile like the one they'd grown up in.

"The land doesn't go with it. It's tenant farmed." Thea chuckled. "For some reason, I can't see Drake milking a cow."

"He's actually very good at it," Jocelyn muttered as she stared at the large house. "He sings to them."

"Drake Fletcher *sings to cows*?" Amelia's wide smile sparkled, making her rosy cheeks resemble apples. She looked to Bob, who was sitting beside her. "Did you know that?"

"That he could sing? Yes. The cows? No."

Jocelyn had surrounded Bob with pillows to keep him comfortable. Now it just worked to muffle his voice. She was lucky he hadn't been smothered to death on the trip.

Alfie, who was next to her, stared out the window. "Look at all those trees."

Would you please take Alfie with you? He needs somewhere to run and someone to look after him like our mother would have wanted.

She couldn't have said no to Tommy after that. Alfie, for his part, seemed fine with the arrangement. Though it might be because Tommy had told him it was temporary.

"Shall we?" Thea opened the door without waiting for an answer. "They'll be in the back garden working on the cricket pitch."

Jocelyn followed her, then Amelia. They all helped Bob descend, with Alfie bringing up the rear. They made for an unusual parade.

Jocelyn's heart thudded against her ribs like a fish in a trap. "Do the others know we're coming?"

"Oliver does," Thea said.

"Richard doesn't." Amelia's giggle tinkled like ice on snow. "I owe him one after the whole *Jocelyn is a madam* story he forgot to tell me." Her eyes flew to Bob. "I'm sorry. You did know that, didn't you?"

He patted her hand. "I believe she is retired."

"I tell you that line goes right here."

Drake's thundering voice sent the fish in Jocelyn's chest upriver and into her throat. Tears clouded her vision.

"I tell you that it goes there, if you measure from the stick thing," Richard yelled back.

"It's a wicket!" Drake shouted.

"That's croquet, isn't it? Why do they call something the same thing in two different sports?" Richard asked. "Let me see the book."

Jocelyn rounded the corner of the house, expecting to see her favorite crow in the garden. She had to search for him.

"You have seen the book three times already, and you keep misreading it on purpose."

Drake wasn't in black. He wasn't in a waistcoat. Despite the temperature, he had his shirt sleeves rolled to his elbows. He had a book in one hand and a hammer in the other. His hair was ruffled in the wind, and there wasn't a cravat in sight. Richard was reading the book over his shoulder, an impish grin on his face.

"See, it goes there. If it hadn't snowed last night, you'd see it. Why can't we just wait—"

"Because tomorrow is goddamn Christmas, and this is Nicky's goddamn Christmas present." Drake marched past where Richard had pointed. "The line goes *fucking here*."

Oliver waved at the ladies from the sidelines, his laughter carried on the wind. "Gentlemen, the ladies have arrived."

Jocelyn didn't care who said what or where they stood. She didn't even care if she did the correct introductions or if she ignored a duke.

All she cared about was the wide-eyed man crushing the rules of cricket in his left hand as she drew nearer. His nose was red from the cold. When he didn't move toward her, her knees trembled.

"Hello."

Drake's gaze flicked to the crowd near the house as he coughed to clear his throat. "Why are Alfie and Bob here?"

Jocelyn's stomach plummeted. "Because Tommy thinks Alfie should live in the country, and Bob thinks you need help with the boys. Plus, I might have bribed him with a knowledgeable herbalist who needs a gardener."

His throat convulsed, like he'd taken a bite of something too large to swallow. "All right. Harry will be happy to see Alfie. There aren't a lot of children his age here. We can try—"

"Drake Fletcher, do you not care why I'm here at all?" Jocelyn asked.

He darted his tongue along his bottom lip. "I'm afraid to ask."

Her heart crumbled. "You think I came all the way to Norfolk because I got into a scrape I can't manage? That I would risk—" It didn't matter what she'd risked. It was too late. It didn't matter. She turned on her heel. "I knew I never should have—"

His fingers closed over her wrist. "I'm afraid you're going to tell me that you're only here to bring Alfie and Bob so they didn't have to travel alone," he whispered. "I'm afraid you're going to say you're only here for Christmas, or that you came to see the house, or the boys, or…" He closed the distance between them and rested his head against hers. His breath tickled the back of her neck. "I can't watch you walk away from me again, Jocelyn."

His words melted her. She turned easily in his grasp and let him see her tears. "I came because I love you, you infuriating man."

The hammer thudded to the ground as he snatched her to him and sealed his lips over hers in a scorching kiss that curled her toes. Between wicked swipes of his tongue, she could feel his smile.

She also might have heard cheers from up the hill.

"I love you." Drake kept her close to him, his hands running over her body as though ensuring she was real.

"Da will get out of prison eventually," she warned him.

"We'll deal with it together."

"When we're in London, people will likely stare," she reminded him.

He kissed her nose. "As they should."

"I can't promise I won't get into scrapes, but I will try." Maybe living in a village surrounded by grass would help.

Drake's eyes sparkled. "Darling, this sounds very much like a proposal."

"It does, doesn't it?" She gulped. "Could you be married to a retired madam?"

He locked his hands behind her back. "Could you be married to a reformed smuggler who fell in love with the first woman he took to bed?"

Jocelyn tangled her fingers in his hair. "The *only* woman you'll take to bed."

"Sounds about right to me." Drake's lips hovered over hers. His smile was all she saw. "And I think a scrape here and there will be just fine."

ABOUT THE AUTHOR

Peri Maxwell has lost herself in reading romances all her life. She began writing as a challenge to herself and wrote her first historical romance on a dare, and now she's hooked. She prefers to write heroines who can stand toe-to-toe with a hero, challenge society's rules for good reasons, and find love with heroes who admire an equal (even if it's a little reluctantly).

She enjoys history, humor, and a good mystery. An armchair historian, she also has a background in women's studies.

Peri lives in Arkansas with her husband and the two cats who rescued them. When she's not writing or reading, she's working her day job or spending time with her family and friends (the same ones who dared her to write a historical romance).